CURSED: BROKEN

CURSED: BROKEN

BOOK ONE

X. Aratare

RAYTHE REIGN PUBLISHING, INC.

Copyright ©2016 X. Aratare

All rights reserved. This book or any portion thereof may not be reproduced or used in any manner whatsoever without the express written permission of the publisher except for the use of brief quotations in a book review.

Raythe Reign Publishing, Inc.
raythereign.com

CURSED: BROKEN–BOOK 1

A M/M, Modern Retelling of Beauty & the Beast

Nick Fairfax vows to do whatever Lord Bane Dunsaney desires for one year. In exchange, Nick's family gets a chance to regain their fortune. Is this the worst mistake of Nick's life, or will it lead to a love only found in fairy tales? A modern, M/M retelling of Beauty & The Beast.

Sensitive, aspiring photographer Nick Fairfax wants nothing to do with his family's corporate business, or their vicious, cold-blooded lifestyle. Intending to give up his inheritance and pursue his art, he arrives at his father's office, only to find that Fairfax Industries has fallen to a scarred man in a hooded cloak.

The man is the reclusive billionaire Lord Bane Dunsaney, and he is bent on destroying the Fairfaxes. But when he sees Nick *everything* changes. Bane offers the Fairfaxes the chance to regain their fortune if Nick will reside at Moon Shadow, his secluded mansion, and do whatever the billionaire wants for a whole year. Nick has no real choice other than to agree to Bane's terms.

At Moon Shadow, Bane lords his power over Nick, going even so far as to take Nick's phone, computer and beloved camera away. The billionaire claims such measures are to protect his *privacy*, but Nick is convinced they are so Bane can control *him*.

Each is determined to see the worst in each other. But as time passes, Nick glimpses a Bane that is much more than the cold-hearted figure that he met in his father's office. He discovers that Bane is a man betrayed by love and no longer believes in it.

But what Nick comes to know about Bane is *nothing* compared to the man's true secret. Bane is *cursed*. He is a tiger-shifter who has *no control* over his beast. And that beast wants Nick. Sign up for our list!

Raythe Reign produces escapist, romantic M/M shifter, fantasy, scifi, adventure, and urban fantasy books and graphic novels. We also are frequent bloggers!

Sign up for our mailing list, and not only will you get the first book of our M/M series, The Merman, free, but you'll also be the first to to...

- Participate in discussions
- Take polls (both silly and serious)
- Be invited to our ARC list for future releases
- Take advantage of any book sales

http://welcome.raythereign.com/get-transformation-book-1-of-the-merman-series-free/

CHAPTER ONE

THE DEAL

Nick Fairfax turned off his motorcycle's engine. The whirr of crickets and the soft whoosh of night wind through the grass and trees replaced the motorcycle's throaty growl. He looked at the gates before him.

They were huge and still bore the remnants of being wrapped in thick vines that must have just recently been cut down. Vicious looking spikes stabbed towards the brilliant night sky from the gates' arched top. Two words were created out of thick, curving iron bars that stretched over that arch: Moon Shadow.

That must be the name of the house. Not a house. A mansion. A magnificent ruined mansion in the middle of nowhere, Nick thought then added, *This is Bane's mansion.*

Nick looked through the gates at the mansion beyond. It was three stories and made of dark stone with dozens of mullioned windows. The panes looked like they were painted with quicksilver. They perfectly reflected the first quarter moon that hung high in the sky. The same vines that had been wrapped around the gates covered much of the front of the house. No one had taken a knife to them just yet. Their dense leaves fluttered in the wind. He saw that there was a tower in the far back corner of the house with a bronze roof that had long ago taken on that gorgeous aged green patina. Perhaps the tower had been built so that the owners could stargaze.

Nick's gaze dropped to the overgrown garden in the front of the mansion. There was a large weed-choked fountain in the center of a circular drive. Flowers bloomed in profusion, spilling down the fountain's sides like water must have long ago. Though it was night and he couldn't see the colors of the flowers that bloomed there, Nick imagined that in daytime this place would be riotous with reds, whites, yellows and pinks.

There was a soft click and the hiss of static came from the intercom box to his left. Nick's head snapped towards it. His heart raced even faster and his palms became slick with sweat.

"Nicholas Fairfax," Lord Bane Dunsaney's English-tinted voice came through the speaker. "Are you ready to honor your part of the deal? One year of your life in servitude to me in exchange for the *possible* return of your family's fortunes?"

Nick's mouth went dry and cottony, but he stabbed the intercom's reply button and responded firmly, "I agree to your terms, Bane. Open the gates."

CHAPTER TWO

THE CHOICE

Earlier that day...
"You either give up photography or you lose every cent of my money. You'll have no home. You'll have no family. You'll be out on the street. Is your art really worth all that?" Nick imitated his father's baritone in a passable voice.

"You're kidding me! Your father did *not* say that!" Nick's best friend Jade Lessitor rocked back in her chair and laughed, clearly certain he was joking. After all, what father truly said such super-villainish things to their son? Charles Fairfax evidently did. But even though Jade knew his father's character, he could tell that not even she believed Charles would sink that low. When she saw that he was serious though the laughter died and she asked, "He didn't *really* say that, did he, Nick?"

They were seated outside at a corner cafe in wealthy Winter Haven. The June sunlight on his skin felt like a warm blanket. He watched as streams of well-dressed, beautiful people walked past them, oblivious to anything but their cell phones. Yet even with his best friend with him Nick felt alone in the crowd.

"He really said that," Nick finally answered her and took a sip of his fizzy water with lime. Telling her like this—so cool and calm—stopped him from feeling the aching pain of his father's dismissal not only of his art, but of *him*.

"Please tell me that you punched him!" Jade's spiked black hair quivered. Under the sunny June sky, Jade looked like a creature from another planet. She had skin as white as chalk and wore dark crimson lipstick and kohl black eyeliner to make her green eyes seem even more cat-like than normal. Her black babydoll dress and combat boots with pink laces truly made her seem otherworldly and out of place among the conservative couture that flowed by them.

"I was too stunned to really say or do anything. I just walked out of the dining room and grabbed a few things. Not all my stuff. Just what I could fit in my motorcycle's saddlebags. Dad had already gone to work by the time I left." He tilted his head towards his motorcycle at the curb. Only one of the saddlebags was filled with clothes. The other one had his laptop and beloved Nikon D7100 DSLR camera. He realized that he had left a ton of the Nikon's accessories back in the house and he sighed. Hard to make a quick exit when not all your stuff would fit in your ride.

"Your father really thought that he would *win* this bet? Let's see, what would anyone choose when presented with a cold-blooded reptile like your father who thinks of you as another one of his minions or your art that gives you peace and pleasure? Yeah, real hard choice!" She shook her head violently.

"It isn't just him who thinks I'll give up photography and join the family business. My brothers think the same thing. They believe my obsession with photographing ruins is a passing fancy that will go away."

Nick grimaced as he remembered his oldest brother Jake actually *chortling* about how lame photography was in general. Steven, the middle brother, had just said something dismissive about how *rare* it was for even a truly *talented* photographer to make any money at it, leaving the impression that not only was Nick *not* talented, but he *certainly* could never make a living doing what he loved.

Jade did the usual thing when he spoke of his two older brothers. She looked like she was sucking on something incredibly bitter. "I'm not surprised about Steven. I mean the guy is practically a robot."

At twenty-five, Steven was four years older than Nick and as different from him as night was to day. They both shared the same slender, muscular build, platinum hair and gray eyes, but that's where the similarities ended. Nick was moved by beauty and intuition. Steven believed in figures and facts only. Steven thought that imagination was the refuge of the weak and easily gulled. Nick thought imagination was the closest one could get to the sublime. Steven had immediately joined their father's venture capital firm after graduating Harvard, eager to use his skills with numbers to strip other companies of all their assets and leave the dregs—the actual employees that had made those companies great in the first place—behind.

"You started your diatribe against my brothers with Steven. I'm surprised. I thought Jake was your *favorite*." Nick chuckled.

"Because I wanted to save the *best* for *last*." Her green eyes narrowed. "Jake is a snake, Nick. He is another cold-blooded serpent in your family. I wouldn't be surprised at all by him laughing as your father said those horrible words to you. I swear I think you're a changeling! You don't belong in that family at all."

Twenty-eight year old Jake was a clone of their father with his shark-like smiles and ultra-tailored suits in dark blues and blacks like bruises. He had a lean hungry look and their father's coloring, including dark brown hair and eyes and a sensual, almost predatory mouth. Jake was second-in-command at their father's firm and took great pleasure in destroying people's lives as he padded his own bank account.

"So your brothers just bobbed their heads like the automatons they are as your father threatened to disown you?" Jade confirmed.

He nodded. "Yeah, but—and I can't believe I'm saying this—they're not as black as they seem."

"Really? Enlighten me?" She crossed her arms over her chest.

"None of them really think I'll do anything other than give up art and join the family business after I graduate college next year anyways so they don't believe that Dad will actually have to go through with his threat and disinherit me." Nick let out a thin laugh. "They really don't understand what my photography means to me. Their one goal in life is simply to make *money*. They've found a way to make loads of it while satisfying their desire to *kill* even if it's only in the sense of killing companies. In their eyes, there's *nothing* better than what they do for a living."

"You really are lowering my opinion of them even more, you realize?"

Nick sighed. "They are what they are. Sometimes I think I'm the only one that took after Mom."

"I wish I had known her." A pall fell over Jade's expression.

His mother Emma Fairfax had died when he was just nine of heart failure. She'd had a heart defect that simply couldn't be fixed and, though she was on the organ donor list, no heart had come up for transplant in time. He still missed her.

Jade suddenly let out a soft laugh and shook her head. "Why would your father or brothers *want* you in the firm anyways? Forgive me, Nick, but you're *not* the business vulture type."

"No need for forgiveness. I agree with you." He leaned back in his chair and groaned. The sunlight splashed onto his face and he relished the light and heat. The winter had been very dark and deep. Spring had been rainy and gray. The cusp of summer was now here and he wanted to drink in every moment of it. He looked back at Jade, feeling a little sun drunk. He wanted to be *really* drunk, but it was too early to be starting on the martinis. "Even if I had any *desire* to rape and pillage companies, I have no *aptitude* for it. But it doesn't matter to them. Dad just wants me under his thumb forever."

"Do you want to be?" Jade asked. Her piercing green gaze was upon him.

"What do you mean? Want to be—"

"Under his thumb, Nick? Or are you prepared to be done with him? Strike out on your own? Live your life? Like your *mother* would have wanted?"

He looked over at the saddlebags on his bike. Most everything he cared for was in there and the person opposite him was his best friend. This was all he needed. Did he have the courage to admit that and leave all the extraneous stuff behind? His right hand curled tightly around his drink.

"I'm ready," he said. "I'm done with them. I want to get out."

"That's AWESOME!" Jade leaped up out of her seat and embraced him. She smelled of clove and oranges. He held her tightly.

He laughed and asked, "You're happy that I'm going to be disowned by my family?"

She released him and sat back down in her own seat. "No! I'm happy that you're going to be *free*."

"Free? That sounds so unreal to me." He shook his head. "Family obligation is worse than any other obligation. Because those bonds—though invisible—are like *steel*."

"I wouldn't know. My family is you, Nick, and I've *chosen* to be bonded to you." Jade smiled brightly even though her words were rather grim. Both her parents had died in a car accident when she was fifteen. She was raised by her grandmother who had passed away just a year ago.

"I'm sorry, Jade—"

"Don't be sorry! You are the best family there is!" she assured him.

"And so are you."

"Do you know where you're going to stay?" Jade's green gaze focused on him. Before he could answer she was clapping her hands together and grinning. "You're staying with me, of course! Lauren moved into Jason's apartment last week so I have a free room that has your name on it."

"Jade, I don't have the money to pay for half the rent at your place!"

Jade's apartment was a cramped two bedroom in the heart of Winter Haven, which was why it cost the earth. His only option if he were to stay in the expensive city was to rent the second garbage can from the left in the dirtiest alley. To live in Jade's place was more of a dream than he could have hoped for. Jade was able to live there, because of her substantial inheritance and her eBay business.

"You don't need to pay anything. At least, not in *cash*. You can take pictures of the merchandize I'm selling on eBay. That will be more than enough to cover rent and I will pay you on top of that," she assured him. "The photos you've taken for me before have doubled what I've gotten in the auctions."

"I'm happy to do that for *free* for you like I have been," he pointed out.

"Well, now you're going to get *paid* for it. You have no choice, but to take my cash."

Jade scoured every pawnshop, estate and garage sale for antique clothes, jewelry or whatever else had value. He would photograph her purchases in the most attractive way possible and she'd sell them for gobs of money compared to what she spent. Living in Winter Haven with all the rich people's castoffs helped hugely.

"I guess I can't argue with that since I had no idea where I was going to sleep tonight after I shoved off from the family home." Nick smiled at her. "Roomies?"

"Roomies!"

They shook on it and both of them finished their drinks.

"Shall we go back to *our* place and have actual *alcoholic* beverages?" Jade asked.

Nick could think of nothing better, but he shook his head, which had her raising her eyebrows.

"I'm going to see my father and brothers at Fairfax International." Nick smiled grimly "I'm going to tell them my decision. I'm choosing art and friendship over them."

Jade grinned. "Damned straight. They're not going to know what hit them."

CHAPTER THREE

BANE

Nick slipped through the rotating doors of Fairfax International. He caught sight of his reflection in the glass. Platinum blond hair, high cheekbones, wide gray eyes and a slightly fey look peered back at him. He tried to firm his expression, but he just looked scared.

I can do this. I can walk away from the family. They don't want me anyways.

He let out a silent huff of laughter. He knew that last line sounded like a child feeling sorry for himself. He'd never fit into the family. Only he and his mother had connected in any way. But she was gone and he was more alone than ever in the Fairfax home. It was time to leave and be the person he was meant to be, not to hang onto old hopes of finally having his father and brothers accept him, let alone love him.

Nick's footsteps echoed loudly as he walked through the cold chrome and marble lobby to the elevator bank. His father and brothers' offices were on the forty-sixth floor. The entire black, steel skyscraper was named after them because his father paid a ton to make it seem like he owned the whole building.

Money my family's made from buying and then picking apart other people's businesses.

As corporate raiders, Fairfax International took over various companies when they were at their weakest. They loaded the companies up with debt then bailed out. They left pensions unfulfilled and workers suddenly without jobs. Yet as his father had pointed out many times, how could he judge when he had enjoyed the fruits of his father and older brothers' raiding for years?

But that stops now. I'm going to free myself from all of this.

Nick was going to make it on his own. He had already scraped together enough loans, grants and work-study to get through his last year of university. And now that he was staying with Jade he would have a roof over his head and food, too.

Shooting for her was fun and now profitable, but his true twin passions were taking photographs of ruins and nature. He lovingly photographed any fallen down structures he found, the more overgrown and remote the better. He would make up stories in his head about the people who must have lived there. His ultimate desire was to travel all over the world and record the past with his camera. But he wasn't naïve enough to think that anyone would necessarily pay his way for that. He would have to earn the money himself and convince people of the beauty and value of his art by showing it to them after he had created it.

Or I'll have those photographs for myself if no one else appreciates them. Either way, it's in my soul. I have to do this.

The elevator's doors whooshed open with a cool hiss of air. He stepped inside the car and swallowed. The elevator doors whispered shut behind him and rocketed him upwards. As each successive floor lit up on the elevator panel Nick drew his worn leather jacket tighter around his slender frame. His hands were slick with sweat and there was the bitter metallic taste of fear on the back of his tongue. He knew he was making the right decision for himself.

And for Dad, Jake and Steven. Like I told Jade, I'd never be any good to them in the business anyways. I couldn't bear to do what they do. Yet I still feel sick like I'm betraying them somehow.

The elevator slowed as floors forty-four and then forty-five were highlighted on the elevator's electronic panel. Finally, the car stopped on floor forty-six. There was only the slightest shudder before the doors opened and the sterile, black-tiled reception area of Fairfax International was revealed.

Now or never.

Nick stepped out of the elevator. The lights were dimmed to save energy during the evening hours. The office felt like it was sleeping. Sarah Westwood wasn't manning the reception desk with her perfectly coiffed hair, red-lacquered nails and frosty smile. She had automatically known what his father and brothers still didn't, which was that Nick was going to be an artist and, unless he struck it big somehow, he would never be making anywhere near the type of money that the corporate raiders, financiers, and attorneys who floated through this office made. He was, therefore, *uninteresting* to her even if he was the youngest son of the owner.

Nick passed by her empty glass and chrome receptionist desk and padded into the hallway beyond. This hallway led to his father and brothers' offices. His father had the largest office on the right. It was the ultimate corner office with floor to ceiling windows facing towards the glittering downtown of Winter Haven.

Nick wasn't surprised that all three offices had their lights on despite the fact that it was late on a Wednesday night in June when the air was warm and sweet and the bars and restaurants were filled with the rich and beautiful people of Winter Haven eating, drinking and laughing. His family lived purely for business and, from the recent conversations that Nick had overheard, he was pretty sure that they were in the middle of some big deal.

Something to do with a company—or maybe a person—called Bane. Dire sounding name.

Nick could tell from the sound of their voices that all three of his family members were in his father's office. His stomach clenched as he realized that his father would force him to make his decision known in front of his brothers. He could already hear Jake's sneer that Nick wouldn't last a week without their money. Steven would push his wire-rimmed glasses up to the top of his nose and list the costs of living on his own in Winter Haven, the likelihood of him making any money from his photography and so on and so forth. Part of Nick was tempted to sneak away then, to put off telling his father altogether. But he imagined Jade's disappointed expression and he kept on.

As he neared his father's office, he realized that there was something *off* in the way everyone sounded. He frowned. He had never noticed that shrill tone in Steven's voice before. Jake sounded like he was pleading, which his eldest brother had never done in his life. His father's voice, too, which normally was so authoritative held a note of plaintive disbelief in it. Nick couldn't yet make out any of the words that they spoke, but he knew that something was wrong.

Maybe I shouldn't go in there. Whatever they're talking about is business-related. There's nothing else that would make all three of them this on edge. They won't appreciate me interrupting them.

But just as Nick had that thought he stepped into the warm pool of light that spilled out of his father's office onto the hallway's carpet. Nick froze in place as he took in the scene before him.

His father was leaning against the front of his desk as if he needed it for support. Jake sagged beside him on the arm of a sofa. His blood red tie, the one he always wore when they were going to close a deal—*or make a killing*—was half undone and looked like a noose around his neck. His normally perfect hair was standing up as he kept running his hands through it with nervous strokes. Steven stared down at a tablet in his hands as if he couldn't quite believe whatever he was seeing on the screen.

Then there was the fourth man.

Nick guessed it was a man from the sheer size of him, because the man was wearing a cape with a hood, hiding himself entirely in a swath of darkness. Even for Winter Haven, which had its share of eccentrics, a cloak and hood were unusual clothing to wear. The man's shoulders were immensely broad and he stood over six feet tall. He was by the windows, back to Nick, looking out at the glittering city of Winter Haven as if it were his domain. There was something in his stance that had the air of command. Nick shivered.

Who is he? And what's going on here?

Just as Nick was about to back-peddle out of the room, certain now that he was interrupting a business meeting, his father's head lifted and he looked directly at Nick. Charles Fairfax was a robust man of fifty-eight. He still had a thick head of dark brown hair with just the slightest touch of frost at the temples. His face was handsome even if his jaw was a little too square to make him pretty. It gave him the appearance of crunching rocks between his molars. He normally swaggered rather than walked. His expression was usually one of conquest as if all would fall before the force of his personality or the dollars in his wallet. But now, he seemed shrunken and there looked to be more gray in his dark brown hair. His expensive suit was rumpled. Lines creased his face that Nick would have sworn hadn't been there this morning.

A prickle of unease went through the young man. Again he thought, *What's going on here?*

"Nick," his father said, his usually booming voice was just a whisper now. Cracked, dry, and pale as paper.

Jake looked over at Nick then and his eldest brother threw his arms into the air. "Fuck, Nick, what are *you* doing here?"

Steven let the hands fall to his sides. His gray eyes scanned Nick and nodded as if something in Nick's face or body told him everything he needed to know. And he was right, too, as he said, "I believe Nick's here to bid us adieu. Take his chances on his art rather than our money. As it so happens, he has the right idea."

The cloaked man's reaction to Nick being there was to stiffen slightly. But he did not turn around. Instead, Nick realized that he was watching Nick's reflection in the glass. Nick watched the man back. The hood of the cloak mostly obscured the man's face, but Nick did catch sight of a powerful jaw and sensual mouth.

Nick stepped fully into the office and voiced the question that had been spinning in his head, "What's going on here?"

"What's going on *here*? *What's* going on here? We're fucking ruined is what's going on here!" Jake's voice rose up into almost a shriek.

"Normally Jake's hyperbole would cause me to correct him," Steven said, his voice more robotic than usual. "But Jake is correct. We *are* ruined."

"What?" Nick breathed. His gaze darted from one man to the next until he focused on the cloaked man. He knew that whatever had happened here, the cloaked man was clearly the one behind it.

His father pushed off of the desk. His legs tottered underneath him for a moment. Nick hurried over to him and steadied him with an arm around his waist. He led Charles over to the black leather sofa in the corner of his office. His father collapsed on the couch, nearly dragging Nick down with him.

"Thank you, Nick. I—I feel a little unwell." His father's skin was gray and there was a sheen of sweat on his upper lip.

"Dad, what is going on? Who is that guy?" Nick asked the last very softly as he tipped his head towards the cloaked figure.

His father went grayer. He rubbed the back of one hand over his mouth as his gaze flickered over to the cloaked figure and away again. He opened his mouth and shut it several times, but nothing came out. Nick's unease grew greater and greater.

"Fuck, fuck, fuck, this can't be happening!" Jake paced. His hands worked convulsively at his sides.

Steven took off his glasses and polished them with a linen handkerchief from his pocket. His hands were trembling. "It is happening, Jake."

"What is happening?" But even as he asked that he knew that his father and brothers wouldn't come to the point so he got up from his father's side. He stalked over to the cloaked man and asked, "Who are you?"

There was a long pause, but then a low, smoky English-accented voice answered, "My name is Bane."

CHAPTER FOUR
THE DEAL

My name is Bane ...
Under other circumstances that voice would have skated down Nick's spine and left a pleasurable tingle in its wake. But not now. His family was in pain and *Bane* was the cause.

"Don't you have a last name? Or is it *just* Bane like Cher or Madonna?" Nick grated out.

The man laughed. "It's *Lord* Bane Dunsaney, but you may call me Bane."

Nick was *not* honored to call the man by his first name. "What have you done, *Bane*?"

The cloaked man's shoulders began to shake. At first, Nick thought he was having a fit, but then the gales of laughter broke out. Rich, velvety laughter that caused his father to hold his head in his hands and his brothers to shrink down. Anger suddenly burned in Nick's belly.

"What the hell is so funny? I don't see anything funny!" Nick snapped. He was tempted to grab Bane and spin him around to face him. Though Nick was probably only three-fourths Bane's size, he wasn't afraid of a fight.

The laughter subsided to chuckles. Bane shrugged the cloak more firmly around his large frame. "Forgive me. I can see that you truly do not understand the *irony* of your question."

"What irony?"

"Your family attempted to take over one of my businesses. They *failed*," Bane answered simply.

"It was a trap," Jake added. "A damned dirty trap."

"Yes, it was," Bane agreed. "But you did not have to take the bait. You could have acted *honorably*. Instead, you let greed lead you. And now you have *nothing*."

Jake dropped down onto his haunches and wrapped his arms around his knees. "You were *waiting* for us."

"He's taken our company over, Nick," Steven explained dryly, but his hands were still trembling as he continued to clean his glasses.

"It's all gone," his father whispered. "We put all we had into acquiring Bane's company and we were acquired instead."

Nick blinked. "I don't understand."

"I own Fairfax International," Bane said simply. "More than that actually. Your family has overextended itself. They are *broke*."

"We're not broke!" Nick scoffed. "We have other investments—"

"No, we do not. I should say that our investments have gone terribly south. We invested in real estate," Steven said. "We've been running in the red for some time."

Nick couldn't believe this. He hadn't noticed things being leaner at home this past year. In fact, they had seemed to live even more luxuriously than ever before. A new car for Jake. A fabulously expensive new sound system in the house for Steven. His father had indulged in his wine collection extensively buying rare vintages that he had only dreamed of owning before. Everything they had done had made Nick think that things were going wonderfully, better than ever, in fact.

"What about the house?" Nick asked. Their house in Winter Haven was worth at least a few million. That might not seem a lot to his family or to Winter Haven residents in general, but it still made them incredibly wealthy to the rest of the world.

"Mortgaged to the hilt," Jake said with a mirthless laugh. "The bank owns it."

"What about your bank accounts?" Nick struggled to find something that his family had left.

"A few hundred dollars at most," Steven answered.

"We're done, Nick," his father said.

The words seemed to sink like stones into a still pond. Silence fell for long moments. Nick didn't pretend to understand how it had happened, but he realized with a sick lurch that it wasn't just him who was poor. His father and brothers were, too. Not by choice, but the end result was the same.

"It's much worse than that," Bane suddenly said, breaking the silence with his smooth as molasses voice. "I intend to make sure that your family will *never* prosper again."

"What? *Why?*" Nick knew his expression was taut with shock and disbelief. He could see his reflection in the glass just as Bane could since he continued to keep his back to them as if they were not worthy of his notice.

"I've watched your family's business. For years. Vultures circling around and around. No mercy. No compassion. Just pick, pick, pick until all there is left of the businesses they buy are bones bleached under the sun. The more workers displaced the better," Bane said. "Haven't you, yourself, seen them celebrating their accomplishments over rare beef and red wine? Like hyenas over a kill."

Nick swallowed shallowly. He *had* seen them do that. Some of the imagery that Bane had just used to describe his family he had used himself, but to have a stranger state it so bluntly and with such distaste had Nick's back up.

"Save your judgment!" Nick snapped. "I don't want to hear it!"

"Of course, you don't! You are a spoilt, beautiful boy! You don't want to know what has funded your fun and free lifestyle! Who cares at what cost it has come?" Bane nearly spat.

Nick reared back as if he had been physically slapped. "You don't know me! You don't know *anything* about me!"

"Don't I? It seems to me that *who* and *what* you are is written in that pretty face and lovely body," Bane taunted.

Nick spun away from Bane. His heart was thundering in his chest. Rage caused adrenaline to spurt into his veins. He wasn't sure what he would do to Bane if the other man continued to speak to him in that way. So instead, he kneeled down in front of his father. That arrogant yet boisterous man seemed so small and insignificant now.

"Dad, it'll be okay. It can't be as bad as he says." Nick clutched his father's broad hands in his own. Charles Fairfax was trembling. That his father should tremble pushed the world off its axis.

"I haven't overstated the peril your family is in," Bane said and his voice seemed to suck all the oxygen out of the room.

Nick scowled. "Talk about wanting to lord it over people! Why the hell don't you leave? You don't have to be here! You can go!"

His father clutched Nick's hands. "No, Nick, no. Just—just be respectful."

"Dad, don't you see what he's doing? Hear what he's saying?" Nick cried.

His father's shoulders curled inwards. "It doesn't matter."

"It matters!" Nick yelled. His voice echoed in the deep silence that had fallen. Apparently, no one agreed with him.

"Still hoping for mercy, Charles? Still hoping that things can be turned around?" Bane asked.

"Are you capable of mercy? Is there still a way things can change?" His father's voice was hoarse.

"Dad!" Nick gasped. To him, asking for something from Bane was like asking the Devil for a favor. He'd just as soon laugh in their faces as assist. And there would always be a price, one that would, undoubtedly, be too dear to pay.

Bane slowly turned towards them. His cloak swirled around his long legs, revealing a well-cut dark suit underneath the thick, black material. Nick found himself looking immediately up to Bane's face. This time instead of just the slice of jaw and mouth, Nick saw far more. The hood fell back for just a moment. Bane had dark hair that curled in waves to his shoulders, striking Siberian blue eyes, a noble nose, as well as expressive full lips and a strong jaw. But that perfect beauty was horribly marred. The right half of his face had the imprint of what almost looked like a handprint burned into his flesh. Puckered skin, reddened and coarse, marked that terrible injury.

What happened to him?

Bane noticed Nick's gaze and he stiffened. For one moment, shame coursed through those liquid blue eyes. It felt like just the two of them caught in that moment like insects in amber. Bane shuddered, but then anger clearly took over and subsumed any other feeling he had.

"What would you do, Charles, to save *yourself*?" Bane asked.

"He won't do *anything* bad!" Nick cried.

"Let your father answer," Bane hissed. He pointed a gloved finger at Charles' chest.

"Dad has nothing to say to you!"

But then his father lifted one hand and Nick found his heart tumbling into his feet even before his father spoke. Bane's lush mouth curled into a smile already anticipating success.

"What—what are you offering? There's always an offer, isn't there? We're businessmen after all," his father said with a strained smile.

Nick's hands left his father's and dropped down into his lap. He felt numb. His father had just failed a test that he didn't even know he was taking.

"An offer?" Bane tapped his chin.

Jake rose up on shaky legs. "Yeah, what *are* you offering? You want something in exchange for giving us a second chance?"

Bane's blue eyes narrowed. They were locked on Nick. The young man felt a thrill of deep unease run through him as if he were in the sights of a gun.

"It is logical that you would want something. Mere censure could not possibly be your goal," Steven said, always logical.

Nick felt like they had once more stepped into another trap. But his family kept forging ahead as if they didn't see it or didn't care.

Which is worse?

"Yes, I suppose you *would* think of that. An offer. A bargain. A *deal*. Something—*anything*—to keep you going. For you know I intend to destroy you. You'll never get work anywhere. You'll be out on the street," Bane purred.

"You can't do that! You don't control everyone and everything!" Nick scoffed.

"Oh, but I *do*. You see your family has made a lot of enemies. A lot of powerful people have been looking forward to their fall. One word from me and they will close any doors that might have just cracked open," Bane chuckled. "They'll be lucky to work at a fast food restaurant after I'm done with them."

Nick burned with anger and hate even as he had to acknowledge what Bane said was true about the Fairfaxes having enemies and lots of them. His lithe body shook. His family had earned the enmity of many people as Bane had said. Bane was using his family's weakness against itself. He saw how the cloaked man was playing them, but none of the rest of his family did.

They're desperate. They're in shock. They're fooling themselves.

But a part of him knew that maybe this wasn't the whole explanation for why his brothers and father were willing to believe Bane. They thought that, at the core, everyone was as greedy and grasping as they were.

"He's not going to help us!" Nick yelled as a last ditch effort.

But they were not listening. They didn't even look at him.

"What are you asking for?" His father rose up from the leather sofa.

Bane's expressive mouth widened into a toothy smile. "I will make you a *deal*, Charles."

"What is it?" Jake asked.

"Yes, what do you want?" Steven chimed in.

"We'll do whatever you ask," his father gasped.

Bane's gaze swung to Nick again. A cruel smile crossed his beautiful yet marred face. "I want your son. I want Nick."

CHAPTER FIVE
THE DETAILS

The office was so quiet. The phrase "could hear a pin drop" suddenly made sense to Nick. Then everyone was talking at once. Jake shouted about Bane not being serious even as his gaze flickered over to Nick like he wished Bane *were* serious and he would give Nick over in a heartbeat. Steven claimed that such a deal couldn't be legal in his dry, pedantic way. His father loudly proclaimed he would never sell his son! Nick was sure that he said something like "no way!" but his voice was lost in the babble. Bane merely smiled.

"Truly, you won't even consider it?" Bane wheedled, his smooth as smoke voice rising above the others effortlessly even though he wasn't shouting.

"*Sell* you my son? Are you *mad*?" His father shook his head.

His brothers nodded their heads in agreement, but their eyes showed that they didn't *completely* agree with him. Nick glowed with pride though. His father really seemed to be sticking up for him, recognizing him as someone valuable, as a part of the family. For one bright shining moment, Nick felt connected to them in a way he never had before.

"You won't give up Nick for a single year?" Bane spread his arms expansively. "Think of it as an internship. He'll even get *paid*, which is so very rare these days. His payment will, of course, be the chance for your family to be rich and powerful again."

"I don't understand. What are you offering here?" His father's brown eyes suddenly had that predatory look he got when he was assessing a deal.

"Dad, don't listen to him! We aren't doing this no matter what he says!" Nick cried, but a small sliver of ice formed in his belly.

Could his father really be considering this? The man had just gone from "never!" to "well, wait, what are you offering?" He glanced at his brothers. Jake looked up at their father with that faintly desperate, avaricious look. Steven had this alert expression on his face, rather like a ferret.

They're all wondering the same thing as I am. No, they're wondering if Dad IS listening to him because he's interested.

"I just want to know what crazy plan he's offering, that's all, Nick." His father exuded that false bonhomie that he used on underlings that sensed they were about to get a shit job.

His father put an arm around Nick's shoulders, but instead of feeling warmed by the act, Nick felt trapped by it. But shrugging off his father's arm in front of Bane would show weakness. It would reveal a crack in their family facade. Bane though seemed to know exactly how Nick felt anyways. He pulled the hood up to more fully hide his face, but the knowing smile on his full lips was still visible.

"What I am *offering* is simply this. Nick will stay with me for one year. He will live on my estate and do *whatever* I ask—"

"*That's* what this is all about?" Nick laughed. "You want a sex slave?"

"Do not *flatter* yourself. You are not to my *taste*. And you would *not* be a slave unless you consider doing hard work *slavery*." Bane's lips writhed back from his teeth. They were white and sharp. But the heavy-hooded looks he had given Nick since the young man had walked into the room belied those statements. Not to mention calling Nick "beautiful" and "pretty" several times.

Nick threw up his hands. "What the Hell am I even worried about? We're not doing this so it doesn't matter what little fantasies you've got going on in your head!"

His father squeezed his shoulder and said, "Let the man finish, Nick. I think it's clear that he's not looking for—ah, *companionship* in all of this. Please continue, Bane."

But Nick burst out, "We're not—"

"I notice that you keep saying 'we' as if your family is involved in this decision," Bane said to Nick.

"Well, I guess it's *my* decision, but I mean, we're *family*," Nick said as if that would convey some Norman Rockwell-esque flavor to his very dysfunctional clan.

But I do feel this way even if they don't. Even if they run me out. I keep hoping that things will change. Maybe the change is acting like we're a family and they'll go along with it.

Bane tilted his head to the side. "So you are devoted to your family? You want to see them do well? You certainly don't want to see them out on the street, begging for coins with tin cups in their hands?"

"No! But I'm not going to be your sex slave for a year to—"

"I see. Your devotion only goes *so far*. Interesting." Bane leaned casually back against his father's desk.

"You've got to be kidding! You're trying to turn this around on *me*?" Nick's shoulders straightened. Was Bane questioning his motives? "You're the one who—"

"Who has *absolutely* no duty to help *your* family. I have quite the opposite feelings for them. They are *my* enemies, after all," Bane said.

"Nick, Nick, it's all right. Don't get yourself all worked up here," his father said.

Nick did shake off his father's hand off that time and took a few steps away. His skin was twitching between his shoulder blades. Why was his father even *indulging* Bane in this way? Was he recording this conversation for blackmail later? He knew that his father had done something like that at one point.

Maybe he's letting Bane dig his own grave. Fine. I can play along with this.

But he still felt panicked. His nostrils flared and the urge to flee was heavy upon him. His brothers were standing still as statues while his father drifted over to the silver serving cart where the cognac was kept. He poured himself a snifter full, but didn't offer a drink to anyone else. Nick felt like he wanted to upend the decanter into his mouth.

"I don't think your son likes it when you discount his feelings," Bane remarked mildly.

"I'm not. But the thing is that I already know what Nick is going to—*understandably*—say, but I admit that I have no idea what *you* are going to." His father took a large swallow of cognac.

"And you always want as much intel as you can possibly have, don't you, Charles? Or maybe it's because you either listen to my offer or start packing your bags. But be sure they're not too heavy to carry in your own two hands, because the cars aren't paid for either." Bane's Siberian blue eyes flared with mockery.

Do we own anything? Even the clothes on our backs?

Nick felt a wave of despair hit him. He had always assumed that his father and brothers understood money. But now it seemed all they understood was debt and how to rack up so much of it that it became a tsunami of bills.

"I'm always willing to listen, Bane. You might not appreciate my business practices, but surely you've noticed that I'm not a one-trick pony. I can adjust. My strategies are not set in stone," his father said. There was a hint of Charles' old business flair in his tone and behavior.

He's really acting like this is a deal he can make!

"You truly are such a *fluid* creature, Charles," Bane murmured.

"So lay out your offer in full. Let us hear it." His father spread his arms expansively.

"Right to the point." Bane chuckled then he began to pace in a short line, changing direction with every point he made. "Nick works for me for one year. He lives on my estate. He does whatever I ask of him. He is at my beck and call twenty-four seven, three hundred and sixty-five." Bane's gaze slid over to Nick. "Which does *not* include sharing my bed as that has no benefit to *me*."

Jake snorted. Nick glared at his older brother. Steven made a tutting sound.

"And what would we receive for this in return?" His father took another long swallow of cognac.

"His payment is that the three of you will be given a chance to prove your worth to me. I will give each of you a division of one of my companies. You will have one year's time to show me that you understand my business philosophy and can put it in practice profitably," Bane ticked off the terms on one of his large hands with surprisingly delicate movements. "If you *fail* you will *lose* everything. If Nick *fails* to stay with me and live up to his part of the bargain you will lose everything. You will be right back *here*, but there will be no third chance."

Jake's head jerked up as he heard the deal. He had that hungry, lean look on his face that reminded Nick of a street kid who hadn't eaten in a long time. Steven was seemingly frozen in place, but his eyes showed his brain furiously working.

"And obviously nothing bad would happen to Nick? He would be well taken care of? Not harmed in any way?" his father questioned.

"He would have to actually *work* for a living, but I would not ask him to anything that would harm him. Anything but his *pride*, that is," Bane answered.

Nick bristled. What the Hell did this man know about him? He acted like Nick was some kind of spoiled little prince! Maybe he'd had it easy compared to a lot of people, but it wasn't like he was afraid to get his hands dirty.

"What happens if we don't take your deal?" Steven asked, ever the practical one.

Bane smiled. It wasn't a nice smile. It was a tigerish grin. There was something almost feral about the man. Despite a veneer of good breeding, the remnants of a posh accent that hinted of high-class English schools and the well-cut suit, Bane's nature seemed quite wild.

"You'll be out on the street tomorrow," Bane said.

"But there are rules against stuff like that!" Nick protested. He turned to Steven. "They can't just kick us out of the house even if the bank foreclosed tomorrow! Steven, tell him!"

But Steven pressed his lips tightly together as if to stop any words from flowing out. He shook his head.

"You've lived in Winter Haven all your life and you *still* think that the rules apply equally to everyone?" Bane asked softly. "Or perhaps you've just been used to being on the *winning* side of those rules so long that you can't even comprehend how unfair and unequal they can be applied?"

"You don't have the power to get around the laws!" Nick yelled.

He looked at his brothers and father, expecting them to show the same level of incredulity as he was. But none of them would look at him. Jake kept rubbing his mouth with the back of one hand. Steven stared down at the tablet he held listlessly. Their father's gaze was on the floor. They believed Bane. They believed that no matter what the law was that Bane would have his way. Nick's mouth went dry as the desert.

Bane drew himself up to his full height again. His voice was low and dangerous, "I *assure* you that your family will not have a home tomorrow. What little is left in their bank accounts will be frozen. No friends will take them in. If they *had* any friends, that is. No one will give them a job. Not even at the corner market. And even if they could scrape up the coin to go to another city or town it will be the same there, too."

Nick jerked back as if physically struck by the man's words. "Why are you doing this?"

"Do you think that your family hasn't done the same to countless others? The suffering that they have caused around the globe has lined their pockets for many years. I am just *paying* them back," Bane said with a tight smile. "Think of me as Robin Hood."

Nick swallowed the bile that had bubbled up in his throat. He had tried not to know the cost of his family's business practices. He wouldn't even look at the news about jobs lost, lives ruined, and pensions disappeared by keeping his gaze always on the horizon and the time when he would be free of them.

"We're not the only ones that do business that way, you know," Jake said suddenly. "Why pick on us? I mean it's clear to me that you were luring us in all the time!"

Their father gestured for Jake to keep silent. Jake recoiled and seemed to curl in on himself.

"No, you're not the only ones. And you're not the only ones that I've destroyed for the same thing," Bane answered. His frosty blue gaze swung back towards Nick and there was something unreadable in it. The beautiful marred face seemed rather mask-like at that moment. Then Bane was turning away towards the windows to look at Nick's reflection instead of head on. "But you are the *only* ones I've given a second chance to."

"Why?" Nick asked.

"I don't honestly know," Bane answered.

"You don't seem like a man who doesn't know what he's doing." Nick frowned. "Though I'm not sure what's worse: that you planned this out or that you're destroying our lives on a whim."

Bane sounded almost sad as he said, "You think one year of hard labor too much for your family's well-being? If that is your answer then—"

"No, I didn't say that! Just—just give me a minute," Nick begged.

Silence fell. There was nothing left for anyone to say except for Nick. His gaze swung around the room at all of his family. What he saw on their faces was fear. Raw, unbridled fear.

There's no recording device. They aren't trying to trick Bane into anything. This is real. This is absolutely real.

Could they all fit into Jade's two bedroom apartment? Maybe for a night or two, but then what? At that moment, he could very well believe that Bane's reach was infinite or that the businessman would make it so. Like an avenging angel he would follow them and make sure his vengeance was meted out.

Is he insane or just really pissed that my family tried to take his company? Does he think of his workers? Does he care about them or is all this just an excuse to vent some anger?

His family wouldn't look at him. He wondered then what they were thinking. If they were given this offer would they accept it to save the others? Some part of him doubted it. He could walk away from them now. Bane didn't seem to be threatening his livelihood, just his brothers and father's. He could leave them to their fate or he could take the deal and save them.

One year of working for Bane. How bad could it be?

He looked at the powerful line of Bane's shoulders and back. He shivered in spite of himself. Bane was beautiful and the exact kind of guy that would have appealed to him in the past. But not now. Bane was poison.

"If I do this," Nick began and he saw his father flinch. Was there a look of hope or dismay or perhaps both on his face?

Bane's head rose. "If you do this…"

Nick tried to read the businessman's expression in the glass. The full lips were slightly parted as if Bane wanted to capture Nick's next words with his teeth. The Siberian blue eyes gleamed in the low light. The puckered, ruined skin of his scar seemed to glow.

"If I do this, they'll be okay?" Nick gestured towards his brothers and father.

"They will be given exactly the things I promised," Bane answered.

"And you'll give them a *real* shot, right? You won't stack the deck impossibly high against them or anything?" Nick pressed and he saw a flash of Jake's eager face, wanting this chance, wanting to prove that he could do the impossible.

Bane let out an earthy chuckle. "The deck is always stacked against people somewhat. But yes, they will get a *fair* chance."

"And whatever you're asking me to do won't be illegal? It won't be to hurt someone else or myself? And it won't be to sleep with you—because, believe me, that so isn't happening." Nick sliced his hand through the air.

Bane let out a sharp laugh. "From the sheer *amount* of times you've brought up sleeping with me, I might begin to think that you are, in fact, *interested*."

Nick's cheeks flared with heat. "Ah, *no*. But that's usually what is the main part of these *arrangements*. It's normally the reason for them, right?"

"You've heard of many of these arrangements?" Bane suppressed a laugh.

Nick flushed hotly again. "Not in real life, no. But I'm sure they happen."

Bane chuckled. "The rich and powerful *always* have someone under duress, don't they? I'm sure you have seen *lots* of that."

Nick bridled at the implication that his family was completely avaricious. "My family has never had a live-in slave—or should I say *intern*, thanks."

Bane lifted his hands in the air as if in surrender. "I see. I am lower than them then in your eyes."

Steven gripped his tablet tighter and Nick knew that he was worried that Nick was going to blow the deal if he kept on being so aggressive.

"I just want things to be clear between us," Nick ended.

"You have been *crystal*," Bane said the word as if it had a piquant taste.

Nick advanced on Bane. He saw the man's large shoulders stiffen in surprise as he approached. His family shot worried glances at him, but he ignored them. Bane slowly turned to face him. Nick stopped a foot from him. Bane was so much bigger than he was. The man could engulf him in those massive arms. There was the slightest scent of sandalwood and cinnamon rising off of him. Exotic spice. Nick looked up into that hooded face and didn't blink. Other than the terrible burn scar, Bane was as beautiful as a Greek sculpture come to life.

"If you *break* any one of your promises to me or to them, you forfeit my family's company and fortune. It *all* goes back to them. Are we *crystal* on that, too?" Nick asked.

"You think you are in a position to make any terms?" Bane's heavy-hooded blue eyes stared right back into his.

"I think that you fancy yourself *honorable* in some weird, twisted way," Nick guessed and the slightest flicker of emotion on Bane's face confirmed that. "I think you don't intend to break any of your promises so what's the harm in putting that on the table, too?"

Bane studied him for long moments. "All right. Agreed." The big man was suddenly spinning away from Nick and heading towards the doorway. He called over his shoulder, "I will send you my estate's address. I expect you will be there later this evening. Do say your goodbyes. You'll all be too busy for guests. Your family's new positions will be emailed to them in a few hours."

"But what about a contract? Surely, we should write this all down!" His father cried, reaching out towards Bane.

Bane laughed. "A contract? In writing? Your son in exchange for potential prosperity? I think not. Your son is wise. I will honor my promises so long as you and he honor yours. That is more than you deserve."

Bane then strode from the room, without a look back, as if he was certain everything would go exactly as he wished it.

CHAPTER SIX
MAGNIFICENT RUIN

"You're crazy, Nick. Certifiably *insane*," Jade's voice buzzed angrily through the earpiece of Nick's cellphone. Even with his motorcycle helmet on and the engine roaring, he could hear her rather well as she was almost yelling.

"I know," Nick sighed.

"And you called me on the phone *instead* of coming back to the apartment—*our apartment*—because you knew that I would convince you not to go through with this crazy plan!"

She was right. He had specifically avoided going back to *their* apartment, but instead immediately headed towards Bane's country estate. The address had popped up on his cell phone a minute after Bane had left. He hadn't given Bane his number so it was a little creepy—okay, a *lot* creepy that Bane knew it.

"It will be *our* apartment, just a little later than we'd hoped," Nick said.

"I can't believe that even your father would stoop this low! To sell his son?!" her outrage reverberated. "That's what this is, Nick! Your family *sold* you to Bane!"

"I *agreed* to be sold," he corrected her.

The truth was if she knew half of what had happened after Bane had left she would never understand why he was doing this. He feared he didn't understand it either. If he had gone back to the apartment, he would have told her everything. He would have told her how his father had promised to pay his way through art school and get some of his art dealer friends to take an interest in Nick's *undoubtedly* incredible photography after the year was up.

"It'll be over before you know it, Nick!" His father had slapped his back and grinned at him avuncularly.

Nick would have had to tell her how his brothers and father had then turned their backs on him to feverishly check for Bane's emails on their phones. Steven and Jake had already been researching Bane's companies by the time Nick had slowly turned his own back on them and headed for the door. His brothers were trying to predict which divisions they would be put in charge of and already vying over who would get the better company. If he'd been in the apartment, he definitely would have told her how his family had hardly noticed when he had gone away.

"Why did you do this, Nick? Why would you agree to anything like this?" she asked, her voice sounded choked with tears now. No longer angry, but afraid and upset for him.

He blinked. The curving, two-lane highway spooled out before him like a length of ribbon cutting through the nighted forest. As he looked at that serpentine road, he struggled to explain why he had done this.

"I couldn't let Bane destroy them. He was going to do it, Jade. There's no doubt about that," he explained.

"Nick, they *chose* how they were going to run their business. Maybe they *earned* this. But you're the *only* one really paying for it. Bane set them up at his companies to do what they love to do best!" she protested.

That was true. Nick was really getting the short end of the deal. Like always. But he still wouldn't have made a different choice.

"I did it, because I wanted to be *free*," he finally said.

"What? What do you mean? How can being a slave make you free?"

"I do this and I'm really *done* with my family. No doubt. No guilt. No looking back," he said.

"And you couldn't have done that by telling them to piss off and becoming an artist instead of Bane's *slave*?"

He could imagine her shaking a fist in the air in front of her face as she paced her apartment. Underneath the anger in her voice, he heard the overwhelming worry. *This* was how people who loved you were supposed to react. He hardly felt the miles between them even as he left the city far behind and traveled into the countryside. Vast forests surrounded cosmopolitan Winter Haven. There were only a few homes tucked deep in the woods. Bane's was one of them.

"Just think of it as an internship, Jade. That's all," he said and winced. Not even he could quite keep a straight face at the idea of this being an *internship*.

"Internship in what? Wait, don't answer that! Because you'll tell me *again* how you're not sleeping with him!" She let out a harsh exhale of air. He imagined that it puffed up her black bangs. "I thought that the worst thing that could happen tonight was that you would lose your nerve and give up on your dream to be a photographer and become a corporate vulture-like your brothers—"

"I would never do that," Nick interrupted her. He gripped the handles of his bike harder. He heard the leather gloves squeak in protest. His photography seemed more like a lifeline than ever before.

"Oh, what a relief! You'll *never* give up photography, but you *will* give up your freedom!" She was quiet for a moment before she said, almost despairingly, "Nick, I can't believe you've done this. Maybe you can undo it."

"Unless you want my father and two brothers crashing at your place *forever*, I'm pretty sure I have to do it. Besides Bane may destroy your eBay business for helping us," Nick said the last with a sardonic smile.

"Doesn't that freak you out a little bit? That the guy would go to those lengths? I mean it's crazy! Almost pathological!"

"Considering I'm crazy, too, in your mind, Bane and I should get along swimmingly," Nick reminded her.

"How can you be so calm about this? It must be shock. It's got to be shock!"

Nick watched as the moon rose up before him. It silvered the trees on either side of the road. The only sound besides Jade's voice was the roar of his bike. The vibrations from the road and the pleasant warmth of the motor flowed up his body. He was calm. More than calm. He felt at peace.

"Maybe it is shock," he answered her, surprised at his own feelings. "Or maybe now I get to live my life without guilt or what ifs."

"You mentioned this lack of guilt before and I really don't get your reasoning here."

"When I was going to leave my family before, I felt like I was letting them down," he said. "I felt selfish about going away like I was taking something from them."

"Oh please! Those three don't care—all right, I'm not going to say it. I'm not going to argue with you about it. Go on." He imagined her pulling her pink sweatshirt tighter around herself as if it were a straight jacket on her feelings about his family.

"They may not deserve what I felt, but I did feel it," Nick explained. "And now...there's no more guilt. No more worry. One year of cleaning Bane's toilets and I'm done with my family's business for good. I feel *free*, Jade. Seriously, free."

"You think Bane is going to make you clean his toilets?" she asked after a beat.

Nick laughed though it wasn't a happy laugh. "From what he said about how he views me—essentially, as a rich pretty boy who's been waited on hand and foot—my guess is that he's going to have me cleaning his toilets with my *tongue*."

Jade made a gagging noise, but then he heard another serious huff of breath. "I really hope that's the worst thing he makes you do, Nick. You've given him so much power over you."

"I didn't give him *anything*. My family did. I'm just cleaning up their mess this time," Nick corrected her.

He followed what he guessed to be a final curve of the road before his destination. He knew he was getting close from the directions he had looked up online before he left his father's office.

"Well, I'm going to come see you this weekend at Bane's place," Jade said. "I need to make sure you're okay."

"Let me ask and see if it's cool for you to come," Nick cautioned. "I don't—holy shit!"

"What? What is it?"

The screech of the motorcycle's brakes drowned out every other sound as Nick skidded to a halt in front of an iron gate wrapped with ivy. But it wasn't the gate he was looking at or the drive beyond it. It was the house.

"I've found it," Nick whispered.

"Found what?"

Nick actually laughed as he answered her, "A magnificent ruin!"

CHAPTER SEVEN
MOON SHADOW

Nick had gotten off the phone with Jade, promising to call her back as soon as possible and to let her know about the weekend visit. He'd intuited from her muttering that she planned on coming no matter what he said. And then there had been that rather formal—and *unnerving*—exchange with Bane over the intercom.

"Nicholas Fairfax," Lord Bane Dunsaney's English-tinted voice came through the speaker. "Are you ready to honor your part of the deal? One year of your life in servitude to me in exchange for the *possible* return of your family's fortunes?"

"I agree to your terms, Bane. Open the gates," Nick had responded.

The gates had then whispered open and Nick's chest had felt tight.

A year of servitude. To Bane. What have I done?

As he put up his kickstand and guided the motorcycle onto the property he told himself that he could always back out of this. But he knew that was a lie and not a very comforting one at that. Bane would destroy his family so fast that Nick's head would spin.

Maybe it won't be so bad. Maybe Bane's a real sweetheart under all that bastard. Yeah, right, and the Easter Bunny is real.

The surface of the ground changed from smooth asphalt to gravel under his feet. Though it was clear that people had been driving on and off of the property, nature still reigned supreme here. Flowers and tall grasses bloomed wherever there was a bare bit of earth. The flowers' perfume hung heavy in the night air. He felt almost lightheaded from it. The massive mansion, looming ahead of him in the moonlight, wasn't exactly a ruin. It was more the overgrown nature of the garden that gave it that appearance.

Still, what would Bane want with an old wreck like this? I love it. But him? This isn't what I expected.

He'd imagined Bane in one of those French country chateaus that was perfectly stocked with antiques that some designer had chosen. He'd believed that Bane's mansion would be as impersonal as it was fashionable. He didn't think Bane would want to take the time to do something as *frivolous* as pick out furniture for his own home. But Moon Shadow hinted that the person who owned it had to have *character*. It might even indicate the owner must have *depth*.

This is the home of a romantic. Nick then huffed. *Bane, a romantic?! Not likely.* Nick, though, *was* a romantic and he itched to get his Nikon out and take shot after shot of Moon Shadow. *But I don't have the carbon fiber tripod. A shaky camera during long exposures will kill the photos. I'll ask Jade to bring it up with her along with the cable release, wide lens, flashlight, and external flash this weekend.* He grinned as he imagined Jade rolling her eyes at the amount of things he needed, but she'd still bring them all anyways. *If Bane allows her to come.*

He was startled out of his thoughts when he saw a chink of light appear between the double front doors of the mansion. The doors were beneath an elaborate stone portico. That chink soon became a slash and then an almost blinding rectangle of light. Nick shaded his eyes from the warm, yellow glow. He blinked a few times and, finally, he could make out the figure of a tall, slender man dressed in a white suit. The man had bronze skin and a bright smile. It was *not* Bane.

"Uhm, ah, hi. My name is Nick Fairfax. I'm the *intern*," Nick explained. He winced at the use of the word "intern." It had sounded almost like a joke in his father's office, but now, he didn't want people to know that he was an indentured servant. He dreaded their reactions.

Though this guy works for Bane so maybe he's used to having young men "intern" at the house.

There was a moment of silence and Nick swore he heard a sigh come from the man, but then the man spoke in an Indian singsong accent, "Yes, yes, of course. I was told to expect you."

"Oh—oh, good. So Bane told you about—about me. Uhm, I didn't catch your name," Nick stammered.

"My name is Omar Singh, but please call me Omar, Mr. Fairfax," the man said in his pleasant accent that immediately had Nick smiling and feeling brighter just for hearing it.

"Thanks, Omar, and please call me Nick."

"I am glad that you were able to find your way here. It is not an easy route and Moon Shadow does well disguising itself as an uninhabited ruin," Omar said with a gesture at the overgrown courtyard. There was a frisson of dissatisfaction in his friendly features as if such disorder displeased him. "There is much beauty in nature, but I, personally, like it better when it is contained in neat little beds."

Nick looked over his shoulder at the sprawling wild flowers and rampant vines, which stirred in the breeze. "I don't know. The overgrown look gives this place a kind of mystique."

"Yes, it indicates a haunted house or abandoned property," Omar quipped.

Nick grinned at the other man. "You say that like it's a bad thing." The other man smiled back. Nick then patted the handlebars of his motorcycle. "I'm not sure what to do with this. Should I keep it out here or is there a garage where I can store it?"

"There is a large garage around the back that has just been constructed. I am sure there will be plenty of room for your motorcycle. We cannot let such a beautiful bike get wet. Let me show you the way." Omar stepped outside and carefully closed the doors behind him. He immediately took the lead, gesturing for Nick to follow after him.

Something made Nick look back at the house just as they were passing around the corner. He realized that one of the curtains for the nearest room had been pulled aside and someone was looking out at them. He just caught a flash of a face before the curtain was jerked shut again. A beautiful, marred face.

Bane.

Nick's stomach did a strange flip. Suddenly, he realized that being alone in this man's house was a whole different thing than being with Bane in his father's office while his father and brothers were present. He was going to be alone here with this strange man. The image of Bane's full lips writhing back from his sharp white teeth flashed through Nick's mind. He shivered. Anything could happen. Anything at all.

But one look at Omar's back and he felt slightly comforted. Though he had little reason to think it yet, he already felt as if Omar wouldn't let anything bad happen.

"I hope that the drive here was not too stressful," Omar said. He laced his long fingers together at the base of his spine and slowed his gait so that Nick could keep pace with him while pushing the heavy bike.

"Not at all. I love riding at night. It's peaceful," Nick answered and silence fell again. Deciding that it was foolish to beat around the bush and wanting some intel before he saw Bane, Nick asked, "Did Bane tell you *why* I'm here?"

A flash of displeasure, almost pain, crossed Omar's handsome features. He nodded. "He did."

Nick decided to take the bull by the horns and asked, "Am I the first *intern* to work here? Or does Bane do this a lot?"

Omar let out a hiss of air between his teeth. "No, you are the *first* and I sincerely hope the *last*. Not that Moon Shadow could not use a youthful presence, but...well, it is as it is."

Nick read a lot into that statement and asked, "You aren't so keen on the deal that we've made then?"

Omar didn't answer. They stopped outside a garage that looked very new and modern yet still somehow went with Moon Shadow. It was a six car garage. Four of the large doors were shut and two were open. Through one of the open doors he caught sight of the chrome gleam of a Mercedes' bumper. Omar gestured for him to leave the motorcycle in the adjoining empty area.

"I will endeavor to make sure that your time here is as pleasant as possible," Omar answered, which wasn't an answer at all.

"I appreciate that." Nick rolled the motorcycle into the garage and brought down the kickstand. He hung his helmet on the handlebars and then unclipped the saddlebags. He slung them over his right shoulder. He paused and met Omar's gaze steadily. "Despite what Bane might have told you, I'm not afraid of hard work. I'm happy to be of use in any way that I can be. I want to make sure that Bane honors his part of the deal with my father and brothers."

Omar nodded, but his unhappy expression grew rather than lessened as if Nick's willingness to work hard made it all the worse. "There is no shortage of work to be done here."

"Then I take it that he wants me to help with the house and the garden?"

Nick brightened at the thought of bringing the house back to life and he would have plenty of opportunities to take pictures of it in its current dilapidated state and then after when it was redone. He did feel a twinge of pain though at the thought that he would be destroying what nature had wrought so beautifully. But the grounds really weren't livable the way they were. He would have to bring some order to that chaos.

Question is: am I the man for the job?

Every houseplant he'd ever had he had killed. Even cut flowers seemed to die faster with him around. He would under-water plants or over-water them. He would give them too much sunlight or too little sunlight. He hoped that this job didn't require actual knowledge or a green thumb, because he had neither. Hopefully, there would be a lot of weeding, raking and cutting to do. Those things he could be trusted with. Anything else and he would need close supervision.

Omar's gaze became shadowed. "He wishes to tell you himself what his plans are for you."

Nick felt a slight tremor of unease at that. "Oh, well, I guess he has a flair for the dramatic. So we'll play it his way."

Omar nodded slightly. "Let us go inside. Bane has asked that I bring you to him right away. After you have spoken with him, I will take you to your bedroom. And if you are hungry, I can have a tray made up for you."

Nick stomach gurgled at that moment. "Food sounds great."

"I will endeavor to make something that will satisfy," Omar said.

They walked back towards the front doors. With every step, Nick's apprehension began to grow again. Omar made no more conversation. He seemed troubled and Nick guessed that he wasn't sure what to say.

Did Bane tell him how my family is awful and I deserve this? Is he wondering why Bane chose to offer us this opportunity, instead of just destroying us and moving on anyways? Does he think that I'm going to be sleeping with Bane? Nick let out a soft huff. *Who wouldn't think I'm going to be sleeping with Bane?*

With these unpleasant thoughts running through his head, Nick decided that he needed to hear someone else's voice other than his own. "How long have you worked for Bane, Omar?"

"Oh, my family has cared for his for over a hundred years," Omar answered.

"Really?" Nick wondered if this family connection is what caused a nice man like Omar to stay with the moody, irascible, intern-hiring Bane.

Omar nodded. "We first took care of his family in India then we accompanied him back to England and finally here to the United States."

"So your father and mother worked for him and your grandparents, too?"

"It is more than *work*. It is a *calling*."

Nick blinked. The way that Omar said "calling" made it almost sound like a *spiritual* calling and not a job at all.

"Oh," was all Nick could say.

"And my grandson will replace me," Omar said with a proud smile. "He is just two now. But I am certain that he will be eager to begin as soon as he can walk."

Nick couldn't imagine anyone wanting to serve Bane, but Omar seemed so enthused about it. "Is Bane married? Does he have children?"

Omar's expression enclosed up. "No, he is alone."

Nick was struck by Omar's tone. It was so final. It was so sad. Not that Bane had shown himself to be anything but a complete bastard, but still, somehow Nick felt sorry for Bane for a second. He was sure that the feeling would pass as soon as he was speaking to the billionaire and being insulted again.

"Bane's a very successful man. I'm sure that when he has a mind to be with someone, he'll have a lot of people to choose from," Nick answered awkwardly.

"Real love does not work like that," Omar answered softly. "And that is the only thing that can save him."

Nick blinked in confusion at Omar's words. But there wasn't time for further conversation as they were before the front doors of Moon Shadow. Nick's chest tightened. His palms were sweating. He knew his knuckles were white as he clutched the edge of his saddlebags too tightly.

Omar opened the doors and again that blinding light spilled out. He motioned for Nick to precede him into the house. Nick stopped a few feet inside and waited for his eyes to adjust. He let out an awed breath when they did. The foyer was huge with a domed ceiling high above them. The floor was black and white marble laid out in a compass design. A mahogany table stood in the center of the design and a gigantic bouquet of white and red roses seemed to gush out of the vase that sat on top of it. Their subtle, sweet scent was intoxicating.

Nick slowly turned around to take in the rest of the space. The walls were covered in dark wood paneling. Watercolor paintings of birds and other wildlife were hung on the walls. These were clearly originals and very old. There were three exits from the foyer. The one straight ahead led to a magnificent staircase that stretched up into the upper recesses of the house. Then there were two doorways, one off to his right and one off to his left respectively. But Nick's inspection came to a screeching halt as the left doorway was suddenly filled with Bane's massive form.

Bane no longer wore the cloak or hood. He had on a pair of tailored black pants and a crisp white button-down shirt without a tie. The first three buttons of the shirt were undone showing a hint of his muscular chest. A curtain of dark hair fell across the marred side of his face while he had tucked the hair on the other side behind his ear. Only one of those striking Siberian blue eyes could be seen. He was staring at Nick, unblinking. Nick stumbled back in surprise.

"God! Where did you come from?" Nick gasped out.

"My study." Bane frowned in consternation at the Indian man. "I told you to bring him to me *immediately*, Omar."

Omar finished locking the doors calmly and without any rush. He was seemingly immune to the displeasure in Bane's voice and demeanor. Nick was surprised to see no less than five deadbolts and two heavy chains being slid across to lock the doors.

"Yes, sir," Omar said. "I would have brought him to you immediately, but we had to put his motorcycle away in the garage. It looks to rain this evening and it would not do to have it get wet."

Bane grunted. "I see." His gaze though was still suspicious. He was evidently fully aware of Omar's displeasure with the internship. Bane turned his gaze again on Nick. "I admit that I am very surprised that you showed up. But the hard work hasn't started yet. You haven't been asked to get those pretty hands dirty."

Nick fought not to react to that piercing gaze and taunting words. He consciously stood in a relaxed position and allowed an unconcerned smile to linger on his lips. "I intend to honor my part of the bargain. Do you intend to honor yours?"

Bane's lips twitched into a smile as if amused at Nick's boldness and answered, "I do."

Silence fell again and Nick knew that he would soon start squirming under Bane's gaze if it continued so he asked, "You wanted to talk to me?"

Bane straightened up to his full height and Nick was struck again by how massive he truly was. Yet his movements were graceful, almost feline. "Come to my study. We must discuss the rules of this house. Omar, you do not need to attend us."

Omar's expression was neutral as he said, "But, sir, perhaps I could assist—"

"No," Bane spoke with finality. The word seemed to echo in the room. Again, his gaze fixated on Nick as he said, "I will speak with Nick *alone*."

CHAPTER EIGHT
RULES

Bane led Nick down a short hall to his study. The door was ajar. Even though it was June, he had a fire going as Moon Shadow was cold inside even on the warmest of days, and especially on cool evenings such as this one. Candlelight provided the only other illumination.

Bane didn't look back at the young man as he strode over to the high-backed chair by the fire and languidly sat down. He stretched out with tigerish grace. He didn't offer Nick a seat, but instead watched the young man out of hooded eyes.

Nick stood awkwardly in the doorway. His gray eyes flickered over the room's interior as if trying to glean something about its owner from the contents. What did he make of the many worn, leather-bound books that lined the walls? Did he rightly guess that Bane found more comfort in books than in people? And what did he think of the sleek laptop that glowed softly on the desk? Did he notice that stacks of journals filled with his precise penmanship sat alongside it? Nick couldn't know that Bane still hand-wrote everything, because when he was growing up there were no such things as computers. They hadn't even been a gleam in someone's eyes.

And what did Nick think of the white Bengal tiger's pelt that adorned the floor by his feet? Its glass eyes gleamed and its teeth were bared. It looked like it was growling at the snapping fire. Nick's gaze dropped to it and a slight ripple of disgust crossed that lovely face. Clearly, he did not like hunting. How ironic that Nick didn't know this pelt had nothing to do with celebrating the destruction of this brilliant beast, but as a reminder of Bane's own past arrogance and the pain he had caused. It was also a reminder of what he truly was inside.

A beast. That is what I am. And I have brought this beautiful young man here like a beast might a prey animal to its den to be devoured.

Bane pushed away that thought. It sounded too much like how Omar would characterize the *internship*. Except his servant would go on to claim that Bane had brought Nick here *because* of his beauty and maybe even *because* of the danger it posed to his self-imposed isolation. Omar would claim that he was starved for company, but more importantly, for *love*, for the love that would supposedly free him of his curse. But Bane thought that ridiculous. Love was an illusion. A cruel one built on hormones and other base needs that soon faded.

So I will never be free. I will be cursed forever.

And he had not brought Nick here to disprove those simple statements of fact anyways. Nick's presence here was to punish the Fairfax family, nothing more than that. Nick was lovely to look at, but there were many lovely things in his home like paintings and vases. Nick though had a mouth and opinions that made him less beautiful than those silent objects.

Bane refused to acknowledge Omar's phantom voice floating through his mind and asking him why this particular punishment involved having Nick live with him for a year. Couldn't Bane have required the young man simply to work at his home during the day and leave at night? Wouldn't that have been safer for all involved? Especially when the full moon came and his curse became active? Bane had no answer to that.

"Well, what did you want to talk about? What are these rules?" Nick truculently asked, thrusting his chin out and interrupting Bane's thoughts.

"Shut the door," Bane ordered.

He did not want Omar to watch them or overhear what he had to say. He could see the Indian man in the hallway already dusting a *clean* vase with assiduous attention. If Bane had pointed out the fact that Omar had a perfect view into the study from that dusting position, this fact would have been scoffed at by his servant, but it would have been quite true nonetheless. Bane snorted softly.

Omar had already made clear to him his extreme distaste for this "internship." Bane indulged Omar, allowing his servant—*the beast's priest*, a voice whispered in his mind—to give him his views on various matters as Omar was as close to family as anyone could be to him. Omar was even, at times, very wise. But Bane would not be gainsaid in this matter with the Fairfaxes. He saw Omar shake his head and heard him sigh just before the door shut with an audible click. Nick continued to stand by the door though, not coming near him. Bane felt his chest tighten.

What do I expect? He dislikes me intensely and what I am about to do will not endear me to him. But it must be done.

Yet still the slight hurt remained. It aggravated Bane all the more and hardened his heart for what would be his next betrayal.

"May I see your phone?" Bane extended one hand towards the young man.

Nick frowned. His plush lips pulled down at the corners as he stared at Bane's well-manicured hand. "What for?"

"Please."

Bane saw how his simple use of the word "please" moved the young man. Nick's expression softened and the look of suspicion drained away. That was unexpected. He thought that Nick would be used to people being polite because of his wealth and status. Maybe Nick just hadn't expected such niceties from Bane since his language had been anything but polite since their introduction.

"I still want to know why." The young man fished out his phone from his tight jeans' back pocket and handed it over.

Bane put the phone into his top desk drawer, closed the drawer, and turned the brass key in the lock. He then placed the key in his pants pocket, well out of Nick's reach.

"What the hell?" Nick shouted. "What are you doing? Give me my phone back!"

"What is in there?" Bane gestured towards the saddlebags, ignoring the young man's squawks.

"Give me back my goddamned phone back!"

"No. What is in your saddlebags?"

They had a stare down. Nick was the first to look away. He shook his head, a kind of wild shock written large on his beautiful face.

"You're crazy, you know? I want my phone back or I'm leaving!" Nick shouted, his free hand fisting at his side while he shifted his saddlebags so that they were half-hidden behind one of his long muscular legs, as if that would keep their contents from Bane's control.

Foolish boy.

"Fine. *Leave*," Bane said with a wave of his hand.

He picked up the glass of Scotch he had abandoned when the young man had arrived. He took a large swallow, relishing the burn as it ran down his throat. It made it easier to ignore the fleeting tightness in his chest at the thought of Nick actually walking away from him right then and there. He had gotten the young man here, which was more than he had truly expected. He didn't want to lose now.

Lose? Lose what? Lose him? He means nothing. I could call and have a dozen more beautiful than him lifting their asses in the air. What does he mean compared to them? Nothing at all.

"I don't see you leaving," Bane remarked.

There was a beat of silence, but then Nick asked, his voice strained, "What about my family?"

"What *about* them?" He took another large swallow of smokey Scotch while he stared into the fire instead of at the lovely young man with the worried face opposite him.

"If I leave will you still give them the chance to get back their business?"

"No." That word fell like a stone tossed into a still pond between them.

Nick let out a soft, bitter laugh and ran a hand through his short platinum hair. "Why are you doing this? Do you want to keep me captive here? What do you *want* from me?"

There was a hint of fear in Nick's voice that caused Bane to freeze. "You are not a prisoner. But there are *rules*. My privacy is sacrosanct to me. I do not wish it *violated*." He flicked his hand towards the desk where Nick's phone was locked away. "Such gadgets make violations more likely than not. You will be allowed to use the phone—*in my presence*—once a week to call your father."

Nick's mouth opened and shut like a goldfish's. "Once a week just to call *Dad*?"

"Don't you want to keep in touch with your loving family?" Bane smirked. "Or at least make sure that they are keeping up their end of the bargain?"

"My father will do his best for you. He *likes* making money. He'll make you a ton," Nick said. "I'm not worried about that."

Money is not everything. I wonder if he will realize that before the end of the year?

"So what are you worried about?" Bane asked.

Nick ran a hand through his hair. It stuck up rather adorably. "I have friends who I have to talk to."

"You *have* to?"

"Yes," Nick ground out the word. "I *have* to talk to them. They'll worry about me if I don't check in."

"As with your father, we will arrange a time for you to contact them as well—in my presence." Bane told himself that he could have cared less about Nick disparaging him to his undoubtedly equally rich and useless friends and that this restriction was based purely on making sure the young man did not tell any *truths* he might learn while he lived here. Truths that Bane did not want to get out. But still he felt that pain at the thought of Nick's sweet pink mouth spitting out epithets with his name attached. He added, "Need I remind you that you are here to *work* not to engage in conversations with your friends?"

"Am I working 24/7?" Nick challenged. "Are you going to give me time to pee and eat? Or will I have to catch both on the run? What about sleeping? Will I be allowed to sleep?"

Bane scowled at the young man. "You will be given *appropriate* rest periods and nutrition."

"How kind of you! I am so grateful for your thoughtfulness!" Nick scoffed and tossed his handsome head.

"You will not be allowed to be lazy and self-indulgent though," Bane's voice rose slightly, aggravated at the young man's dismissive tone.

Nick let out a laugh. "I'm guessing that you don't have many friends if you think talking to them is lazy and self-indulgent."

Bane went silent for a moment at that well-aimed jab. He had few friends and none of them knew him really. How could they? How could he let them know him? Time traveled on, but he did not. He looked the same as he had when the curse first fell upon him. He was immortal so that its torment could be visited upon him for eternity. All he had to do was look into the mirror at his unchanged face with the horrible scar and he would be reminded of all he had done. He finished his drink while Nick looked surprisingly discomfited at his win against him. It was almost as if he felt badly for Bane, but then the young man hardened his expression as his eyes dropped to the locked drawer that contained his phone.

"Now, the saddlebags. What are in them?" Bane asked.

Nick's gray eyes narrowed. He would not be so trusting as he was with the phone. "My clothes. Why?"

"No computer? No camera?" Bane asked. There was the slightest flicker of concern in Nick's eyes when he said "camera" so Bane knew the young man had one. That needed to be rectified. "Give me your camera."

"You're not taking my stuff. It's *my* stuff." Nick's eyes snapped with indignation and the slightest bit of alarm.

Does the camera mean so much?

Bane stood up and walked over to the young man, crowding him against the door. He often used his larger size to intimidate others. Nick's back thumped against the door even as he tried to look unimpressed. The young man was half a head shorter than he was. But he made up for it in spunk. Nick's breathing quickened and his nostrils flared like a horse's did when it was afraid. But Nick kept his gaze steadily on Bane's face and a tight hold on his saddlebags.

Brave boy.

Bane leaned down so that his eyes were mere inches from Nick's. He could see the flecks of blue in them as well as hints of silver. He caught the young man's scent: clean and woodsy like the forest after a rain. He stopped himself from leaning down lower to nuzzle the soft flesh behind Nick's ear. But he found himself unwilling to draw all the way back either.

"You have a camera in your bags. Give it to me," Bane demanded.

"No," Nick responded just as determinedly.

"I will not have you taking pictures of me and mine—"

"It's for my art!" Nick cried. He shoved Bane back with surprising strength and sidestepped around him. Nick kept a few feet of distance between them.

Bane slowly circled the young man. The beast inside of him delighted in the nervous twitches of Nick's shoulders. Nick clearly sensed that Bane was more than he seemed but the young man didn't know—couldn't even have imagined—what Bane really was. Bane knew he should stop this, pull back and calm down, but Nick's pushing him away had set something off inside of him.

"Your art?" Bane taunted. "You are an artist? Really?"

Was Nick some kind of dilettante rich boy artist? His daddy's friends buying his prints and promptly tossing them into a dark corner once the sale was complete? But the faint memory of Bane's mother painting in the long Indian afternoons intruded on his unkind thoughts. He remembered how her eyes had come alive when she was in the middle of a painting, eager but anxious to show the finished product to him and his father. But then Bane remembered just as clearly watching the light fade out of her eyes when his father disparaged her hard work with a few dismissive words. But Nick was nothing like his mother. He wasn't a true artist. He was undoubtedly just trying to avoid the responsibility of earning a living by hiding behind his "art".

"I'm a photographer," Nick said, but there was a slight uncertainty in his eyes that wasn't there when he had talked of other things. It was almost as if this was something that was so close to his heart that he wasn't sure if he deserved that title.

"Again, you are here to *work* not engage in foolish pastimes," Bane said.

Nick let out a sharp laugh. "God, now you sound just like my father!"

Bane stiffened. "He doesn't approve of you taking pictures?"

"He doesn't approve of anything except making money! I was going there tonight to—look, it doesn't matter. But..." A wild light entered Nick's eyes. "I can't give photography up! You can't ask me to! It would be like cutting off my limbs to give up my camera. I don't expect you to understand that, but you have to believe me."

Bane stared down into that lovely face and did believe. But there was a problem. He could not risk Nick photographing him when he was changed, when the curse transformed him into a beast.

"It is impossible," Bane murmured.

Nick reached for him. It was so unexpected that Bane froze as that hand rested for a second on his shoulder before fluttering away. "I wouldn't violate your privacy! I would ask before I took a picture of anything! I could—could *document* the transformation of Moon Shadow!"

"Transformation?"

"You're planning on redoing the house, right? I could take before, during and after pictures," Nick suggested. His face was taut with emotion, more emotion than even the taking of the phone had brought.

"I…"

He could have the camera during some days, but never at night and not at all around the full moon. It could be done. I would then have a history of Moon Shadow, too. If he is any good …

"Please," Nick begged.

Those luminous gray eyes gazed up at him, pupils wide and dark like the sea and Bane found himself relenting and withdrawing himself physically from the young man. He retreated back to his chair and poured himself more Scotch with a surprisingly trembling hand. He downed half the glass and immediately wished he hadn't. Alcohol did not harden his heart. It only made him soft and lonely. He set the glass down unfinished. He would not look at Nick as he spoke.

"I will allow you to have the camera at certain times—*after your work is done*—but I must see every picture you take. You do *not* have permission to take pictures of anything you like. You must check with me first," Bane said.

Nick's shoulders relaxed. "Right. No problem. I—I go crazy when I can't use my camera."

Bane experienced another flash of memory then. Again he remembered his mother as she had sat unseeing in the mental institution after his cursed nature made itself known to her. He had lost control, transformed into the beast and killed his father right in front of her. Her easel and paints had sat in the corner of her room untouched for the rest of her life. His actions had killed her spirit just as they had killed his father's body.

"You need to give me your camera now though. I will take good care of it. If you work well, you may be allowed to take some pictures in the next few days. I am having some people come for the weekend for business. I don't believe they would wish to be photographed," Bane said. He quickly shut his lips as he was suddenly sure he would offer more to the young man if he kept talking.

Nick put his saddlebags down on the ground. He kneeled beside them and opened one of the packs. The young man's unique woodsy scent mixed with the smell of clean clothes rose up. Bane drew in a deep breath He knew Nick's scent would be in his nose all night. A wave of heat went through him. He gripped the arms of his chair and held himself still. He would not lean down and lick a stripe down the back of Nick's neck. He would not nuzzle Nick's fine platinum hair. He would not push the young man onto his back and ravage him. He would sit and do nothing else.

Nick gently, almost reverently, pulled out a camera in a black leather case. Bane knew nothing of cameras, but he was sure it was expensive, and he was suddenly sure that the worth of it to Nick had nothing to do with its price tag. Nick reluctantly held it out to Bane. For one moment, Bane imagined how they must look at that moment: Nick on his knees, arms outstretched with the camera in his hands, as if offering it as a sacrifice to his feudal lord.

Bane took the camera from Nick more harshly than he intended and the young man winced as it was handled so roughly. Bane made sure to place it carefully down on his desk.

"I will keep it safe," Bane repeated.

Nick nodded slowly.

"Do you have a computer?" Bane asked.

Shoulders sagging, Nick pulled out a laptop and handed it over as well. Bane placed it beside the camera. Nick repacked his clothes, straightening out the simple t-shirts, shorts and a few pairs of jeans. Bane frowned as he took in the casual contents. Clearly, there were no suits in the saddlebags.

"You do not have any suits or formal evening wear," Bane said more than asked.

Nick stood up. "Uhm, no. I'm a college student. Not a lot of call for formal evening wear."

"We dress for dinner here," Bane said.

"You mean like suits and stuff?" Nick's eyes widened.

"Yes," Bane answered.

"You want me to wear a suit and have dinner with you *every* night?" Nick asked slowly as if he wanted to make sure that he understood what Bane was saying.

"I do. It is expected. Do you have suits at home?" Bane asked.

"Maybe one or two. I don't know if they even fit," Nick said with a shrug. "I'm sure I have some slacks and a nice shirt or something."

"Suit coats are required. You will need them. I shall have my tailor come and—"

"You're going to have your tailor make me clothes?" Nick's eyebrows rose up into his hairline.

"I will not have you wearing ratty t-shirts and too tight jeans." Bane tipped his head to Nick's current apparel.

"My jeans are not too tight! They're perfect," Nick argued.

Bane bit back any further remarks as he found himself focusing too avidly on how the jeans encased Nick's long, muscular legs and pert ass.

"What's going to happen at these dinners?" Nick asked.

"We will *eat*."

"You want us to *talk* during these dinners, too?" Nick was really grinning at that moment.

"Only if you have something worthwhile saying. Otherwise, *silence* will be preferable," Bane retorted.

"I see."

"I do not think you do."

"And will these dinners be lit by candlelight?" Nick asked.

"I enjoy the softer light candles give." Bane frowned then, realizing he was walking straight into a trap.

Nick bit his lower lip as if stifling a laugh. "Oh, okay."

"What?" Bane snapped.

"You want us to have romantic, candlelight dinners together where we dress up in our best clothes. That doesn't sound at all *odd* for intern and employer to you?"

Bane had not intended the scenario to be romantic. Not consciously. It was how he always had dinner. The fact that he would now be sharing it with someone was irrelevant.

It might even be annoying and less pleasurable than being by himself.

"There is no *romance* between us, Mr. Fairfax. As I have made clear, I have no desire to bed you. And your constant assertions otherwise make me quite sure you wish my thoughts were different on the matter." Bane scowled at him though as there was that slight thrill of heat in his loins.

Nick's cheeks colored, but he didn't look away as he said, enunciating every word, "You've made me your indentured servant for a year. You're threatening my family with destruction. You've taken my phone, computer, and camera away from me, making me a virtual prisoner here. I can *assure* you, Bane, that I want *nothing* more than for this year to be *over* as quickly as possible."

Again there was a stare down, but this time it was Bane who looked away. It was not foolish, useless guilt that plagued him. It was not cringing from how hard and wrong those facts sounded being laid out like that. Not at all.

Bane shouted, "Omar!"

The door to the study was immediately opened, which confirmed Bane's suspicion that Omar had been listening at the keyhole the whole time.

"Yes, sir?" Omar asked.

"Take Mr. Fairfax to his room," Bane instructed curtly.

Omar nodded and reached for Nick's saddlebags. Nick fended him off. "Oh, that's okay, Omar, I've got it. No worries."

"It is not a problem at all, Nick. I am eager to show you to your room. It has a beautiful view of the rose garden out back," Omar said.

"The rose garden?" Bane straightened up, anger flaring his nostrils. That was not the room that he had instructed Omar to prepare for Nick. The young man's room was supposed to be on the side of the house overlooking the garage. "I told you to put him on the west side, Omar."

"Oh, sir, I am so sorry, but I must not have heard you. You know how my hearing is," Omar said with a shrug.

"Yes, *selective*," Bane growled. The room that Omar chose was likely one just a few doors down from his own. What was his servant thinking?

"I have already prepared the room. The other is not fit for habitation," Omar said breezily.

Bane scowled at him. "I *see*."

"You will, sir. I promise that you will." Omar bowed before leading the beautiful young man from Bane's sight.

CHAPTER NINE
A ROOM WITH A VIEW

Nick followed Omar up an impressive set of broad curving stairs to the second floor of Moon Shadow. He was awed by how huge and spacious the stairwell and hallways were. Everywhere he looked were antiques and oil paintings, tapestries and silver. They were of such high quality that they should have been in a museum, but they also had a "lived in" quality to them. They belonged here. They were meant to be used and touched instead of simply looked at behind glass.

"These things...are they..." he stopped as he wasn't quite sure what he was asking.

"They are Dunsaney heirlooms. Every single piece here is from the family's estates or things Bane has picked out himself over the years. That is what you were wanting to ask, yes?" Omar looked over his shoulder with a knowing smile.

"Yeah, I kind of was," he admitted with a laugh. "Every time that I think that Bane is this cardboard cutout villain I learn something about him that contradicts that."

Omar stopped outside of a closed oak door. His expression was pained. "What you have seen of Bane...well, he is not at his *best*."

"Is this his worst? Wait, don't answer that, because if you say 'no' I'm going to be really freaked out," Nick laughed nervously. He thought of the trick that Bane had used to get his phone from him and the fact that said phone was now locked in Bane's desk. And his camera...A black hole seemed to open in his chest for a moment at the thought of his camera being out of his hands.

Omar gave him a weak smile, which had Nick's heart tumbling into his feet and he'd been quite sure his heart couldn't fall any farther. The Indian man cleared his throat and put one hand on the door handle. "This is your room."

Omar turned the handle and pushed the door open. The ceiling fixture—an elegant chandelier shaped like an upside-down layer cake—was already turned on and cast a beautiful crystalline light over the entirety of the massive room.

Nick stepped inside and his saddlebags slipped from his shoulder and onto the highly polished wooden floor. To his left was a king-sized four-poster bed with dark blue hangings, piles of pillows and the plushest looking comforter he'd ever seen. To his right were two high-backed chairs separated by a slender-legged table. They faced a marble mantle where a crackling fire danced merrily.

The chairs looked so deep and comfortable that Nick wanted to sit down on one of them right at that moment and warm his hands by the fire. He imagined sitting there on a rainy day with his legs tucked underneath him and a blanket over his lap. There would be a book hanging loosely from one of his hands as the fire popped merrily. And just as he thought this, his imagination offered him something unexpected.

He imagined turning his head to the chair next to him and seeing Bane sitting there. Bane's hair was drawn into a ponytail at the base of his skull. It no longer shaded half of his face. It didn't need to. There was no disfiguring mark there. But it wasn't the lack of scars or the fact that he'd pictured Bane in the chair beside his that shocked Nick. It was the *expression* on Bane's face that he imagined. It was soft and tender. It was an expression that Nick was *certain* would never be aimed at him. It was love.

Bane was a bastard and he could *never* look like that. Certainly not at *Nick*. And Nick didn't *want* Bane to look that way at him. Bane was the phone-stealer and camera-taker. He was the man that took pleasure in the destruction of the Fairfax family and was enjoying the thought of bossing Nick around for a whole year. Heart hardened, Nick could now look at the chairs and not imagine himself, let alone Bane, in them at all. He doubted he would get much chance to sit down and read a book anyways. Bane would, undoubtedly, consider that the height of laziness.

"There is an adjoining bath," Omar's voice snapped him out of his thoughts. The Indian man had walked over to another oak door at the other side of the room. He opened that door, too, and switched on a light. Inside was a gorgeous bathroom tiled all in white quartz with a huge claw-footed tub and a separate glass-enclosed shower.

"Beautiful," Nick murmured, meaning it.

The whole bedroom was gorgeous and totally unexpected. He turned and headed towards the drapes that covered two sets of large windows and pulled one of them back. He saw the windows were twice as tall as he was, curved at the top, and looked out onto the garden in the back. He squinted and could see past his own reflection to the ground below.

"Is that a...*rose garden*?" he asked.

He could see what looked like a sea of rose bushes. There were just the barest traces of gravel paths between the clumps of bushes. It must have been magnificent when it had been cared for. Even now, in its overgrown state, it was impressive in a natural, wild in tooth and claw sort of way.

"Yes, Bane wishes to have it completely redone. He is very fond of roses," Omar said. He stepped over to Nick's side and looked out himself, or maybe he was just studying Nick's face in the glass.

What is he looking for? He seems so kind. Not at all like the type of person that would be around Bane.

"Is that what I'm going to be doing? Gardening?" Nick's earlier fears of killing every plant came back.

"Perhaps, though it is much too big a job for one person." Omar put his hands around his back. "How would you like to help me get Moon Shadow ready for a party of friends?"

"Bane's having *friends* over?" He couldn't quite keep the absolute disbelief out of his voice. "I thought they were just business associates. That's how Bane described them anyways."

Omar sighed. "Yes, I suppose they *are* business associates and, not exactly, *friends*."

"Well, either way, I'm sure you'll need help and I'm happy to give it. When are they coming?"

"Friday. So I'm afraid that we must be up bright and early tomorrow as we only have one day to prepare. How does 5 AM sound?"

Omar looked so hopeful and had been so friendly that Nick didn't have the heart to tell him that the only time he saw 5 AM was when he stayed awake all night. But with all the enthusiasm, he could muster, he said, "Sure."

I better get used to the early morning hours. I'm sure that Bane won't let me stay in bed until 8 AM. He would probably consider getting up that "late" lazy and entitled. Maybe it is for most working people.

"Excellent!" Omar placed his hands together in a prayer gesture and actually bowed to Nick. "Thank you so much for your future assistance!"

Nick blinked and did a little bow back himself. "I don't think you have to thank me, Omar. I'm pretty sure that helping you in any way I can is part of the *internship*." When Omar winced at that term, he added, "Not that I mind this part of it. Seriously, I'm happy to give you a hand in any way."

"You are most kind."

Afraid that Omar would bow again, Nick asked, "Why—why did you give me *this* room?"

"I do not understand." One of Omar's hands fluttered up nervously near his exquisitely knotted tie. "Do you not like it?"

"Oh, no, I like it. I *really* like it. This room is *beautiful* and it's perfectly to my tastes." Nick pointed to the neatly stacked pile of books on one of the side tables by the chairs near the fire. He could see from the titles that they were some of his favorites. One by H.P. Lovecraft, another by Robert E. Howard and a slender volume of Sherlock Holmes stories. "Did you give me the nicest room in the manor to make up for the internship?"

Omar played with his perfect tie and wouldn't quite meet Nick's eyes. "Yes...and *no*."

"What's the 'no' part?"

"If Bane was thinking properly, he would *want* you to have this room. He would know you were *meant* to have it."

"I'm pretty sure that if Bane had his way I would have been occupying a broom closet under the stairs," Nick said dryly.

Omar let out a distressed sound. "You must not judge him so harshly even if it appears he deserves it."

"You like him. There must be something good about him. Or maybe you're a saint." Nick grinned. "I'm voting saint."

"No, I am just a humble priest," he said.

Now this shocked Nick totally. He would not have thought Bane religious at all, but to have a priest on staff would indicate something quite different.

"A priest? What kind?"

"Oh, I belong to a very small sect. My village in India is the only one that follows the old ways now," Omar explained and pinked.

"And they don't mind their priest being half a world away?" Nick's eyebrows rose up.

Omar gave him a smile. "You must not concern yourself. I am exactly where fate has ruled I should be."

"I admire that kind of certainty," Nick said.

"You will find your own. I can see it in your eyes." Omar smiled at him in such a confident manner that Nick could almost believe that even though his life was a mess right now he would come out the other side of it and know exactly what to do.

"Is Bane...a follower of your religion?"

Omar almost looked *alarmed* at that question and Nick wondered if this was part of the "privacy" that Bane didn't want to be violated. Maybe Bane was into some weird, freaky cult which sacrificed animals or forced followers to dance naked under the moon. The last image had him biting his inner cheek to stop from grinning. He knew that this was all nonsense, because Omar did not seem the type to be a part of anything like that. Still, the Indian man's discomfort was severe.

"Bane is...I mean to say that he is...well..." Omar dithered.

Nick put a hand on Omar's left forearm and assured him, "It's okay, Omar. You shouldn't reveal any secrets to me. Especially not if it will get you into trouble with Bane."

Omar relaxed slightly and gave him an uncertain smile. "It is not that I wish to keep things from you but—"

"You don't have to explain. Really. It's fine," Nick said with full conviction.

Omar took in a soothing breath, smoothed down the front of his white suit and said, "I will go now and prepare a little supper for you, if that is all right."

"Of course, it is. Thank you so much."

Omar performed that bow again. Nick was so flustered that he just waved, which had Omar smiling and bowing again. After Omar had closed the door silently behind him, Nick looked around the room and let out a low breath. He looked at the chair that he'd imagined sitting in near the fire. He wanted to go over to it, but his eyes darted to the *other* chair where he'd imagined Bane perched and stayed where he was.

He tilted his head back and said to the room, "What have I gotten myself into?"

CHAPTER TEN

TIGER, TIGER BURNING BRIGHT

Bane was acutely aware of Nick's presence in Moon Shadow. The beast let him hear Nick's movements no matter where Bane was in the mansion. His study. The kitchen. The porch. And now, finally, in his bedroom down the hall from the young man.

He is just three doors away from me. That's a leap away for the beast.

Bane tried to shut out his awareness of Nick. After all, Omar had shared a home with him for decades and Omar's father had before that. He'd also had many houseguests and even *bedmates* who had laid right beside him and the beast had never focused so intently on them. But with Nick it was different. The beast simply would not obey him. The beast was *fascinated* with Nick.

He heard Omar bring the young man supper—taking ridiculous amounts of care to make it delicious and attractive in Bane's opinion—but if that made Omar feel better about the *intern* situation then so be it. He heard Nick eating the meal. The scrape of his spoon against the bottom of the soup bowl was like the banging of a gong. The drag of the knife over the plate seemed as loud as a marching band. The click of the fork as Nick placed it down, food finished, was similar to the final cymbal crash at the end of a piece of music.

A rush of *something* went through him though as he heard the young man unbuckle his saddlebags, open the drawers in the dresser and put his clothes away. Nick was preparing to stay. He would be in Bane's home and in the room that Bane had provided for him for a whole year.

Omar might have chosen that particular room, but all of Moon Shadow is mine.

Nick would live in his home. Nick would eat the food that Bane gave to him. Nick would perform the tasks he proscribed. Nick was *his*...for one year at least.

Bane tossed and turned at these thoughts. These were the beast's desires. They were basic, animalistic, and possessive. Yet they caused a hot, wild feeling to run through him that he craved more of. Bane wanted to stretch out his claws and knead the mattress. He hadn't felt this *alive* in a long time.

Bane heard the slither of Nick's clothes leaving his body and the creak of the bed as the young man laid down upon it.

He sleeps naked just like I do.

Both of them now were stripped and under the sheets. With his senses on alert, Bane felt so close to the young man that he almost believed he could stretch out one hand and run a finger down Nick's spine. Arousal prickled between his thighs and he turned onto his side, facing away from Nick, but the beast's attention was still directed fully towards the young man. In his mind's eyes, he pictured the beast standing up on the bed, ears pricked, ice blue eyes narrowed, and tail swishing.

Now another sound subsumed all others: Nick's heartbeat. The beast's tail paused in its swishing. Its ears, though still pricked, held less tension. Its eyelids slid half-way shut. The beast found the sound of Nick's heart *comforting*.

Bane thought of Poe's *The Tell-Tale Heart* as he listened to the now steady rhythm of Nick's heartbeat. But instead of being wracked by guilt over a murder by the ghostly beating of a dead heart, he was being haunted by a live one.

I have done nothing wrong in bringing Nick here. He will be treated properly. I am giving his family a second chance. One they do not deserve. That is all.

But why was he doing this at all? Why had he insisted on having Nick live with him? Why did he want the young man under his roof, eating his food, dependent upon him for safety? Those were the questions that Omar had asked him again and again in words and with looks. And he had not allowed himself to know the full answers until now.

Regret. Revenge.

Tonight was not the first time he had seen Nick Fairfax. The first time was right after he had realized what the Fairfaxes were up to in regards to taking over one of his companies. He was in downtown Winter Haven, just near Fairfax International, when he received the email confirming that Charles, Jake and Steven was trying to buy up controlling shares in one of his companies. A feral smile of anger had crossed his lips as anger bloomed in his chest. He would destroy them. He would make sure that they never had the opportunity to make another dime again. They would rue the day they had gone up against him.

But in the midst of these rage-filled thoughts, he had seen Nick directly across the street from him. He hadn't known who Nick was then. A beam of sunlight caught the young man in its embrace. Nick was *gilded* by its stunning golden light. Bane's breathing stuttered. He forgot about the email and the takeover. He forgot about destroying the Fairfaxes. The beast inside of him went perfectly still, too. Both of them had been *transfixed* by Nick.

The young man turned his head and smiled up at the sun in sheer pleasure at the beauty of the day. Bane's heart slammed against the interior of his chest and he started to walk towards Nick. Though the scar on his face usually made him *shy* about meeting people for the first time, he did not think about the disfiguring mark at all as he crossed the street. He wanted to know this young man that the sun seemed to bless.

But right at that moment, Charles Fairfax emerged from the building behind Nick. Bane's steps slowed. Charles swung an arm around Nick's shoulders. Bane stopped.

"So, son, where should we go to lunch?" Charles asked and the spell had been broken.

Bane realized then that the young man that had captured his interest in a way that no one else had was Nick Fairfax. The one person he could *never* have as no one and nothing could stop him from destroying the young man's family. Nick was undoubtedly a spoiled, thoughtless, empty-headed young man *at best* anyways. The beauty he wore on the outside had to be only skin deep. Anyone who had the Fairfax name would be that way. So what he had felt that day on the street was *nothing* more than an illusion.

Yet...

Yet Nick's beauty haunted him and he hungered to see it again. Even if it was a thin veneer it was still arresting. And then Nick had actually walked into the office at the very moment that he was celebrating his victory over the Fairfaxes. It had felt like fate had intervened and, for once, was on his side. The idea of the internship had come to him almost instantly. It seemed so perfect. He would get to punish the young man for being a Fairfax, but still admire his outer beauty.

Yet...

Yet Nick was different than he had imagined. The issue with the camera had shocked him—still shocked him—because it went against his belief that the young man was vacuous. And the beast's utter, ultra awareness of Nick was more than a little disturbing, too. The beast normally was more quiescent when there were still two weeks before the full moon. But the beast was acting as if the full moon was only a few *days* away. It was Nick's fault that this was happening.

Though why? Omar would say it is because I yearn for love. Love! What a bitter illusion that is! And to love a Fairfax? Absurd!

Yet here he was, awake in his large bed, silk sheets drifting over his bare skin, unable to forget that Nick was near. Every restless movement had silk sliding and tangling around his long, muscular limbs. It felt like hands caressing him and with his constant awareness of Nick it felt like *Nick's* hands caressing him. The beast growled low in his throat, taking over his vocal chords for a moment and Bane froze. He swallowed and forced the beast back down.

I am in control. I am a man. I am not a beast.

He closed his eyes and forced his body to go limp. He was certain that he would never fall asleep and for *hours* he didn't. But finally between one moment and the next, he slipped into a dream. He knew he was dreaming, because instead of his night-shadowed bedroom around him there was the bright green jungle of India.

Sweat trickled between his shoulder blades beneath his white linen shirt as the jungle's steamy heat embraced him. His khaki pants clung to his thighs. The exotic, sensual scent of flowers and ripe fruit filled his nostrils. The buzzing of insects teased his hearing.

India. My India.

His hunting rifle was in his hands. The gun was as familiar to him as his own limbs. He ran his fingers over the smooth wooden stock and felt the engraving of his name on a metal filigree.

It was easy to believe that the dream was reality when every one of his senses was so sharp. But this dream was one he'd had a thousand times before. It always felt incredibly real, perhaps because it was a recreation of an actual moment in his life. This was the dream of when his fate had been irrevocably changed, when he had become *cursed* and the beast had come to inhabit this body with him over one-hundred years ago during the British Raj in India. He welcomed the dream this night for it meant he would not think of Nick.

His hands were slick on the rifle's barrel. Night was coming, but the air was still hot as an oven. He and his faithful servant, Tarun, were biding their time. They were hiding in the tall grass near a watering hole to catch a white Bengal tiger that the local people claimed was the *spirit* of all tigers. They had seeded the ground with bird lime—a concoction of mustard oil and latex, which the tiger would undoubtedly lick. It would stick to the tiger's face. In order to rid itself of the sticky stuff the tiger would rub its face with dirt and leaves, blinding itself, making it easier to kill.

"It will come soon, sahib," Tarun whispered. "Night is falling fast."

"I wonder if this magic tiger is bulletproof." Bane gave him a grin.

"Jalal is a villager, sahib. He knows nothing. Tiger spirit indeed! So foolish!" Tarun shook his head in disgust.

Tarun was referring to an argument Bane had had with a local villager, Jalal.

"You must not hunt this tiger," Jalal had said when Bane revealed his plan to track the beast. Jalal was also a servant of the Dunsaney family, but unlike Tarun, he had been with Bane only a short time so Bane did not know him well. Bane remembered how his nut-brown face, worn with the lines of years and hard labor, had looked so fiercely at him. There was none of the meekness of most servants in this man.

"Why not? It will be a fine trophy," Bane pointed out.

Jalal's chin lifted and he looked noble as he proclaimed, "This tiger is *not* for hunting. It is the spirit of *all* tigers. It *must* not be killed or all tigers will be harmed."

"That's superstitious nonsense!" Bane shook his head with amusement. He turned to his other servant, "Tarun, do you believe this? Is the tiger we track a *spirit* of some sort?"

Tarun had been with him since he was a boy and Bane trusted the man implicitly. Tarun's full mouth pursed as he looked with distaste at Jalal. "It is superstitious nonsense, sahib. Do not listen to him. He comes from a village in this valley. It is cut off from the world. Everything is *magical* to them."

"You do not know everything because you come from the city!" Jalal shot back. "You have lost much by leaving the land behind." He switched back to speaking to Bane, pleading with him, his dark eyes luminous with the desire to make Bane understand. "To hunt this tiger is bad, but to do so with anger in your heart is *worse*. If you succeed, you will be *cursed*. I know that your heart aches now—"

"Enough!" Bane snapped. His face flushed an angry crimson under his tan. His heart thundered in his chest. Did even the servants know of his transgressions? And how he had been abandoned despite the lengths he had gone to? Of course, they knew. Servants *always* knew. But to say something to him? *Unforgivable!* Tarun looked murderously at Jalal. Bane pointed a finger in Jalal's face. His voice was low, "You will go with the others back to the estate. When I return, I will determine whether you still have a place in my household any longer."

"Since you are intent on hunting this tiger, sahib, I cannot remain with you." Jalal pressed his hands together in front of him and bowed. "For your sake, I hope you do not succeed in this hunt."

And before Bane had been able to respond, Jalal had melted into the forest. Now, with sweat running down his face, stinging his eyes, Bane scoffed at the man's words. Even though he knew this was a dream, he always seemed to forget that Jalal was right. If only he had only listened to the man back then things would be so different! But he had not. And there was no changing the past.

Bane heard the softest sound of a tongue lapping water. His head jerked up. The beast was there! He peered through the grass towards the watering hole. The white Bengal tiger was magnificent. Its coat was the snowiest white with onyx stripes. It was huge. Even down on all fours, it was tall enough for its whiskers to reach his shoulders. The length of its body was one and a half times his height. Its paws were the size of his head. It was the most incredible beast he had ever seen. And it would be his kill.

He raised the rifle to his shoulder. He had a clear shot and...

The dream changed.

It had never done that before.

No longer was it the white Bengal tiger at the pool. It was *Nick*.

The young man was naked. His beautiful sculpted body was covered in sweat. There were streaks of mud on his long legs. There was a cut on his right cheek that had Bane growling low in the back of his throat at the thought of someone hurting the young man. The cut had likely come from running through the jungle, but the sight of blood on that fair skin caused his heart to clench. At first, he didn't know why he felt this way. It was merely a scratch. But nothing so beautiful should be marred. And Nick was *his* to protect. No one and nothing should hurt him. He was under Bane's control and, therefore, under his *protection*.

Bane went to lower his rifle, but he realized he was no longer carrying it. He no longer *could* carry it. He was the tiger. He was the beast. And he had sighted his prey. His Nick.

Nick dipped one cupped hand into the water and brought it up to his pink lips. He drank the water down greedily. Nick dipped his hand into the pool again, but this time, instead of raising it to his mouth the water dribbled off of his palm. His head jerked up and he scanned the long grass where Bane was hiding. Nick let out a gasp and his eyes grew huge when he spotted Bane.

Bane had involuntarily stepped out of the grass and into the open ground by the pool. The look on Nick's face was terror mixed with admiration. The young man met his gaze and he saw Nick's nostrils flare.

You are mine, Nick. Do not even think of running from me. I shall chase you down and make you regret it.

Nick, though, clearly had other ideas. Bane knew the moment Nick's limbs tensed with the intention of springing up and dashing off into the trees. He lunged before Nick had the chance to get halfway up from his haunches.

Nick let out a strangled yell as Bane—in one single leap—had pinned him on his back on the fragrant jungle floor.

Nick was naked and he squirmed beneath Bane's monstrous tiger form. Arousal flooded Bane and he roared, which had Nick going utterly still beneath him. The entire jungle went still at the cry of the singular predator that Bane was.

The young man's breathing came in frantic gasps as Bane leaned down and licked the column of the young man's pale throat. He tasted the salt of Nick's sweat and beneath that the indescribable taste of Nick himself. Male, musky and yet almost sweet. His mouth watered and he let his long, pink tongue slither out and lap up the pool of sweat that had formed in the hollow of Nick's throat. The young man moaned in fear and pleasure. Since this was a dream and not real life he had no fear of harming Nick. He could *indulge*.

Bane's tongue continued its journey down Nick's chest. He tasted the pretty pink nipples that beaded into tight nubs after two licks. Then he had Nick's stomach muscles jumping as his tongue traced the hills and valleys of the muscles there. Nick drew in a sharp breath and did not let it out as Bane's tiger tongue went *lower* still to the treasure trail of hair leading down to his pretty cock.

The young man's cock was not engorged with blood. It was limp, flaccid. At least it was until his tongue ran along its length and then it plumped gorgeously. Nick bucked and looked down at where a tiger was so near his most delicate organ. The young man's horror and fear though soon became tinted with a desperate desire as Bane licked his cock again and again. That rough yet agile tongue curled all around the width of Nick's rose-colored cock, which rapidly became harder and more eager, dripping with arousal. Nick's precum bathed Bane's mouth and the earthy taste had him growling with such hunger that Bane saw black spots. Nick tensed, but then Bane was licking him again and the fear was clearly overwhelmed by *pleasure*.

Seemingly against Nick's will, the young man's hips rose from the ground towards the tiger's fierce mouth. Nick shivered as the length of his cock ran along the sharp point of one of Bane's fangs. Bane realized he wanted to close his mouth over that sweet organ, but in his tiger form he would harm Nick.

Unlike in the real world where changing between tiger and man was fraught with difficulty, he shifted effortlessly. The paws on either side of Nick's quivering thighs changed to arms and hands. His tigerish snout was gone and his human face was there once more. The young man's cock was still in his mouth, which was now free of dangerous fangs. His torso and legs had totally transformed as well. He was naked and erect. His penis leaked precum onto the already moist and fertile ground.

Nick caught sight of him as a man and there was a strange look in his eyes. Almost *more* fear than when Bane had appeared before him in the guise of a tiger. Clearly, this was Bane's guilty conscience pricking him and he tried to shake it away and direct the dream in the direction that he wanted it to go, but it would not obey. Instead, the young man tried to scramble backwards, but Bane lightly grazed Nick's cock with his teeth and Nick froze once more.

You're mine. You'll stay mine whether I am a beast or a man. Do you understand? I will pleasure you. You will submit.

Though these statements were only thoughts, Nick reacted as if he had heard him and didn't try to escape again. The young man trembled beneath him as he grasped Nick's hips. His fingers curled around Nick's powerful ass muscles while he relaxed his throat and slowly—oh, so slowly—sank down on the young man's cock. He only stopped when his lower lip brushed the top of Nick's balls. The young man was panting and staring at him with wide, shocky eyes. Nick's pink lips were parted. A sheen of sweat glistened on his lithe body as he shifted with need.

Many people thought that the one receiving the blowjob was the one in control. Depending on how it was done that could be true. But Bane knew that the one *giving* it, if they were strong, could make the receiver's control seem like a paltry wisp of cloud. Nick's expression told him that the young man did not feel in control at all. Bane grinned around the hard, hot cock in his mouth.

He kept his eyes on Nick's face as he sucked on the young man's cock like it was a straw. Nick's head fell back against the jungle floor again and he let out a gasp. His hips strove to ride up, but Bane kept them flat against the ground as he drew up and down on Nick's cock. He kept up the suction as he drew off, letting his tongue swirl over the head of Nick's cock. Precum gushed into his mouth and he eagerly swallowed it down.

Nick's hands beat a tattoo on the ground in frustration as Bane's mouth lingered on the head of his cock. He barely rasped his teeth against the sensitive skin and Nick was still again but let out a sob of frustration. The young man wanted release. *Needed* release.

Will I give it to him?

Bane trailed his tongue over the slit and he was rewarded with more of the young man's precum. He could tell that Nick was on the edge and that was where Bane intended to keep him for as long as possible.

Bane's own cock ached. It felt like a heavy iron bar between his thighs. Keeping one hand on Nick's hip, he let the other slide down between his own thighs. He grasped his cock and stroked himself. That ache increased. His balls drew up tight against his body. He stroked himself in time to his sucking on Nick's cock.

The feeling of Nick's cock straining inside of his throat was mirrored by the feeling of his own cock plumping in his hands. He stroked himself almost viciously, twisting his wrist as he drew up. His tongue pushed against the prominent vein on the underside of Nick's cock as he sank back down onto it. With only one hand holding Nick's hips against the forest floor, the young man was able to lift his hips up and his cock sank deeper into Bane's throat. Bane swallowed around it, his throat muscles closing in on Nick's shaft, and the young man cried out in abandon.

A quick glance up at Nick's face showed that he was on the final cusp of that wave before his orgasm would crest and break over them both. Bane wanted them to cum together. He drew his thumb over the head of his own cock, spreading his slit, causing a sharp, almost electrical ping to arc down his shaft and into his balls. He was ready. He would cum the moment that he felt the splash of Nick's semen on his tongue.

He sank down once more fully onto Nick's cock. He sucked hard and long, but just as Nick was about to cum, he gripped the base of the young man's cock and *squeezed*. That stopped Nick from cumming. He had to keep up the pressure though for Nick was right there at the very edge. Nick's fingers left the earth and dug into Bane's hair. This was the first time he had voluntarily touched Bane and Bane let out a growl of approval around the young man's cock. This vibration nearly had Nick screaming.

"Please!" Nick's voice rose up for the first time, raw with need. His eyes were rolling back into his head. "Bane! *Please!*"

Bane's eyes fluttered shut. Hearing Nick *beg*. Hearing Nick say his *name*. This was what he needed. He released his hold on Nick's cock and felt it swell one last time in his mouth before that first hot gush of semen coated his tongue and the back of his throat. He drank down most of the young man's seed before pulling off and letting a few spurts hit his lips and chin. He licked some of the drops of creamy liquid up and wiped the rest away. Part of him wanted Nick to lick it off, but the young man looked to be too much in a haze. Bane, on the other hand, was still tight as a drum with arousal. He had not cum. He was holding back. The beast inside of him wanted to mark Nick, even if this was just a dream.

He straddled Nick's hips. The young man's head was lolling to the side. Nick's eyes were halfway closed and his gaze was distant from being spent. But when he felt Bane move, Nick's eyes focused in on him. Tension filled that limp, spent body. Nick's gray eyes widened and his breathing sped up. Bane found himself reach and cup Nick's face before making a soft, soothing sound. The tension slowly drained out of the young man.

With his gaze locked on Nick's, he grasped one of the young man's hands and slowly drew it to his cock. Bane's cock was so hard that it curled up towards his heavily muscled stomach. He held Nick's hand an inch away from his hard member and waited to see what Nick would do. It was his dream and yet Nick seemed as willful and untamed as he did in real life. Bane grunted in pleasure as, after a long moment, Nick's hand curled around his cock.

Bane's eyes hooded as Nick slowly stroked up and down his length. He was at the tipping point. One more stroke and he would cum all over Nick's beautiful body. His scent would be on Nick's skin. Nick stroked him firmly and Bane fell forward, catching himself at the last minute with his hands on either side of Nick's head, as he came. His face was inches from Nick's. So close. So very close.

As spurt after spurt of his cum painted pearlescent trails over Nick's body, his head dropped down farther. They were breathing in each other's air. As the last shuddering gush of cum left him, his lips descended onto Nick's. It was the barest brush of mouths, but somehow it was more thrilling than it had any right to be.

Bane was about to deepen the kiss, but when he moved to do so, Nick was no longer beneath him. He was alone in the jungle once more. He had paws instead of arms again. He glanced at himself in the pool's reflection and saw a tiger staring back at him. He was the beast once more and he was alone. He let out a roar of sorrow, of loneliness. He sprang into the leafy vastness of the jungles in India that he could only see in dreams intent on forgetting the past and his present.

CHAPTER ELEVEN
BREAKFAST IN BED

Nick woke up to the sound of Omar's cheery greeting, "Good morning, Nick!"

Then the Indian man yanked open the heavy brocade curtains and it seemed to Nick that there was *nothing* good about this morning. Nick groaned and pulled the blankets over his head to protect himself from the faint, but damnable light of the rising sun.

His head was foggy with sleep. He'd had the strangest dreams all night and still felt them clinging to his mind like sticky cobwebs. His face immediately reddened as he remembered one of them that involved a giant tiger that transformed into Bane sucking him off. That one had ended just as he and Bane had begun to kiss, which had felt far more intimate than the blow job. He ran a hand down his bare belly and chest. He felt some dry remnants of ejaculate and he quickly—and hopefully surreptitiously—wiped away the evidence of it.

Oh, God, I can't believe I'm dreaming about that bastard. Though he had a great mouth. He'd be so pissed if he knew I dreamed he went down on me though.

"This is 5 am, isn't it?" Nick muttered to Omar as he peeked out from under the covers. "It didn't sound so very early last night."

"Yes, but who can sleep when it is such a *beautiful* day!" Omar answered briskly as he tied the curtains back.

Omar then brought a silver breakfast tray over to Nick from the side table. Nick tried bringing the comforter down, but his eyes immediately watered as it seemed frighteningly bright outside. The sky was a peerless blue. He could actually hear birdsong. He smelled the freshness of grass and blooming flowers. He pulled the blankets farther over his head. Omar pulled them down.

"You cannot eat under the covers." Omar lifted off the domed lid on the tray and the heavenly scent of eggs, bacon and toast wafted out.

Nick sat up, the covers tumbling fully off of his head, and Omar placed the tray over his legs. "Thank you, Omar. Really, you didn't have to do all this. I could have come downstairs and made toast."

"Nonsense. Breakfast is a very important meal. It will give you strength for the rest of the day."

Nick's eyebrow rose up. "Why do I think you mean more than simply *physical* strength?"

"Bane is already up and in a foul mood, I'm afraid. We will have to get to work quickly. My *selective* hearing with him only goes so far," Omar cautioned.

"So you admit that you do have selective hearing then?" Nick let out a laugh.

"Sometimes it is best to only hear certain things and not others with Bane," Omar answered. "But sometimes I must carry out his instructions to the letter."

"Like waking me up at the crack of dawn?"

"I have been up since 4," Omar said a grin.

"You're a morning person. Chirpy and aggravating to all of us who are night owls."

Omar just laughed in response.

Nick scrubbed his face. His eyes felt filled with sand. He hadn't slept well, other than the tiger/Bane dream, he'd tossed and turned for hours in the comfortable bed. The bed looked old, but it was sturdy and it had one of those ultra-modern foam mattresses so he should have fallen asleep right away. But without something to distract him from the stresses of the day—*like my phone*—Nick hadn't been able to shut off his mind. Instead, he had gone over and over every single thing that had happened.

Groggily, Nick looked down at the plate of food, but he perked up as he caught the heavenly scent of rich coffee in the individual-sized press pot. "This really looks amazing. Thank you again. Last night's dinner was awesome and now this? Bane thinks this whole experience is a punishment, but it feels more like being in a resort with this delicious food and breakfast in bed."

Omar flashed him another smile. "I am glad to be of service."

Nick quickly took a bite of eggs, moaned in pleasure, and wolfed down half the plate without breathing. The creaminess of the eggs and the sharp salt of the bacon had his mouth watering for the next taste. The sweetness of what suspiciously looked like homemade jam on the toast was the perfect accompaniment to the saltiness of the eggs and bacon.

"I can't believe how good this tastes. You're a fantastic cook!"

"I am so glad to see someone enjoying it."

"Bane not eating breakfast today?"

Omar sighed. "No. He just picked at it."

"He's probably just upset that you're being kind to me," Nick guessed with a wince. "Maybe you should let me fend for myself. I can make a pretty mean mac and cheese."

Omar shook his head and cut the air with his hands. "No! Please you must let me take—take care of you."

"You're trying to make up for the *internship*, aren't you? But, Omar, this isn't your fault," Nick said.

"It is truly my pleasure to make you comfortable here and to have you look upon Moon Shadow as your home," Omar said firmly.

"I don't think Bane wants me to think of this place as *home*."

Omar took in a deep breath and laced his fingers behind his lower back. "Bane is a *complicated* man, but he is a *good* man."

"He hides the latter part pretty darn good." Nick grinned.

Omar's answering smile was weak. "I know it must seem that way to you. No, not *seem*. That is not accurate. He has *been* that way with you. Truthfully, he has not been his best in some time. I am hoping he will *remember* what it is to be the good person I know he can be with you here."

Nick carefully put his fork down next to the plate. "I highly doubt that I'm the man you're looking for if you think I'm capable of pulling Bane out of his—ah, shell, or whatever."

"Why do you say that?"

"I just want to get through this year and then escape and start my own life. I've been holding back for a long time. I'm not here to do anything, but help my family get out of their financial hole," Nick explained. "I'm *not* here to help Bane. Maybe he's a good guy deep down, but...I'm not here for him."

Nick winced a bit at how cold that sounded. But then he shrugged it off. He liked Omar and wanted to help him. Bane was another matter altogether. The man was a right asshole and no amount of nicey-nice was going to change that.

Besides, there's no way I could reach the guy's heart even if I wanted to. His face looks like he smells something bad when he sees me.

"Sometimes Fate has other plans for us than we intend," Omar said, not seeming offended by Nick's answer at all.

"I promise to try my best not to bring out the worst in him, but that's all I can promise," Nick told him.

"That is all one could ask of you."

"I just have to keep things as simple as I can."

"Yes, yes, of course." Omar paused and then said, "I should tell you what your tasks are for today. Bane wishes you to clean the bedrooms and adjoining bathrooms on this floor."

Nick bit his inner cheek to stop from laughing. When he heard the word "bathrooms" he thought of the toilets that he'd told Jade he'd be cleaning with his tongue. It appeared like he was right. He nodded.

"I can do that," he said.

"Good, I was certain you would be more than capable. I will help you with the first one and you will see how it should be done," Omar said.

Now that his eyes were not watering, he could look past Omar and out the window. Even from his bed he could see the rose garden. Red, white, pink, purple, and yellow roses bloomed in profusion everywhere. It was an ocean of roses. He hoped that Bane would let him spend some time outside today. It was going to be a beautiful day.

If only I had my camera. His jaw clenched as he remembered that it was locked away somewhere. *Bane better not damage it.*

"Also, Bane has arranged for his tailor, Mr. Fioretti, to come this afternoon to take your measurements," Omar said.

"He's serious about the formal dinners, isn't he?" Nick had forgotten that part of his conversation with Bane. He really wasn't sure what he made of the dinner arrangement. Sitting opposite Bane in an uncomfortable suit with candles glowing and Bane glowering at him wasn't his idea of a good time.

Maybe it will go so badly after the first night that he'll give it up. I'm sure he'll have to go into town, too. Maybe I'll hardly see him. Right. Sure. Just keep telling myself that.

"He is rather old-world," Omar said noncommittally. "Also, I understand that your father will be sending some of your things over today. I will be on the lookout for them."

"Yeah, I packed pretty light. Can't fit much in my saddlebags."

"And you had very little time to prepare as well." Omar's head tilted to the side.

"That's not exactly true. I already was planning to stay at my friend Jade's so I was already packed."

"Does she live in another city?" Omar's forehead furrowed.

"Oh, no, she lives in Winter Haven," Nick explained. Seeing the perplexed look on Omar's face, he felt the need to explain.

"I went to my father's office last night to tell him that I was leaving."

Omar's brows puckered. "Leaving?"

"Leaving the family. That's the choice my father gave me, you see. Either give up my photography and join the family business of making money and ruining lives or leave the family with nothing. I chose door number two," Nick said.

Omar regarded him quietly. "Surely your father would have relented. A child should be allowed to follow where his talents lead."

Nick swallowed the last of his coffee and shrugged, covering up the surprising stab of pain at Omar's honest bewilderment about his father's actions. "Things don't work that way in the Fairfax family. You're either with us or against us. There's nothing in between."

Omar's forehead furrowed even as the perplexed expression remained. "Yet you came *here*. You are sacrificing a year of your life for them."

Nick gave him a pained smile. "It's not exactly as selfless as it seems. I feel *guilty* about leaving my family. It seems like a selfish thing to follow my own dreams. And if I left them in this bad spot while going off on my own I wouldn't feel right about it. So here I am. I do this and then I'm free of any guilt and any burden of staying with them forever after."

"I think you give yourself too little credit for the sacrifice you are making. You are acting honorably for your family even if they—and forgive me, I may be wrong in this—would not do the same for you," Omar said.

"They probably wouldn't." Nick shook his head. "They *definitely* wouldn't. But they're more...cold blooded, I guess, is the way to put it. They probably think I'm weak for doing this. Thankfully for them, I don't agree."

"I am glad that you are away from them then," Omar said. His expression was still so disturbed that Nick felt a wash of warmth and liking for the man. Omar was clearly a gentle soul.

"Me, too, and I'm never going back. What about your kids, Omar? What are they like?" Nick steered the conversation away from his own family.

"I have a son and daughter." Omar immediately warmed to the subject. "My daughter is an engineer and my son is a doctor."

"Wow! You must be so proud," Nick said.

"I am exceedingly proud. My grandson is my daughter's child," Omar explained. "Bane ensured that my children went to the best schools in the world. They are able to pursue the dreams that are in their souls. My grandson is like me. He wishes to be here. My granddaughter is a poet. Her faculty with words is great. I am excited to see them grow into their gifts"

Nick couldn't imagine even the taciturn Bane being immune to Omar's goodness. Who wouldn't want to help the Indian man? He imagined that Omar's children were just as kind and worthy as he was. Nick couldn't even envision having family support him like that.

"I have pictures of them. I will show you later," Omar said with enthusiasm.

"I'd like that. I'm glad Bane has been good to you and yours."

"As I said, he is a good man," Omar answered.

"I can tell you think so," Nick said noncommittally.

"Finish your breakfast and when you are done, come find me downstairs. I will be in the kitchen," Omar said.

"Be there real quick," Nick promised.

Omar smiled and left him to his thoughts.

It wasn't long before Nick strode out of his room, showered and dressed with the breakfast tray in his arms, and found the carved oak staircase that led down to the first floor. Moon Shadow was large, but it was laid out simply enough that he could easily find his way. He was on the top of the steps when he heard voices raised below. He slowed his pace.

He realized that one of the front doors was open and there was a wash of sunlight flooding the foyer. He saw that that one of the voices was Omar's. He was speaking to a man on the front step. The man was dressed in dusty boots, faded jeans and a flannel shirt. He looked to be about fifty-years-old. His face was flushed with anger, but also it looked to be the face of a heavy drinker to Nick from the veins and mottling around his nose.

"You tell him what I've said!" The man was sticking a finger at Omar's chest. His tone was belligerent and spittle flecked his lips. "Every time he comes around here more of our livestock go missing. When we find what's left of them, they're in little pieces. They've been mauled and eaten by some large animal."

"We have no large animals here, sir," Omar's voice went high in protest.

"It *only* happens when Bane's here. Never when he's not. We're sure that he's brought some animal from foreign parts here!" The man's gaze raked Omar up and down as if the Indian man, too, were some kind of animal from foreign parts.

Nick's hands tightened around the tray as he raced down the stairs to Omar's side.

"What's the problem here?" he asked sharply.

Omar half-turned in surprise as Nick appeared at his elbow. "It is all right, Nick. Mr. Brennan was just going away."

Another pudgy finger was stuck in Omar's face. "You tell Bane that we're setting traps and waiting with guns. If his *pet* comes near our farms again, we'll be sending it back to him in pieces!"

"Hey! Don't use that tone with Omar! You have no right—"

Nick was interrupted by Bane's dark voice, "Mr. Brennan, *you* have been told before not to *grace* my property with your presence. If you do so again it is *you* who will be meeting the wrong end of a gun."

Nick spun around. Bane was standing half in the shadows of the hallway, looking like some hulking beast in the half-light. He had a hunting rifle in one hand, but that seemed less dangerous than the rest of him.

Mr. Brennan turned so red then that his skin looked purple. "You've been warned, Bane! Don't say you haven't been!"

"Shut the door, Omar," Bane said simply.

Omar closed the door in Mr. Brennan's face. Nick could see from the shadows underneath the door that the farmer hesitated for long moments before he finally left the doorstep and lumbered away. Nick's shoulders slumped in relief.

"Who *is* that guy? And what wild animal is he talking about?" Nick asked.

"There *is* no animal. It is all in Mr. Brennan's drink-addled imagination," Bane answered coolly. "Aren't you supposed to be working? I am not saving your family just to have you hanging about in my hallway."

"I was trying to help. I wasn't being lazy!" Nick snapped, taken aback by Bane's dark mood being aimed at him.

Bane stared at him. His face was in shadows so that Nick couldn't read his expression. The edge of the handprint burn was visible. It looked raw and red this morning. An angry color. Almost a fresh color. Nick felt a sympathetic prickling along his own skin.

"He was indeed trying to help, sir," Omar said softly.

Bane shook his head. His long hair falling loose around his shoulders. "We do not *need* his help against the Brennans of the world. I just need him to do as he is told."

And with that, Bane strode away, leaving Nick gritting his teeth and thinking it was going to be a very long year.

CHAPTER TWELVE
PHOTOGRAPHS IN THE ATTIC

Bane sat in his study with the door open. He was pretending to do business. He had his laptop on, but he hadn't touched it in so long that it was about to go into sleep mode. He was far more aware of the glass of Scotch. It wasn't his first glass. It wasn't even his second. Alcohol didn't affect him like it did humans. He didn't get drunk and sloppy. It just dulled his keen senses a little bit and today he needed that little bit badly. He needed it because the beast's uber-awareness of Nick had grown even worse since last night.

Whenever he saw Nick now he remembered the taste of his cum, the feel of his skin, and the heat of his lips. These were things he only knew from the dream, but it didn't matter. He knew that if he were to lick a stripe down the column of Nick's throat that the taste would be the *same.*

And the beast—who had taken little interest in his human couplings before—was alive with desire for Nick. It kneaded its paws and its tail wagged eagerly from side to side whenever it saw Nick. It had drunk deeply of the young man's scent and Bane feared that its current hunger might be for *meat* instead of for *sex.*

You must stop this, he told the beast.

The beast's ears twitched, but it remained facing away from him in his mind's eye. It was tracking Nick's progress cleaning one of the bathrooms upstairs. He heard the thump, thump, thump of Nick's heart as he crouched low and then the whisk, whisk, whisk as he scrubbed the floors with a wiry brush.

It had surprised him when the young man hadn't made a fuss about doing this kind of menial labor. Bane had expected cries of disgust and a refusal to do the work. At a minimum, he had thought Nick would do a poor job, but he had not. Bane had checked one of the rooms that Nick had cleaned and he had found it spotless. Nick hadn't even asked for gloves before scrubbing the toilets though Omar had insisted on giving him some. And as if to laugh in the face of Bane's assumptions about him, Nick actually *whistled* while he worked!

It is the first day. He is likely thinking of this as a holiday from his usual life. His happiness with doing drudgery will soon fade. He will let his brat show. Any day now...

Bane's gaze snapped towards the bottom of the stairs, which he could see through the open door of his study. No one was there this time, but Omar had already tried twice before lunch to get upstairs to help Nick.

"What are you doing?" Bane had asked the Indian man the last time.

"I am going upstairs." Omar's warm brown eyes flickered away from his guiltily.

"Why?" Bane circled around the man so that he was on the second step of the stairs, blocking Omar's path

"I need something?" Omar made that sound like a question. He was a terrible liar.

"What do you need? I will get it for you." Bane tried not to let the tigerish smile out, but it flashed over his face anyways. It was an angry, triumphant smile though he wasn't sure what he had "won". Omar's determination to help Nick was almost endearing if it wasn't going directly against what Bane wanted the Indian man to do.

Omar lifted his chin up defiantly and said, "I want to see if Nick needs anything and what he would like for lunch."

"If he *needs* something he will come down and ask. He will eat whatever you see fit to prepare," Bane answered firmly.

Omar pressed his palms together as if in prayer as he explained, "I do not yet know his likes and dislikes—"

"It doesn't matter!" Bane burst out, which had the Indian man jumping. Bane lowered his voice, "It doesn't matter what he likes, Omar. Don't you understand that this is a punishment?"

Omar went very still. His dark eyes did not blink as he stared long and hard at Bane. "For who?"

"What?"

"Who are you punishing? Nick? Nick's family? *Yourself*?"

"How could this punish *me*?" Bane let out a shrill laugh.

Omar gently placed a hand on Bane's shoulder. His brown eyes were full of concern and care. "Something is different about him. I can feel it, Bane. The tiger spirit within you is reacting to Nick in a way I have never seen it behave with anyone before."

Bane jerked away from that gentle hand. His back hit the side of the stairwell. His nostrils flared as a shudder of fear ran through him. If Omar sensed it, too, then it was *not* just in Bane's imagination that the beast really was reacting to Nick differently.

"There's nothing *special* about Nick," he said, his voice a husk of its normal loudness. "Nick is—is a spoilt child. I am doing this—"

"Are you certain? Because if he is special this could mean...well, it could mean *everything*, Bane. You know what will end the curse. You know that it is—"

"*Love*?" Bane snarled the word. "*True love*? With Nick Fairfax?"

He laughed so hard that he began to cough. Omar did not laugh. He stood up straighter and crossed his arms over his chest.

"Why could you not fall in love with Nick? Even from my brief interactions with him he seems an honorable young man—"

"He is a spoilt brat!"

"He is not the only one," Omar said under his breath.

"Love—let alone *true love*—does not exist, Omar," Bane hissed. "Your ancestor knew this. She knew when she cursed me for killing the beast's body that I would be like this for all time."

Guilt and grief flashed across Omar's face. "I do not believe that, Bane. She would not have done that to you...or the spirit."

"You hope that, but I know it isn't true." Bane shook his head. "Your ancestor didn't believe in true love. And because of that I shall always be this way and your family will always be trapped, too, unless you finally agree to accept my release and leave me—"

"We will *never* leave you" Omar interrupted. "My family will continue to take care of you. Even if you do not want us. I know that you need us. The tiger spirit does as well."

"The beast needs no one and neither do I."

Bane had stalked back into his office then and drank another glass of Scotch after that. But the alcohol had done little to blunt the beast's attention to Nick. When Nick had come down for lunch—bacon, lettuce and tomato sandwiches on homemade bread with sharp cheddar cheese—the beast had focused in on Nick's voice as the young man took his meal with Omar in the kitchen.

Omar and Nick had chattered gaily with one another as if they were the best of friends. Omar was always friendly, but it was apparent to Bane that the Indian man truly enjoyed Nick's company. A surprising spike of jealousy went through him.

Bane had taken his own sandwich in his study, alone, and hardly tasted it at all. He had thought he'd have to break up the party in the kitchen to get Nick back to work. After all, worthless young men needed to be prodded to do anything, but Nick had gone upstairs after an hour. He'd even helped Omar clean up the lunch things before he went back to scrubbing toilets.

Another hour had passed and Nick's movements had become almost soothing background noise. But then Bane realized that the sounds had changed. Bane sat up in his chair and listened intently. There was a creak of a hinge, then a clunk of something heavy coming down and then the tap-tap of Nick's feet walking up steps. Bane frowned. Where was the young man going? Then he heard a dragging sound and a rusty squeal. That was when he knew where Nick was.

The attic!

Bane jumped up from his chair so quickly that it spun in a fast circle. He flew down the hallway and up the stairs to the third floor. The entrance to the attic was in the main hallway. He saw that the stairway was extended down from the trapdoor in the ceiling. Cold sweat appeared on his upper lip. His things from India were in the attic. His mother's paintings. His father's papers. But most importantly, there were photographs of *him* from one hundred years ago looking the *same* then as he did now.

He took the attic stairs two at a time. The attic had a high peaked roof and was quite airy. The floor was made up of smooth oak boards. Sunlight gushed onto the floor from the dormer windows. Dust motes danced in the sunbeams. Shrouded furniture and paintings abounded. But he had no problem finding Nick. The young man's heartbeat led him right to where Nick was: sitting on the floor before a large trunk. The trunk was open. In Nick's hands were old, black and white photos.

He's found the ones of me...

Time seemed to freeze as Bane's vision zeroed in on the photo that Nick was looking at. It was one of him standing outside the old manor house with his rifle. Nick's face was turned partially to the side and he saw the furrowed brow and faint frown. Nick was clearly thinking that this person in the photo looked a lot like Bane. Bane must have made some sound, because Nick's head whipped around towards him.

"Bane! Damn, you scared me!" Nick gasped out.

Like on that street the first time he'd seen Nick, his heart seemed to stop as sunlight from the windows spilled down on Nick's platinum hair. The young man's hair was curling becomingly around his face, which was damp with perspiration. The white t-shirt he wore clung to his muscular chest and flat washboard abs. The young man's light gray shorts had a few streaks of dust and dirt on them. Nick's long legs were curled up underneath him. His face, which was turned towards Bane, held a trace of guilt.

"What are you doing up here?" Bane demanded to know. His voice was a low deep growl.

That guilt had Nick's cheeks pinking prettily. "The trapdoor was down and I thought I heard something—"

"Heard something? What did you *supposedly* hear?" Bane interrupted.

That pink flush became a much deeper rose and it spread from Nick's face down his throat and disappeared beneath his t-shirt. "I just saw the trapdoor open—"

"Open? Really? It was just *magically* open for you?" Bane took a menacing step towards Nick.

The young man got to his feet. Bane saw his pulse throbbing in the side of that swan-like neck. Nick answered, "Yeah, it was, I—"

"Are you *certain*?" Bane took another step and there was only six inches between them.

One of Nick's hands fluttered up by his throat as he claimed, "Yes, I found it open and thought I might have heard—"

Bane grasped Nick's chin and the young man inhaled sharply. "You were *spying* on me. Looking into my *personal* things."

"No," Nick protested. His nostrils flared.

"*Yes*, you are a little snoop-"

"I am not!" Nick ripped himself out of Bane's hands and took took two steps back. The beast thought that Nick was going to run. When prey ran it had to be *chased*.

Bane lunged at Nick. He hadn't intended to. But he did. It was Nick's mouth. Bane kept remembering the kiss from the night before and seeing those lips moving and lying—for Nick had to be lying! The trapdoor left open? Not likely!—and he couldn't bear it so he found himself slamming Nick up against the attic's wall, his hands on Nick's shoulders, his face inches from the young man's. They were breathing in each other's air.

"You were *snooping*," Bane growled. The beast was so close to the surface that he wouldn't have been surprised if he sprouted whiskers. "Weren't you?"

"How did you get over here so fast?" Nick's eyes were huge and he was clearly shocked more by Bane's speed then the heavy hands gripping his shoulders. "You actually blurred for a second."

Bane immediately realized his mistake. More than one mistake actually. The first mistake was showing Nick his speed—his preternatural speed. The second mistake was getting this close to Nick...and his lips. His own writhed back from his teeth. The beast surged forward in his chest and the scar burned hot.

"Don't try to *distract* me from the fact that you are snooping through my private things." Bane shook Nick slightly.

Nick seemed to realize at that moment that Bane's hands were on him and a spark of anger appeared in those surprised gray eyes. "Let me go, Bane!"

"Not until you tell me the *truth* that you snuck up here to look at my private—"

"Let. Me. Go. *Now*." Nick's eyes blazed.

"And if I won't? What will you do? I am stronger than you. I assure you that there's nothing you can do to make me release you," Bane said with an almost purr in his voice. He could smell Nick's sweat and a touch of musk. He remembered that scent from devouring the young man's cock the night before.

But that was a dream, his mind protested. Yet Nick's musk smelled the same in reality as it had in the dreamworld.

Nick went suddenly limp in his grip, almost as if accepting Bane's greater strength. Bane found himself moving in. Nick's lips were so plush, so pink, so kissable. He wanted to feel them against his own for far longer than he had in that maddening dream. He would drink them in. Rasp his teeth over that lower lip until it plumped. He would slide his tongue over them, wetting them, and then he would just devour Nick. The beast had gone so very still inside of him. It must approve too.

"So *this* is the type of man you are," Nick said, softly, but it had the same effect as if he had shouted it in Bane's face.

Bane realized almost immediately he'd made yet a third mistake. This one far worse than the other two. He was holding Nick against his will to take what he wanted.

What am I doing? I'm hurting him. I'm scaring him. I'm ...

"I..." he began but found he could say nothing. His eyes were focused on Nick's lips again.

Those lips curled into an angry smile. "Omar told me this morning that you were a *good* man, but you *aren't*. Somehow you've fooled him. You're the type that uses his strength to get what he wants no matter what the cost to the other person. You have no honor."

At the word "honor" Bane's hands released the young man. He knew of another man who had no honor, who had taken advantage of a boy, who had gotten what he'd wanted and then...

This is nothing like that! I am not Alastair! Nick is not me!

"You shouldn't be up here. You shouldn't be looking at my things," Bane said tightly even as his skin flushed red and his scar burned like a brand with shame. "I—I should not have touched you like that. I—I apologize. My temper gets away from me at times. It is not an excuse, but it is the truth."

Nick stared at him as if he didn't quite believe Bane's words. His gaze measured Bane's position compared to the trapdoor out of the attic. Bane's scar burned so badly then that he nearly let out a whimper.

"Right. Sure. Whatever," Nick muttered. "I'll just go downstairs—"

"Not with those!" Bane pointed at the photographs that were still in Nick's hands. "You should not have those. They are not yours. They are mine. Private, personal things."

Nick regarded him warily again, but there was a flash of guilt on his face for a moment, too. "I shouldn't have looked in the trunk, but I had hoped that there were things related to Moon Shadow in there. I didn't realize these were your things. The trunk looked so old. But I guess it's one of your ancestor's trunks."

Nick held out the photographs. The photographs of Bane. Bane quickly snatched them away and stuffed them into his back pocket, which had Nick frowning. Clearly, the photographer in Nick didn't want the photos damaged. Bane was realizing now that he needed to likely destroy them. Holding onto the past was dangerous for him.

"You really are a throwback to your ancestor. You're like twins. Omar told me that your family lived in India for a time. I guess that's where these were taken?" Nick asked hesitantly.

"Yes." Bane answered.

Nick doesn't realize that the photos are of me, Bane thought with relief. *That's the funny part about being immortal, you assume people will figure it out, but they don't. Their minds offer plenty of excuses for why you look the same decade after decade. Only Alastair ever guessed the truth, but I wanted him to.*

"Is your hunting rifle the same as his, too?" Nick asked. "The one in the picture looks just like the one you pulled downstairs on Mr. Brennan."

Bane's eyes flickered down to the picture. It was of him and Tarun. He had his rifle slung over his shoulder. It was the day they had set out on the hunt to kill the beast. Amazing that Nick recognized the rifle. The young man was more observant than most.

Before Bane could answer, there were light footsteps on the stairs behind him. He turned and saw Omar appear. The Indian man looked perplexed to find them both in the attic. Then he saw the open trunk and he didn't exactly pale, but he did glance quickly between the two of them.

"Nick *claims* he found the attic door ajar. He came up here looking for information on Moon Shadow," Bane gave the word "claims" all the emphasis he could.

Nick's head shot towards him. "I didn't claim anything! That's what happened!"

"I'm afraid that it is my fault that the attic door *was* open. I was bringing down some of the vases we keep up here for your guests," Omar said. "I must not have closed it all the way."

Bane studied him closely. Was Omar lying to protect the young man? But he immediately saw that Omar was telling the truth. His back straightened and the scar throbbed.

"I see," Bane said stiffly.

"I told you I was telling the truth!" Nick cried triumphantly.

"Seeing an open door doesn't mean you must go through it and rifle through the things inside the room beyond, does it?" Bane asked tartly.

Nick flushed and lowered his head. "No. I—I'm sorry. It's just Moon Shadow is interesting. It would be good to know its history when I shoot it."

"If I *allow* you to take photographs of my home, you mean." Bane did not look at Nick as he said that, but he saw out of the corner of his eye Nick jerk as if slapped.

"But you said I could—"

"I said I would *consider* it," Bane answered curtly.

"I think you *owe* me something for what you did up here." Nick crossed his arms over his chest.

"*What* happened up here?" Omar looked alarmed.

"Nothing," Bane gritted out.

"You're going to give me my camera tomorrow, right? You're going to let me shoot Moon Shadow?" Nick stepped in front of him and met Bane's gaze full on. "That's what I want. Not an apology. A promise."

Bane's eyes flickered to Nick's shoulders. How hard had he grabbed him? Were there bruises? Had he frightened Nick?

Had he made the young man feel unsafe here with him? Of course he had. He was worse than Alastair had ever been. He swallowed down bitter bile.

"You may photograph Moon Shadow," Bane promised.

Stiff-backed, he walked out of the attic, feeling his scar burn with shame.

CHAPTER THIRTEEN
SPIRIT ANIMAL

Nick chewed his inner cheek to stop from laughing at the fluttering Italian tailor, Mr. Fioretti, as he circled Nick with a tape measure in one hand, a tablet in the other and a stylus clenched between his teeth. Nick had been measured once for some suits and a tuxedo, but never by Winter Haven's most famous and eccentric tailor. From what his father had always said getting a private fitting like this from Mr. Fioretti — and on such short notice! — should have been impossible. Yet here Mr. Fioretti was. Nick could almost imagine the type of money that Bane must be dropping in order to have the tailor right here and now measuring him. His father would be envious.

But why would Bane spend that kind of money on me? He must really take his formal dinners seriously! But then Nick remembered all too well Bane's closeness in the attic. The way Bane's eyes had burned like gas-lamps. The way Nick's own heart had hammered in his chest when Bane was leaning in to kiss him. Desire had been like witchfire between them. *So maybe he has a very good reason for wanting to see me in tailored clothes.*

That scene in the attic disturbed him in other ways, too. The photographs he'd found of Bane's ancestor still hung in his memory like frost. The man in them had looked so much like Bane that Nick had, at first, assumed that they *were* of Bane. They were black and white, but that didn't automatically mean they weren't modern. Yet he could tell that the photos were very old simply from the feel of the paper. Bane, therefore, was his ancestor's doppelganger.

Except for the scar. That's the one difference between Bane and the man in the pictures.

"Do you see yourself as a mammal, a fish, or an insect?" Mr. Fioretti mumbled around the stylus, but it broke Nick out of his thoughts about Bane.

With laughter in his voice, Nick asked, "*What?*"

"I am trying to get a gauge on your personality!" The tape measure was expertly put around Nick's upper chest. "So what animal—other than human—are you?"

"Like a spirit animal?" Nick asked, brow furrowing.

"Exactly! You would be surprised at how much how we see ourselves informs our fashion and gives us the best look," Mr. Fioretti explained.

Nick really didn't see himself as any animal. He wondered what that meant about him. As he searched his mind for something semi-appropriate, he realized that Bane must have been asked this question, too. Though Bane seemed to intimidate everyone, Nick had a feeling that Mr. Fioretti in his zeal to make beautiful clothes would have been oblivious to Bane's glowering and would have asked his spirit animal question.

"What's Bane's spirit animal?" Nick asked just as the man himself prowled into Nick's bedroom without knocking.

"Oh, Bane is a tiger. A big cat!" Mr. Fioretti answered, clearly oblivious to Bane's arrival.

Nick's cheeks burned again both with anger that Bane seemed to think Nick deserved no privacy and because whenever Bane found him he was doing or saying something that he shouldn't. He still felt the ghostly grip of Bane's hands on his shoulders from the attic. The man hadn't hurt him. He hadn't even been afraid that he *would* hurt him though Bane had been so damned close up in that stuffy attic. No, there had been a thrill at being so near a man that was so clearly dangerous. An alpha in all ways, which meant a bastard in so many others. Bane held Nick's gaze without speaking. Nick's cheeks burned hotter, but he didn't look away.

Mr. Fioretti twittered, "And what is your animal, Nick? It will help me immeasurably to know."

"He's a rabbit," Bane rumbled. "A beautiful bunny."

Mr. Fioretti's black head bobbed up to look over at the big man. "Bane! How good to see you, my friend!"

The tailor put down the tools of his trade before he went over and cupped Bane's face. He then proceeded to kiss both cheeks in the European fashion. Bane gave him a broad, welcoming smile though he did show a lot of teeth.

Funny that he would have compared himself to a tiger. He is cat-like. Must have noticed it myself and that's why I had the strange dream about him actually being a tiger. Or maybe it's that tiger rug in his study. I should remember the moment he sucked me off every time he says something mean and it won't sting as much.

"How are you, Bane?" Mr. Fioretti twittered.

"Very well and you?" Bane asked.

"I am thrilled! Just thrilled, I tell you! You give me such a beautiful young man to clothe! How could I not be happy?" Mr. Fioretti fluttered back to Nick's side. "I will make for him the most stunning suits you have ever seen."

"You're making me blush here, Mr. Fioretti." Nick laughed.

"That just makes you prettier! Do you not think so, Bane?" Mr. Fioretti asked.

Nick's breath caught in his throat. He wished Mr. Fioretti had not asked that. He almost expected Bane to get angry to be accused of desiring the "spoilt Fairfax". But Bane's response was to have his gaze rove over Nick's body.

Nick only had on a pair of dark gray boxer briefs. His nipple beaded as Bane's eyes lingered on his chest. The man's gaze was like a physical caress. Bane's eyes slid down his legs to his bare feet and then back up again to his groin where it remained for a long time. Bane seemed to be assessing the size of his cock, which had Nick's face burning as hot of the sun and had him wanting to shift his weight from foot to foot. When Bane's eyes came up to his face again, Nick gave him a steady stare in return. Bane did not look away and he did not blush.

"I am certain if anyone can make him *presentable* it's you, Mr. Fioretti," Bane remarked dryly.

"Oh, he is a vision! It will be a pleasure and a challenge to make sure that his clothing is as lovely as he is," Mr. Fioretti waxed eloquently.

Bane leaned one massive shoulder against the wall as he watched Nick through hooded eyes while Mr. Fioretti darted in and out with his tape measure and then scribbled the numbers down with his stylus on his tablet.

"Just as an aside, Mr. Fioretti, my spirit animal is *not* a rabbit." Nick narrowed his eyes at Bane. "It's an…eagle."

"Eagle?" Bane's eyebrows rose. "You see yourself as a predator of the skies?"

He didn't, of course. The idea had just come to him. He had to replace the idea of "bunny" in Mr. Fioretti's head. He had thought it was a choice of animal that even Bane wouldn't scoff at, but clearly he had been wrong.

"I'm a photographer," Nick explained more to Mr. Fioretti than to Bane. "I like to think I have keen vision. What has keener vision than an eagle?"

Bane let out a soft snort, but he was smiling slightly. He almost looked agreeable.

"An eagle it is! I think I have all I need from you today, Nick." Mr. Fioretti slipped the tape measure around his neck and placed the stylus and tablet into his inner suit pocket. He turned to Bane and clasped his hands in front of him as if in prayer. "My understanding is that Nick will need suits for all seasons, yes?"

Bane grunted his assent. "I don't believe he has anything other than casual clothing."

Mr. Fioretti tutted and shook his head. "That is the way of the world these days, Bane. All the young people want to be comfortable. It is only because they have never had a proper suit that they think suits are uncomfortable. I will be able to have a few things here for him tomorrow. The rest will take some weeks as I need to order the proper fabric and other materials."

"Of course, that would be fine," Bane said graciously, which surprised the hell out of Nick as he wouldn't have thought that Bane knew what graciousness was.

At that moment, Omar knocked on the door. The Indian man stepped inside and had with him Nick's suitcase. Nick hopped off of the block that Mr. Fioretti had him standing on and immediately went to take the suitcase from Omar.

"Dad sent my stuff! Finally," he said as he brought the suitcase in and put it on top of the bed. He had few hopes that his father had thought to pack any of his camera equipment. He really needed to call Jade to tell her that he was all right and to ask her to bring his stuff.

If Bane will let her come. Maybe I should ask for forgiveness rather than permission. She'll just show up and he can grouse, but I can't imagine even Bane being able to dislodge her once she's here.

He bit his inner cheek again to stop from laughing at the mental image of Jade as a burr in Bane's tiger coat.

"I certainly hope you have something in there to wear this evening," Bane murmured and Nick jumped. He hadn't heard the billionaire come over and now Bane was right by his side. He was standing so close that Nick could feel his body heat.

Feeling self-conscious and hoping against hope that his father had actually taken some time and care to pack his things, Nick unzipped the suitcase.

Maybe he had Marya do it. Maybe he... He threw back the lid. *Oh shit.*

His father had clearly packed for him and in a hurry, too. Cheeks burning with embarrassment, he felt Bane looking over his shoulder at the clothes that had simply been tossed in, rolled into balls, and crushed into corners. He saw a few shoes in there, too, but none matched. Everything was wrinkled. He picked up one button down shirt with two fingers and sighed. It looked like an accordion.

"Oh, my," Mr. Fioretti said and there was this look of pain on his face at seeing clothes so abused.

"This is no problem! I will get an iron and we will soon put this to rights!" Omar remarked with forced cheerfulness and was about to head to the door to get said iron but Nick stopped him.

He had felt Bane go still when Omar offered to help and he already knew that the man did not want Omar serving Nick in any way. Plus Omar had to cook dinner.

"No worries, Omar," Nick said. "I can do it. I even know where the iron is. You go handle dinner. I'll be down in a jiffy to help you."

"If you are certain, Nick." Omar did not sound certain at all. He lingered by the door.

Nick already felt exhausted after a full day of cleaning toilets. The thought of having to iron all his clothes and put them away had his shoulders slumping. But there was no way he would add to Omar's burden. So he said brightly, "I am. It's all good."

There was another pause as Omar looked at him with uncertainty, but then he turned to the tailor and said, "Let me walk you out, Mr. Fioretti."

"Oh, thank you so much!" the Italian tailor twittered.

"It was nice to meet you, Mr. Fioretti. I promise not to let my father touch the suits you make for me." Nick gave a grin, reached over, took the tailor's hand and shook it.

"Omar is right. An iron and everything should be perfect. It was a pleasure meeting you as well, Nick. I will see you soon," Mr. Fioretti said.

After the two other men had left, it was just him and Bane in the room. Both of them were looking down at the clothes. Nick couldn't help but be frighteningly aware of the man. He smelled of sandalwood and cinnamon again, which was a rather addictive smell. He exuded an alpha aura that was both intriguing and repelling at the same time. Nick wasn't sure if he was safe alone with this man, especially not in his underwear. But Bane must not have been thinking seduction at all considering the next words he spoke.

"Does your father not care at all?" Bane's voice was surprisingly soft and sad.

Nick gritted his teeth. "He's just not really good at stuff like this. I'm sure that he did his best."

Nick met Bane's eyes and the lies shriveled up on his tongue. He found himself quickly looking away. He didn't need Bane's pity at the fact that his father didn't really care about him. Charles Fairfax was doing a great job of making him feel bad all on his own.

If only he realized that Bane would have seen this then maybe he wouldn't have stomped wrinkles into my clothes.

"Charles is a careless man. He is careless of his things. He is careless with his son. I am surprised that you..." Bane broke off. His brows were furrowed as if something truly made no sense to him.

"That I what?" Nick demanded to know.

Bane's dark hair covered the scarred half of his face. Only one of those intense blue eyes could be seen, but Nick was glad for that, because that one eye seemed to see too much. "Why did you come here, Nick?"

Nick's brow furrowed. "To help my family."

"But *why*?"

"Because I care for them. Because they're family!"

"But they do not act like it," Bane murmured.

Nick's shoulders sagged even more. "Sometimes family forgets the niceties, you know? They take for granted that you'll be there. Unconditional love and all that."

"Love?" Bane's voice dripped with disdain. He gestured towards the suitcase. "If love were real this would have been packed with care. If love were real your father would have come himself to bring it. If love were real he would have called to check in on how you were doing."

Nick's heart tumbled lower and lower with each of Bane's valid points. But then the mention of a call had him angry at *Bane*.

With narrowed eyes, Nick snarked, "Maybe he called *my* phone, but since you have it locked away—"

"He didn't. I checked," Bane answered curtly.

Nick felt his heart plummet the rest of the way into his feet. He had told Jade that he wasn't doing this to win his family's love, that it was all about freedom from guilt when he left them, but the sense of despair that ran through him right then told a different story.

"Oh," was all Nick got out. Then he forced himself to say, "He's likely busy making sure he's doing a perfect job for you. That's, undoubtedly, what he thinks is best."

Bane turned to leave, but he stopped mid-way to the door. He turned his head slightly. "I do not know why you agreed to all of this, but I hope, for your sake, that it was *not* out of love."

Bane then disappeared out of Nick's door.

CHAPTER FOURTEEN
ROMANTIC DINNER FOR TWO?

Bane entered the formal dining room, but found it dark and empty. There were no candles glowing, no plates on the table, and no ubiquitous vase of roses. This was not like Omar. The Indian man would have the long, beautiful mahogany dining table set perfectly by now. But it was not.

Nick. Nick has something to do with this.

He slapped his hand against one of his powerful thighs and stalked into the kitchen where he found a very happy Omar, singing as he slid chicken enchiladas into the oven.

"Omar, why is the dining room table not set?" Bane asked.

"Because I thought a meal outside would be better. I have already set the table on the back porch," Omar explained.

Bane saw homemade guacamole and freshly chopped salsa sitting in bright bowls of red and green on the counter. Omar had even fried his own chips. They glistened with oil and salt. They were still warm. Bane's stomach rumbled and the beast's tongue slid out and licked its muzzle.

Omar glanced over at Bane. "You look quite handsome! I am sure that Nick will approve. Now if only your *manners* would match your outfit."

Bane looked down at the lightweight summer suit he had on. It was a soft gray with blue stripes. His button down shirt was a pale blue and his tie a darker ice color in silk. His shoes were polished. His hair was brushed though he still kept half of it covering his scar. The scar was red and raw looking, uglier than usual. It was the stress of having Nick here and the activeness of the beast that was causing that. The beast paced inside of him. Eager to see Nick. *Needing* to see Nick.

"Perhaps I should dine alone then as I do not intend to treat Nick as a *guest*," Bane muttered.

"No, you *will* be dining together. You *will* be charming. You *will* be a gentlemen. You can do that, can't you?" Omar asked as he put margarita glasses on a festive tray and set a frosted pitcher of the tart drink next to them.

"Why should I wish to do that?" Bane turned a narrow-eyed glare onto the Indian man.

"Because I have asked you to. Would you do this for me? Or am I not worth even that bit of courtesy?" Omar stood very still and waited for an answer. He did not look at Bane. He stared straight ahead.

Guilt pricked at Bane. He shifted uneasily. He remembered Nick's comment about *honor* and now this. He cared deeply for Omar. The truth was that the Indian man could ask almost anything of him and he would do it. But why did it have to involve Nick? He knew the answer to that question before he had even asked it. Omar disapproved of the internship in general, but it was also clear that Omar had taken Nick under his protective wing. So unless he wanted to alienate Omar he would have to be polite at dinner.

"I—*yes*, Omar. I will be a gentlemen for you," Bane finally answered.

"Good." Omar picked up the tray and Bane followed him outside onto the back porch.

Bane jerked to a halt. What he saw before him was startling in its beauty. The back porch was awash in candlelight and white roses. Fat, cream candles were on every surface. A small circular table had been set in the corner of the porch. It was swathed in a peerless white tablecloth and set with decorative plates and silverware that would match the Mexican dinner.

There were linen napkins artfully twisted into peacocks. And everywhere was the heady scent of roses not only from the garden but also from the half dozen crystal vases that dotted the porch stuffed with the most delicate white blooms. White roses were some of Bane's favorites.

Omar placed the tray down on the table and set out the glasses rimmed with salt. He then poured the alcoholic drink into both of them. There was a half smile on the Indian man's lips, which indicated to Bane that he was very pleased with his reaction to the porch.

That was when Bane realized something. "Why are there only two chairs, Omar?"

"Because it will just be you and Nick eating out here tonight," Omar answered as he leaned down and sniffed one of the white roses in a vase.

Bane went still. The beast's head lifted up and the very tip of its tail wagged happily. Bane was not happy. It was one thing for Omar to ask him to be a gentleman at dinner when the Indian man was going to be there. It was quite another to force them to dine *alone* and in such a romantic setting.

Bane's voice was slightly pinched as he said, "I do not think that is wise—"

"You *agreed* to be a gentleman for me. You will show Nick tonight that I am not wrong about you." Omar picked up the tray, but left the pitcher out for them to refresh their drinks.

"He gets under my skin, Omar. Whenever I am with him I feel—"

"Yes, you *feel*. That is new," Omar answered. That half smile was now a full one. "That is *good*."

Bane leaned against one of the pillars of the porch and crossed his massive arms over his chest. The beast was looking around eagerly for Nick, ears pricked for his arrival. The young man was still upstairs. He was humming something that had the tip of the beast's tail wagging in time to it now. Bane determined to ignore the beast's reactions to Nick, but he couldn't afford to ignore Omar's behavior.

"What are you planning, Omar? What do you want to happen between Nick and I?"

"Nothing in particular." Omar would not meet his gaze though.

"Your *nothing* is someone else's *everything*. Out with it, Omar."

The Indian man stared at Bane. "Do you not see the similarity between Nick's current situation and your old one?"

"I have no idea—"

"Why do you hate the Fairfaxes so much as opposed to every other business out there? Are they any worse than most? I do not think so," Omar pointed out sharply.

"The Fairfaxes are not—"

"Your father was far more venal than Charles Fairfax. He treated you as if you did not belong in his house, because you valued things other than *money* and *position*," Omar continued as if Bane had not spoken. "Nick is the *same*. And just like you he desperately wants his father's love. He may never get it either."

"He will not get it. Charles sees no value in Nick, I'm certain of that," Bane muttered and a frown tugged his lips as he started to see Omar's points of similarity.

"But instead of recognizing these similarities between you and him and having some sympathy in your heart you treat him like your father treated you! Or worse...you are treating him like Alastair treated you." Omar looked at him fiercely.

Bane's scar had been burning hotter and hotter as Omar spoke. He had remained still and silent until Omar said his faithless lover's name and then he spun away from the Indian man and gripped the porch's railing. He stared blindly out at the mass of rose bushes.

"I'm sorry to have hurt you, Bane. That is the last thing I want, but you are not being as you should with that young man," Omar said quietly. "You could be a help to him. You could save him from some of the pain that you, yourself, experienced. I can only think that you are not doing this, because you will not see the truth in front of you."

"Which is *what*? That I am a spoilt brat, too, who had a terrible, unloving father?"

"Oh, you are a brat sometimes," Omar laughed gently. "But you usually have so many good qualities that it does not matter very much."

"I don't see in Nick what you do, but even if I did, I don't know what you want me to do about it," Bane said.

"You could end this internship," Omar offered.

"No," Bane said immediately as something in his chest tightened.

"Then you should, at least, treat him with respect and open your heart to him a little," Omar suggested.

Instead of responding to Omar's suggestions, Bane blurted out, "Devon is one of the guests that is coming tomorrow. You do realize that, don't you?"

He watched with interest as Omar's shoulders bunched. Devon Wainwright was the heir to a large fortune but his focus was on the environment and other good causes. He and Bane were friends with benefits. There was nothing serious between them. Devon was handsome, charming and generous, but Omar *hated* him and Omar didn't hate anyone.

"Yes, I am well aware of Mr. Wainwright's invitation here," Omar said stiffly. "But I do not see what he has to do with Nick." Omar turned curious brown eyes upon him. "Do you wish to sleep with Nick, too, as you do with Mr. Wainwright?"

Bane cursed himself. Only Omar would see the connection between Devon and Nick the way he had phrased his question. "No, of course not. I was just changing the subject."

Omar let out a theatrical sigh, clearly indicating he believed that Bane was in denial about something. With a rather intense look he said, "I am curious what Mr. Wainwright will think of you having an *intern*."

Bane shrugged. "Why would he care?"

"A beautiful and intelligent young man in your house for a year? What could Mr. Wainwright worry about?" Omar sniffed.

"With you making romantic dinners like this I believe you *want* there to be something for Devon to think about," Bane retorted, but a line of heat went through him as he imagined Nick entangled in his arms. He clenched his jaw to suppress the image. "But it wouldn't matter even if—as in Nick's *heated* imagination—I brought him here to bed him all year long, because Devon and I are just friends. He has no claim on me."

"I do not sleep with my friends," Omar said repressively.

"Do you really object to sex outside of marriage?"

"No, you know I do not," Omar answered and let out a sigh. "Mr. Wainwright distracts you from finding the person you *should* be with."

Bane's expression darkened. "Enough with the true love, Omar."

Omar turned to him. "You should ask yourself why you are fighting so hard against getting to know Nick."

"I know all I need to know about him." Bane tossed his head.

"I truly doubt that." Omar's insightful brown eyes studied his face. "You have created some version of him in your head that is simply not true. I believe you are afraid to know the *real* him, because then—"

"Then I will fall in *love* with him and he will fall in love with me and this curse will be lifted for all of us?" Bane let out a bitter laugh. "Omar, it is not *me* who is not seeing things clearly. Nick is here to pay for his family's bad acts. That is all. Nothing else."

Omar's gaze darkened and his voice was dangerously soft, "Do you believe that a son is responsible for a father's bad acts?"

A flush of shame went through Bane. Omar was well aware that Bane's father had been a *beast* without having the spirit of one inside of him. Lord Richard Dunsaney had been a far worse man than Charles Fairfax, but he defended him, "My father was a product of his time and a victim of drink."

"What does that matter? If he was guilty then *you* are responsible for all he did," Omar said tightly. "That is how you would judge Nick."

Before Bane could respond, Nick stepped out of the back door and asked, "What smells so good?"

Bane turned his head to look at the young man. Both he and the beast stilled as soon as they saw Nick. He wasn't in a suit, but he looked...

Perfect. Like summer.

Nick was scrubbed clean so that his golden skin glowed. His platinum hair curled becomingly around his striking face. He had on a pair of tan slacks and a mint green shirt with Chinese collar along with white sandals. For a moment, Bane imagined he had asked Nick to Moon Shadow for dinner, not for an internship, but just to be together. That somehow he had walked across the street when he had first seen the young man and his last name had not been Fairfax. He imagined his stomach fluttering at the sight of the young man if that were the case. Except he didn't have to imagine it. He felt it.

Seeing that Bane was looking at his clothes, Nick self-consciously ran his hands down his front. "It's not exactly a suit and I'm not sure if I did the best job ironing it, but I think it looks okay."

"You look quite handsome, Nick," Omar enthused.

Bane's tongue stuck to the roof of his mouth. He mumbled, "It's fine. You look fine. We should sit. Omar's good dinner will get cold."

"Oh, let me get the starters," Omar remarked.

"Can I help you? I'm sorry I didn't get down here earlier to set the table—"

Omar made a waving motion with his hands for Nick to stay where he was. "Nonsense! I have everything in hand. You just sit down and relax. You did good work today." Omar hustled inside happily, all his censure from earlier gone.

Bane went over to the table and was about to sit down himself, but then he remembered his promise to Omar. He was to be a gentleman. And he knew how to act like one. So instead he pulled out a chair for Nick. The young man stared at him a moment, but then sat down in the proffered spot. Bane found himself drawing in deep breaths of Nick's scent. He was clean from the shower and there were hints of citrus and spice from the shampoo he had used. His curls looked like burnished gold in the candlelight and Bane imagined twirling a few of them around his fingers. Realizing what he was doing Bane quickly moved away. He sat down opposite the young man and suddenly understood the phrase "pleasurable torment" all too well.

CHAPTER FIFTEEN
LOVE

Nick stared across the small table at Bane. He felt absurdly self-conscious in the outfit he had chosen, but it was the nicest thing he had, and seeing Bane's beautiful suit made him feel under-dressed. The last time he had worn this outfit though was on a rather terrible date where the guy thought paying for dinner meant he got to fuck Nick that night. Being at a table loaded with flowers and candles had Nick feeling like maybe he was on another bad date. Bane, at least, was far better to look at than the last guy, but Bane was also far greater a bastard so the one rather knocked out the other.

Yet Nick could not help noticing how intensely sensual Bane was even when he wasn't trying to be. The fall of dark hair. The full mouth. The strong jaw. The tigrish movements. There was just this sense of alpha surety that had Nick wanting to respond to him in ways he wasn't sure he was comfortable with. The man was untamed and he was so big. Nick would be swallowed in his arms if Bane held him.

And when exactly do I see Bane holding me? Yeah, not happening. I don't want it to happen.

Omar bustled out with the homemade guacamole, salsa and chips just before Nick had to admit the pulse his cock gave as he imagined those massive, muscular arms wrapped around his own slender form.

"Omar, this looks great!" Nick grabbed a chip and dipped it into the thick guacamole. After crunching it and licking the salt off of his fingers, he glanced around and asked, "Where's your chair? Aren't you going to be eating with us?"

"No, I am not. It's just the two of you," Omar answered brightly.

Nick gave Bane a sharp look. The man had wanted to kiss him in the attic by force so was this some attempt to get into his pants by seduction?

But Omar set this dinner up. He wouldn't help Bane do that.

Seeing the unasked question in that look, Bane growled, "This has nothing to do with me. Omar wishes us to—"

"Get to know one another," Omar finished. "If I am here Bane will not talk. So this evening you will both speak and find some common ground."

"Find some common —" Nick got out but Omar was already bowing and going inside. Leaving him and Bane alone.

For a long time the only sound was the night insects. Nick picked up his glass and took a sip of his drink. The margarita was tart and refreshing. Omar had clearly made it with fresh lime juice, a touch of simple syrup and good quality buttery tequila. He took another large sip. He realized that Bane was doing the same. Both of them evidently needed a drink to get through this.

"So for Omar hope springs *eternal*." Nick let out a weak laugh. He couldn't imagine what they were going to talk about for an hour at least.

Unless I bolt down my food and leave. But I don't think that Omar will let me do that.

Bane just nodded.

"He doesn't understand that you hate my family and me so..." Nick goaded, leaving room for Bane to disagree. He did not. "Right." Nick sighed and took another gulp of margarita.

"You enjoy photography," Bane finally said more than asked.

Nick thought about not answering. Photography was hugely important to him. He didn't want to risk Bane mocking it. But then he imagined Omar inside, listening to see if he spoke. Omar might even delay bringing the next course *until* they had talked for a set amount of time. So if he kept silent Omar might *never* come out and this meal would go on forever.

Nick said carefully. "Yeah, I do."

Bane leaned back in his chair. The candlelight filtered through the billionaire's long hair and Nick could see the strange scar between the dark locks. He really wanted to ask Bane about it, but then the man asked him, "Why?"

"What?" Nick blinked and his forehead furrowed.

"Why do you like photography? Because people exclaim over your work? Because it makes you feel important?"

Nick's eyes narrowed in anger. "No, because I *like* creating art even if no one else sees it. It's for *me*."

"You think your photographs are *art*?" Bane asked. One of his eyebrows arched.

"Yes, they are." Nick tipped his chin up.

"Of course, you would think that." Bane grimaced then and looked like he didn't like his own tone.

"You've never seen them," Nick pointed out sharply. How could Bane judge whether his work was art or not without actually seeing them? This was so like what his father would have said that his back was immediately up.

"No, I haven't."

"So *why* are you being dismissive?" Nick asked acidly. "You've *never* seen my photographs. You don't know if they're art or not, but you act like I'm delusional for thinking they are."

"True. I can't judge your work without seeing it." Bane drained his glass and poured himself more of the potent drink.

Nick's heart was beating sickly in his chest. He didn't feel he had a victory out of this conversation even though he seemingly had "won". Maybe it was because he truly wished to not have to argue about this at all. Why did Bane look at him and assume his photography couldn't be art? Was there something about *him* that made people assume that he was just a dilettante?

"You sound just like my father, you know?" Nick crossed his arms over his chest.

"How so?" Bane's voice was curious with just a touch of defensiveness in it.

"He dismisses my photography just like you do. It's useless! It's not a *real* job! What makes you think that anything you create is worthwhile?" Nick repeated his father's words.

"Has Charles ever seen your photographs?"

"No, of course not." Nick let out a bitter laugh. He remembered how he had *tried* to show his father some of them when Charles had made the ultimatum. His father hadn't even glanced down at his portfolio.

"I'm sorry. That must be…disappointing." Bane almost sounded sincere. "I would like to see some of them."

"You will. If you let me take photographs tomorrow of Moon Shadow." Nick made the last statement very pointed.

Bane's burning Siberian blue eyes met his. "I have already agreed to let you photograph the house as…as recompense for my behavior in the attic."

"Do you think that makes me feel good that I had to blackmail you to do it?"

"Does that matter?" Bane crumbled a chip in one hand into powder. "You are getting what you want."

Nick leaned forward in his chair. "I'd like to get the opportunity because you see the *value* in photographing Moon Shadow. I can't prove to you the value of *me* doing it until you see what I'm capable of. But I would *prefer* you agree to this, because it's a good idea."

There was a long silence. Bane's gaze shifted to the garden. His expression was unreadable. But finally he said, "All right.

I want you to take photographs of Moon Shadow. I shall judge whether you should be the official photographer after I see your work. Perhaps I will even agree that your photographs are *art*."

A flutter of nervousness went through Nick as he thought of Bane *judging* his photography at all, but then again, if he expected to live off of it he would have to get used to having a critical audience. He had to believe that his work could stand on its own.

"I know why my father doesn't believe in my photography. He doesn't believe in art generally. But why don't *you*? Are you against art, too, or just against me?" Nick knew that this was a provocative question and he wasn't exactly sure what he expected Bane to say. Nothing good for sure. But it bothered him that Bane had such a low opinion of him for what seemed like no reason.

Yet he still is attracted to me.

"I have nothing against art," Bane answered stiffly.

"Then it's against me. Great." Nick downed his drink and poured himself another. The tequila bubbled in his veins and a warmth was spreading through him, but he was so tense from Bane's presence that he couldn't relax.

"No, not exactly." Bane fiddled with the salt and pepper shakers on the table. "Most children of the rich who go into *art* aren't really artistic at all. It's just a way to waste time and appear busy instead of actually doing something worthwhile.'

Nick's jaw clenched. "So you agree with my father that entering the business world is the only legitimate profession?"

Bane shrugged a massive shoulder. "Why don't you want to work in your family's business?"

"I can't imagine anything further from creating art as my family's business," Nick answered. "They take things apart. I want to build them."

"So you agree that your family's business is destructive?" Bane leaned back in his chair and Nick felt like he had walked into a trap by saying what he had.

"It's not creative," Nick answered stiffly.

"Yet you benefited from it."

"And you've lived a life where everything you've gotten or benefited from was perfectly obtained? No one was hurt in the process?" Nick laughed bitterly. "You're a *lord*, Bane. I'm pretty sure somewhere in your family tree people suffered for your family's wealth and position."

Bane shifted uncomfortably. "It is not possible to live a life without hurting someone."

"And you are in *business*, too. I am *certain* beyond a shadow of a doubt that people have been hurt by you personally. No matter how scrupulous you've been, you don't get to be as rich as you are without hurting people in the process," Nick pointed out.

"Perhaps. But I believe I have done far more good than ill with the way I run my businesses." Bane looked thoughtful. "Is that why you want to be an artist? To stay away from business and hurting people?"

"Part of it, yes. But another part is that I can't help myself." Nick studied one of the chips in his hands. "I *need* to create things. Even if no one sees them. Even if no one else thinks they're good."

"Many people say they are artists for every reason other than for art," Bane finally answered. "My mother was an artist and she spoke as you do about the *drive* to create things."

"Was?" Nick knew nothing of Bane's family. Somehow he couldn't imagine the big man with parents or siblings. Like Athena, he could almost imagine Bane springing fully formed out of Zeus' forehead.

"She died." There was such finality in that statement that it almost hurt to hear.

Nick immediately thought of his own mother. Her heart defect had stolen her life far before she passed away. He remembered her sitting in her chair in the garden, sunlight on her pale face with her eyes closed as she was too weak to stay awake. A wave of sadness went through him. He missed her still.

"I'm sorry. Mine did as well," Nick offered.

Bane went still. "She must have been very young." Nick found that statement very odd as Bane wasn't that much older than him so his mother couldn't have been that much older than Nick's when she died. Yet Bane seemed to think the death of his own parent natural, but Nick's mother's strange. "How—how did she die?"

"She had a heart defect. Didn't get a replacement in time," Nick answered swiftly, not wanting to bring up the years of watching her fail. "And yours?"

Bane went quiet for long moments. "Suicide."

Nick's mouth opened and shut. There was nothing to say to that. Even the ubiquitous, "I'm sorry" hardly seemed enough, but he said it anyways.

"She'd received a…a shock. She saw things that no one should see." Bane's beautiful face was bleak. "And she didn't survive it."

That was such an odd way to describe the reason for a suicide that Nick was struck dumb for a moment.

"That's awful," Nick murmured finally.

"Yes." Bane swallowed down a full glass of margarita and poured another.

"What about your father? Is he still alive?"

"No."

There was no room after that definitive, almost angry "no" for more discussion in that direction. So Nick cleared his throat and asked something that seemed on safer ground, "You were saying that your mother was an artist."

"She was a painter. She would have loved to paint this." Bane gestured to the riotous growth of roses that bobbed in the moonlight. "Once upon a time, Moon Shadow had a very formal rose garden. I can still see the ghost of it, but nature has taken over."

Nick saw a profusion of blooms bursting forth everywhere; a jungle of blossoms and thorns.

"It's beautiful," Nick agreed.

Bane laughed dryly. "One of the projects I will have for you is to make it into what it once was."

Nick's eyes went quite round. "That will be an undertaking. It's beautiful now, but it will gorgeous once its restored. I just hope I don't kill anything. My green thumb is more of a black thumb. I've even killed cactuses."

"Most of it will just be weeding, trimming, cutting, essentially back breaking work in the sun." Bane looked at Nick's skin. "You will need SPF 50 sunblock if you are to help with this."

"More than that. I burn *with* SPF 75 on," Nick laughed and Bane actually gave him a weak smile in return.

"You have English skin. I had the same problems when I first lived in India," Bane said. He actually bit his lip as if he regretted admitting this fact.

"You lived in India?" Nick leaned forward in his chair. "At the same estate I saw your doppelganger in front of?"

Those pictures really *were* eerie. It was like seeing evidence of time travel. Nick wondered if Bane felt that way looking at his ancestor.

Bane took another drink of margarita, perhaps to give himself time to recover. "Yes, I lived there up until my twenties."

"Do you still own that estate? Do you go back there?" Nick was filled with curiosity. He had always wanted to go to India, especially with his camera.

"I still own it and no, I do not go back."

"Why not?"

"Because my business keeps me very busy," Bane's answer was clipped.

Nick leaned back in his chair and the openness that had begun between them seemed suddenly lost. He played with his drink and didn't look at Bane.

"I was scarred there," Bane said, shocking him.

Nick's head jerked up. Again, it was clear from Bane's expression that he wanted to draw the words back into his mouth as soon as they were out. He looked like he was not quite able to believe he had said them. Nick's gaze went to the burned handprint on Bane's face. Bane dipped his head down so that more of his hair covered the scar as if he were trying to hide it.

"How did it happen? It looks so painful," Nick asked.

Bane brought one hand up to his face, but then lowered it. "You wouldn't believe me if I told you."

"Try me," Nick challenged.

"India is an ancient place. Things exist there that exist nowhere else. People have abilities…" He stopped and waved a hand as if it were nothing. "But it does not matter. It makes me peevish to speak of it."

Nick was quiet for a minute and then said, "Fair enough. I don't want you to think of painful things."

Bane glanced up at his face and Nick realized that the man believed he was telling the truth. He looked almost…touched. At that moment, Omar appeared with a pan of bubbling enchiladas. Nick immediately got up to help plate them, but Omar shooed him down again.

"But I want to help," Nick protested.

"You will help me by eating them," Omar assured him.

Both Bane and Nick immediately dug into the gooey enchiladas. The peppers, cheese and chicken worked together to make a perfect savory goodness that had them focusing on food and forgetting everything else. Omar came out once more with sour cream, and then with a pleased look at them, went inside the house leaving them to the food, the crickets, the candles, the night and each other.

After devouring one enchilada and having served himself another one, Bane said, "Your photography…I'm surprised that your father is allowing you to pursue it if he thinks it so worthless."

Nick placed a dollop of sour cream in the very center of a square of enchilada before answering simply, "He isn't."

Bane frowned. "I don't understand. He's paying for your schooling, isn't he? You are still living at home—"

Nick let out a thin laugh. "The night that this all happened." He gestured between them. "I was coming to tell my father that I was pursuing my art career. He had already told me if I did that I would be disowned, but like I said, art means just about everything to me. So if this *deal* or whatever hadn't happened, I would have been living with my friend Jade and paying my own way through school."

"So he was going to disown you when you accepted the deal?" Bane's brow furrowed.

"Yep," Nick answered simply.

"And you were willing to accept the loss of the money and help and—"

"And family? Yeah. I was," Nick answered.

"You didn't think he would relent?"

"No. Dad's not the kind to take losing well. And he would have considered it losing by me deciding to pursue my dreams instead of his."

Bane continued to frown. "But you came here and agreed to my terms to—to *save* them."

Nick shrugged. "You have the same look on your face that I think my best friend did on hers when I told her what I was doing."

"Now it makes even less sense to me that you would come here."

Nick set down his fork and stared at one of the candles that flickered between them. "I told Jade that I was doing this so that when I did break away from the family that I would have no guilt about it. I would know that I had done my best by them. I would be free and clear with no guilt." He paused and continued, "But when you said earlier tonight that you hoped I wasn't doing it out of love...well, maybe I was hoping that my dad and brothers might just feel a little differently about me because of this."

Bane's Siberian blue eyes locked onto his. "You're an outsider to them?"

"Oh, yeah, the changeling in the family. I was more like our mom, but..." Nick shrugged again. "I think they love me as much as they can love anyone, you know?"

"Love? You would do better to put your faith in something else to change their behavior towards you." Bane's mouth compressed into a tight line.

"You don't believe in love?" Nick's eyebrows rose up.

"No."

"I can't let this go at a one-word answer, Bane. Why don't you believe in love?" Nick asked.

The billionaire grimaced and dabbed his mouth with his napkin. "Because as I told you earlier if love were real then your father would have behaved quite differently towards you."

Nick felt a sharp pain in his chest as he said, "Actually, that might just prove that my father doesn't love *me*, but that doesn't mean love isn't real."

"The greatest betrayals come from those who should love us," Bane's Siberian blue eyes seemed to burn with intensity as he said this. "In the end though, love is really another word for *passion* and *selfishness*. We want those who make us feel good to stay with us as long as possible. We try to bind them to us to keep that good feeling going and we call those bonds *love*. But when that person no longer incites those pleasurable feelings we discard them, often in the most painful way possible."

Nick regarded Bane critically. He saw the tension in Bane's jaw. The grim determination in Bane's eyes. The twist of pain in Bane's flattening mouth. And Nick found himself asking, "Who hurt you?"

Bane reared back as if struck. He blinked. "What do you mean? I'm not speaking of anyone specific, but love in general. You asked why I don't believe in love and I answered you."

The reaction, of course, told Nick he was right on the money. "Love is a *concept*. It doesn't hurt us all by itself. *People* hurt us. *People* make us believe or not believe in concepts."

Bane's eyes narrowed. "You are wrong. I—"

"Every inch of you right now shows pain and betrayal. The *idea* of love doesn't do that, but a *person* would. The memory of their betrayal would," Nick pointed out.

Bane regarded him silently for long moments. "I see that you are done with dinner."

Nick looked down at his empty plate. It was practically licked clean and the pan of enchiladas was empty. Confused, he answered, "I—yeah, I guess."

There was a scraping noise as Bane scooted his chair back from the table and stood. He placed his napkin over his empty plate and inclined his head. "Then I will take my leave of you. Goodnight."

And with that, Bane left Nick alone on the back porch amidst white roses and candles and the new knowledge that someone had shattered Bane's heart.

CHAPTER SIXTEEN

CLAWS

After leaving Nick on the back porch, Bane ran into Omar in the hallway as the Indian man popped out of the kitchen ahead of him. Omar had a tray in his hand that held two flans, obviously for dessert.

"Bane, what is wrong?" Omar asked, wide eyed.

"Nothing. Dinner was lovely. Share dessert with Nick," Bane answered curtly and blew past the Indian man.

"But you love my flan!" Omar called after him. "You were getting along with Nick ! You were making progress! So what is wrong?"

Bane did not stop to answer him with another lie. Instead, he headed to his study and shut the door. He poured a huge portion of Scotch and drank down half of it. He leaned back in his chair. The beast prowled in his chest back and forth, back and forth. It bared its teeth and growled low in the back of its throat. It always did this when he thought of his first lover: the man that had been his father's best friend, had taken his virginity and had caused his downfall.

Alastair, I hate you still.

Bane swallowed the rest of the Scotch. He knew that he had left Nick out on the porch flummoxed. Nick's perceptive—if *innocent* question—had dredged up the old hurt and made it fresh again.

One would think that after 100 years that I would be through with thinking of him.

But Alastair had taught him all he needed to know about life. He'd shown Bane how love was a lie. He'd demonstrated how betrayal was easy, even *common*. He'd destroyed who Bane had been and who he might have become with his cruelty. Bane poured himself another Scotch.

I won't think about Alastair.

He wished the conversation with Nick had not gone as it had. He had actually been enjoying the meal and the company. If not for Alastair's unwelcome memory, he would still be out there, perhaps hearing more about Nick's photography and the young man's other dreams. He wasn't alone in his wish to still be with Nick. The beast had stopped pacing and its attention was back on the young man. Bane closed his eyes and let his enhanced hearing tune into Omar and Nick chatting over the flan.

"So Bane said something interesting, Omar," Nick was saying.

"Oh?"

"Well, actually what was interesting was the thing he *didn't* say. We were talking about love and it was clear—well, it *seemed* clear—to me that he'd gotten his heart broken," Nick said.

Bane had been leaning back in his chair, but at these words he sat upright and nearly stood up, ready to storm out there. He was tense as a bow as he thought, *Omar, you will not tell him about Alastair!*

The Indian man gave a sigh. "Most people who reach Bane's age have had their hearts a little chipped."

"*Bane's age*? He's not that old, Omar!" Nick laughed and Bane imagined the young man rocking back in his chair in amusement.

"He has had more experience than you might imagine," Omar said carefully.

Good job covering for your mistake, Omar! Bane slumped back in his desk chair.

"So what happened? Who hurt him?" Nick asked sounding both genuinely worried and curious.

Omar, he does not need to know this. Keep it general, Bane mentally willed, but he knew it would not do any good.

"Bane behaves as if he has no heart, but the truth is that he's—"

"More sensitive than most people? Yeah, I sort of got that." Bane could hear the smile in Nick's voice as he said this.

You think I'm sensitive? No, you have believed me a bastard with no heart...until now. Bane crossed his arms over his chest.

"You realized that, did you? What gave his sensitivity away?" Omar chuckled.

"Uhm, *everything*." Nick laughed so hard he started coughing and Bane heard him take a drink.

What?!

"Okay, maybe *not* everything." Nick's voice was filled with amusement. "But no one could be so serious all the time without being sensitive. It's like the world is a brillo pad on his skin. I, especially, am an *irritant*."

You are a pebble in my shoe, Nick. An attractive pebble, but I am constantly aware of you. Even now the beast fixates on you and I wonder if it is safe ...

"Why do you think that is?" Omar asked.

"Uhm, because I'm a Fairfax and Fairfaxes are *scum*? I don't know," Nick admitted. "For a while there at dinner I thought...I don't know what I thought. I actually sort of enjoyed talking to him. He's clearly intelligent and interesting, but a little *prickly*."

It was a good talk, Nick. I enjoyed it, too. Bane found himself smiling.

"Bane and you are more alike than you know. He's had to create an armor around himself to survive," Omar explained.

The world is a cruel place.

"Yeah, Jade keeps saying that I need to do that, too, but I don't want to lose who I am because of other people, you know?" He heard Nick pouring some more margarita into his glass.

"Yes, I know exactly what you mean. If you change because of those who hurt you—and not for the better—then they have truly won," Omar agreed.

"Was it a lover that *won* against Bane?" Nick asked.

Bane's shoulders tensed. *Alastair did not win. I learned from my experiences with him.*

"Yes," Omar answered finally after a long pause. "The man who hurt Bane was the best friend of Bane's father."

"Seriously?" Nick's voice went high and scandalized.

"You are thinking of some old decrepit man! Not that old men cannot be dapper and attractive."

Nick laughed. "You're very handsome, Omar, and anyone would be happy to be with you."

"Thank you on behalf of all older gentlemen everywhere." Bane imagined Omar bowing at that.

"Still it seems pretty damned sleazy for a friend of Bane's dad to seduce his son. How old was Bane at the time?" Nick asked.

"In his early twenties, but the way he was raised...well, he was more innocent than people of that age now," Omar explained. "And there were greater consequences for being homosexual."

"He said he grew up in India," Nick said.

"Y-yes, I'm afraid my country is not all that progressive in that way quite yet and when Bane was with Alastair it was even less so," Omar explained.

It was a death sentence back then so you had to trust the person you were with absolutely. Alastair sold me out for money. Money...

"I'm guessing that Bane trusted this man?" Nick's voice dipped low.

"Yes, and it was a *poor,* if understandable, choice. Bane's father was very...remote." He imagined from the thumping sound that Omar was drumming his fingers on the table. "More than that. He was *cruel*. And when Alastair showed Bane affection, Bane jumped at it."

Alastair was NOT a father replacement! He was the exact opposite of a father!

"Did Bane's dad...hurt him?" Nick asked tentatively.

Bane's shoulders bunched.

"Yes, he was a physically violent man to both Bane and his mother," Omar said.

"I'm sorry. I shouldn't be asking you this, Omar. I know Bane wouldn't want me to know this about him," Nick said.

"And, normally, I would not reveal these things, but I am making an exception for you, because I think knowing his past will make Bane's behavior more understandable."

"Still trying to get me to save Bane?"

I do not need saving! Especially not by you, Nick.

"Perhaps. But tell me that *you* don't need some saving, too," Omar's tone was gentle, but Bane recognized it as the tone he used with Bane when he was imparting some hard truths.

Nick was quiet for long moments, but then he said, "Maybe you're right. Getting away from my family has been good. Cleared my head. And if Bane lets me take pictures of Moon Shadow it will really be worthwhile."

"I'm sure he will. Oh, Nick, you look exhausted! Go on to bed," Omar suggested.

"The dishes aren't done," Nick protested through yawns.

"I will get them."

"Omar, you *cooked*. I can, at least, clean," Nick protested.

"Do not be silly. I find cleaning very soothing. It will help me get to sleep. Now go to bed," Omar shooed him away.

Bane and the beast listened to Nick's soft footfalls as he went down the hall and up the stairs to his bedroom. He heard Nick undressing. Toeing off his shoes, whisking off his shirt, and dropping his pants and underwear. Then there was the rush of water as he brushed his teeth. These sounds had Bane's eyelids closing. His breathing evened out. There was just one stray thought before he slept and that was an awareness that the beast was not bedding down with him. It was wide, wide awake and listening to Nick's heart beating.

Bane thought he was dreaming again.

He was in the shape of the beast, stalking through the rose bushes, and observing Moon Shadow from the back yard. He looked up at Nick's bedroom window. It was dark. The young man was sleeping soundly. He had worked hard that day and had finally fallen into unconsciousness. It made sense that he should dream of Nick sleeping though he wished Nick were awake and at the window so that he could see him.

I could have stayed with him at dinner, but I couldn't bear it. I couldn't ...

Omar had hoped the dinner would make him understand Nick better and it had. Though he tried to tell himself that Nick's strenuous defense of his photography was merely talk, he didn't really believe that. Nick's passion and desperate uncertainty about his art was so like his mother's. Her paintings had been exquisite. They were filled with emotions that made it very difficult for him to even look at them so he housed them in the attic, covered by sheets. But he couldn't tuck Nick away, out of sight.

Nick made him *feel*. Nick made him *want*. Nick made him *dream*.

So he stared at those black windows and wished...wished...

I want to see him. I want to see Nick. I want to smell him and touch him and lick him. I want to possess him.

Roses bobbed in the night wind, sending their sweet and subtle scent all around him. It was the scent of desire. He climbed the stairs of the porch and looked at the closed screen door. The handle was flat and only needed to be depressed. He lifted one massive paw and the handle moved down and the door popped open. The interior door was ajar. He vaguely remembered dreaming about leaving it open when he had walked out into the garden. Even in dreams he would not transform in the house.

On soft tiger paws Bane glided into the mansion. The interior of Moon Shadow was a vision of velvety blacks and bone whites. All the electric lights were off. Only the moonlight that streamed through the mullioned windows cut through the pure darkness. Bane's enhanced night vision was hardly necessary though as he knew every inch of Moon Shadow by heart. The first time he had set foot within the mansion's walls he had felt at home. He had experienced nothing like that since entering his family's estate in England.

He made his way to the stairs and silently padded up them. In his beast form, he could take the stairs four at a time. He mounted the last step and slipped into the hallway. Nick's room was just fifty feet away. The door was cracked open, which was convenient. His paws would not work on door knobs even in dreams. He nosed the door open and stood in the doorway.

The curtains were parted in the center, allowing a thin stream of moonlight to come in. Bane's head swung towards the four poster bed. He could hear Nick's soft breathing. His head lifted up and he saw the silhouette of Nick's sleeping form. He stalked towards the bed and placed his front paws on top of the mattress. The bed sank down with his weight as he lifted himself up.

Nick was laying on his back. One arm was flung across his eyes while the other was lying along his side His chest was bare. The covers only came up to his waist. A hint of the treasure trail of hair disappeared underneath the blanket. Bane's gaze followed the hills and valleys of the muscles of Nick's belly. He noted how cut Nick's hipbones were. His tongue came out as he saw those cinnamon colored nipples. He was just about to hoist himself all the way up onto the bed and taste them when he heard Nick sigh. He froze. Nick rolled onto his side, facing Bane. Nick's eyes remained, thankfully, closed.

But this is a dream. If he wakes it won't be a problem. It will be like before.

But Bane felt that somehow that wasn't true. He waited two heartbeats to make sure that Nick was deeply asleep before he got down from the bed on silent paws. He stared at Nick for long moments before he melted into darkness.

Bane remembered nothing more of the dream. When he woke up in his bed the next morning, he was still thinking of the dream, still remembering how beautiful Nick looked spread out on the bed, sensual and innocent.

Why can I not dream of him and myself fully in human form though? Why must the beast always be a part of this?

Bane stretched out his legs luxuriously. His feet slipped out from under the covers. He felt something gritty on the sheets beneath his feet. He sat up, moving his hair out of his face, and looked down at them. The bottoms of his feet were covered in *dirt*.

CHAPTER SEVENTEEN
EYES LIKE STARS

Nick had been so tired that he'd barely remembered stripping, brushing his teeth and collapsing on the mattress. The cleaning and ironing had taken more out of him than he'd realized. Just as he'd fallen into sleep he had an uncomfortable thought that Bane would be *amused* that he was achy after the first day of hard work.

A good night's sleep is all I need. I'll be fine tomorrow. Unless I dream of Bane and tigers again.

And he did.

But it was different than before, because he wasn't an unwilling participant, but eager to curl against Bane's side. And no longer was the dream drenched with the exotic spice of India. The dream took place on Moon Shadow's back porch. It was night and the moon was full and heavy in the sky.

Nick was sitting on the couch with his legs tucked beneath him and his head resting on one of Bane's massive shoulders. The billionaire was practically purring. The steady beat of his heart was in Nick's ears. One of Bane's muscular arms was curled around him and he lightly trailed one hand up and down Nick's spine. Unlike in every real life encounter they'd had, there was no tension or anger between them. He felt peace and comfort. He felt like they *belonged* to one another.

Something in Nick's chest seized. Belonging was something he'd never really had.

Nick put his nose against the collar of Bane's shirt and drew in deep breaths. Bane's unique scent of sandalwood and cinnamon filled Nick's nostrils. He found that he couldn't get enough of that smell. Bane let out a rumbly laugh.

"You like my scent, Nick?" The man's Siberian blue eyes were not sharp or cold, but filled with warmth and softness as he gazed down at Nick

"I do," Nick found himself saying. "It comforts me."

One of Bane's large yet elegant hands caressed Nick's cheek. "I am glad. Because you are safe with me."

"Safe?" That was not a word he would have used about Bane when he was awake. He had always felt anything but safe with him, and yet, right at that moment, he could almost believe it.

"I will protect you from anyone and anything," Bane promised, his eyes unblinking as he said it. "Even myself. *Especially* myself. For you are my mate."

"Mate? That sounds a lot like *love*, Bane, and you do not believe in that," Nick pointed out. A trickle of desire wound through him at the word "mate". It was a primal word. It meant belonging, too.

Bane just smiled.

Out of the corner of Nick's eye, he saw something white moving through the tangle of rose bushes. His head lifted up and he was alert, his breath catching in his throat, and his heart beginning to race. Bane though continued to just hold him. Completely unconcerned.

"What's that?" Nick breathed.

"It's the beast," Bane answered.

"*Beast*?!" Nick sat up fully, but Bane pulled him close again.

There was a parting in the rose bushes and Nick saw the head of a massive white Bengal tiger looking at them. It had eyes the color of stars.

"Don't be afraid," Bane whispered in his ear. "It won't come up here."

"Why not? What's stopping it?"

The beast could have ripped through the rose bushes and leaped onto the porch in a single bound.

"You stop it, Nick," Bane whispered again. "You keep it calm. You tame the beast in me."

The tiger made a soft rumble and all Nick could see were its eyes as it withdrew into the darkness of the roses. Nick turned to look at Bane again and forgot about the tiger. The man was so beautiful and powerful and *sensual*. Nick reached up and followed the length of Bane's jaw with his fingertips. His hand moved up into Bane's hair. It was *soft*. He curled the long strands around his fingers and then brought them up to his nose and breathed in more of that citrus and sandalwood scent.

"You like the smell of me," Bane murmured as he leaned in and sniffed Nick's hair. "But I *love* the smell of you."

Nick shivered and arched back to give Bane more access to his throat. "You say that like you want to take a *bite* out of me."

Bane's mouth opened and his hot breath gushed over Nick's neck. "Maybe I *do*."

"You mean you're not just interested in me scrubbing your toilets?" Nick let out a throaty laugh.

"Oh, I *am* interested in that, too." Bane's lips curled into a smile.

"Really? I thought this was *my* dream. Not yours." Nick huffed.

"This is a dream? This feels quite real to me," Bane chuckled as his lips drifted over Nick's collarbone.

Nick shivered and tipped his head back. "Has to be a dream. We hate one another."

"Do we? But dinner tonight was so...*nice*." Bane lapped at the hollow of his throat.

"Yeah, it was. Sort of," Nick murmured.

Bane grasped his chin and tilted Nick's head so that they were eye to eye. "*Sort of?*"

"Until you left."

"I had to leave." Bane buried his head in Nick's curls.

"Why?"

"Because I was in pain and I didn't want to lash out at you."

Nick rested their foreheads together. "You don't have to be alone with your pain."

Bane's fingers trailed down his cheeks. "You would share it with me? Even though I'm keeping you practically prisoner? Your phone and your camera are locked in my desk. Out of your reach. So does one dinner change things between us?"

"You have a point," Nick said without heat. "I should be very angry with you. I *am* angry."

"Yes, I know. But then again...maybe you should think of those actions as me *protecting* you instead of me *imprisoning* you." Bane kissed his jaw. "Keeping your father and everyone else away so it's just the two of us."

"My father doesn't care about me. No one, but Jade does and I *like* her. I want to talk to her," Nick objected.

"Maybe you should just realize I want you all to myself then. That's what this is all about. I saw you on the street and I just couldn't look away," Bane breathed in his hair. "But then I was disappointed when I realized you were with *him*. Charles Fairfax."

"Saw me in the street? I don't understand." Nick's forehead furrowed. But then Bane was kissing him on the mouth.

It was like he was being devoured. Bane's lips, teeth, tongue in him and on him. Feasting upon him. Hot, wet, deep, breath-stealing kisses. Bane pulled away and his Siberian blue eyes glittered like stars just like the tiger's had. Nick trembled.

"You confuse me," Nick said after licking his lips. "You seem to hate me. You act badly towards me. Then tonight at dinner you're different like you finally—"

"Saw you? Yes, perhaps I have a little. I am a selfish creature, Nick. And when I'm disappointed I lash out," Bane murmured.

"You were disappointed because you realized I was a Fairfax?"

"Yes, because I thought it meant I couldn't have you, but now...now I see that's not true at all," Bane murmured.

"You don't *have* me. This is a dream. A weird dream. Tomorrow, I'll be all freaked I had it and—"

"But you're in my arms now, aren't you?" Bane looked up at him through dark lashes. "So perhaps you might as well enjoy it? You can *curse* yourself tomorrow for falling for my charms."

"So no guilt for falling for the bastard Bane?" Nick's lips curled into a smile.

Bane feathered his fingers through the back of Nick's hair. "You might find that I can be *charming*. A gentleman even."

"I'll have to take your word for that."

"No, Nick." Bane's fingers trailed over his lips. "I will *show* you."

Nick put his arms around Bane's neck. "Tomorrow is a new day."

One of Bane's massive hands was suddenly between them. He undid the button and zipper of Nick's pants with practiced ease. The with a tigrish smile, he pulled Nick's cock out into the cool night air. Nick hissed and bit his lower lip. He reached for Bane's pants and undid his as well. Bane's cock was as wonderfully huge as the rest of him. Nick ran a hand up and down that massive, rose-colored shaft. He then dragged a finger along the slit and licked the precum from it.

"You taste like roses," Nick laughed.

Bane's mouth was on his again. His tongue seemed to chase that taste all around the interior of Nick's mouth. Nick was breathing heavily when they broke apart. But he hardly had a chance to catch his breath before Bane caught both their cocks in one of his large hands and began to stroke them.

Nick's fingers dug into Bane's shoulders as he made a keening sound in the back of his throat.

"H-harder," he begged.

Bane obliged. Heat built up in Nick's balls and shaft as Bane's hand squeezed and stroked him just like he wanted. He scrabbled at the front of Bane's shirt when the big man ran a thumb over his slit, spreading it wide. Precum bubbled up eagerly. Bane used it to make the stroking *slicker*.

"Kiss me, Nick," Bane demanded. "I want to feel those lips of yours upon me. I want to know you want me, not just a stranger's touch on your beautiful cock."

"I want you. God, I want you!" Nick cried.

He was trembling all over and felt clumsy as he lowered his lips onto Bane's. At first, it was just a press of flesh. Not an open-mouthed kiss, but closed and tender and rather desperate. Then Bane's lips parted under his. Their tongues slowly tangled together. The taste of Bane had him keening, especially when Bane sped up his strokes. He ground his front against Bane's hard stomach. His balls were already drawing tight against his body. Bane had him on edge. He was *always* on edge with the big man.

"Cum with me? Please," Nick moaned against Bane's mouth.

He raked his fingernails down Bane's back and the billionaire let out a tigerish rumble. Bane's fingers rolled his balls then and Nick bit down on Bane's lower lip, which had the man laughing.

"You are like a *kitten* nipping at me," Bane said.

"A *needy* kitten with *claws*." Nick raked his fingernails down Bane's back again.

"That just feels *good*, Nick."

"Make me feel good then. Please?"

"How can I refuse such a pretty request?"

They kissed again, devouring each other, their bodies crushed together. Bane's hand rose up and down on their two shafts. Heat flared in Nick's groin. His cock *burned*. His balls *ached* with the need to release. The friction of Bane's hand against the velvety skin of his cock was too much. He surged against Bane again and both of them moaned. And then Nick was cumming and so was Bane. All over Bane's hand. All over Bane's beautiful clothes. All over each other.

Nick collapsed onto Bane as the last gush of cum exited him. Bane pressed kisses to his hair, gentling him through the aftershocks. Nick's eyes drifted shut. This was glorious. This was right.

Except for the sticky clothes.

He grinned against Bane's chest. "What do you say about having a shower together—"

There was a rumbling roar in the rose bushes. Nick jerked upright and snapped his head around towards the garden. The tiger was back! Only it wasn't in the rose bushes any more. It was on the porch's steps.

The tiger's coat was pure white with onyx black stripes. It was three times Nick's size. One swipe of those paws and he would be dead. But those paws looked so soft, too. It padded over to him on those paws. It's eyes shone like stars.

"Bane," Nick whispered. He reached for the billionaire, but his hand just found air. He turned his head to find that Bane was no longer beside him. Bane was *gone*. It was just him and the tiger. "Bane!"

Nick rocked up in his bed as he soared out of the dream. The china on the tray Omar was carrying rattled as the Indian man nearly jumped out of his skin at Nick's scream.

"Nick, are you all right?" Omar asked, quickly setting the tray on the night table. He hustled over to Nick's side and sat down on the bed placing one hand on Nick's forehead as if to test for a fever. "You feel a little warm."

"I'm okay," Nick said, still shaky. "I just had a really weird dream."

"A dream? What about?"

"You heard what I...what I screamed, didn't you?" Nick asked.

"Bane's name." Omar's brown eyes were full of trepidation. One of his hands reached up and played with a necklace he had on under his gray shirt. Nick saw it and realized it was a stylized *tiger* motif.

"Tigers," Nick murmured.

"What?" Omar sat up straighter.

"That's a tiger charm. Does it mean something?" Nick asked. He was suddenly so alert. Tigers in his dreams. Tigers around Omar's neck. Tigers in Bane's study.

"Ah, yes, it is part of my religion," Omar explained.

"What part exactly?"

Omar got up from the bed and went over to the windows. He pulled the curtains open. Sunlight streamed in and Nick put up an arm to cover his eyes.

"My people believe that there is an ultimate spirit for every living thing. We worship the tiger spirit," Omar explained as he came back to the side table and placed the tray on Nick's lap. "But we have failed the spirit."

"What are you talking about?"

"The tiger spirit ensures the health and vitality of all tigers, but there are few left in the wild," Omar said as he took off the silver lip to reveal French toast, bacon and fresh squeezed juice. There was also the very necessary press pot of coffee.

"That's not your fault, Omar. That's all of humanity's fault," Nick said even as his gaze focused on the silver tiger charm with diamond eyes that reminded him of stars.

"You would think so. But the spirit that we worship was…injured. Imprisoned." Omar sat down on the bed and he looked so forlorn that Nick's heart ached. "We failed and now every tiger suffers."

"Omar, no, no, don't think that." Nick squeezed the Indian man's shoulder. Though he had little understanding of what Omar meant, and doubted it could be true, he said, "I've only known you a short time, but I also know that faith like yours is rare. I'm sure you're doing more than a million people could do."

"You are too kind, Nick. But you must trust me when I say that I have failed."

"Well, I don't know if it's connected at all to your faith, but I've been dreaming of tigers." Nick gave out an uncomfortable laugh and ran a hand through his hair.

"You have been dreaming of *tigers*?" Omar blinked.

"A white Bengal tiger with eyes like stars," Nick said and let out another uncomfortable laugh. "That sounds so crazy, doesn't it?"

Omar looked almost *awed*. "No, Nick, I do not think that is crazy at all."

CHAPTER EIGHTEEN
HOUSEGUESTS

"He is dreaming of the tiger spirit!" Omar paced in Bane's office and Omar *never* paced. His hands rose up in the air like startled birds and soared down to his sides again.

"He is dreaming of *tigers*. He saw *this* pelt." Bane gestured towards the floor where the white Bengal tiger pelt lay, forever growling. "It means *nothing*."

And yet his heart beat harder at the thought. The beast looked unsurprised, but it was too busy following Nick's progress upstairs.

Omar stopped pacing right in front of him and gave him an incredulous look. "You do not believe that."

"I don't believe it means what you do. I am certain of that," Bane replied dryly.

"It is a *sign*, Bane." Omar began pacing again. "He cried out *your* name when he woke from this morning's dream."

Bane blinked. "He did?"

"Yes, it was quite a *desperate* cry."

"Why was he *desperate* for me?"

"I did not ask him. It seemed too personal to do so. But the *tiger*, Bane! He is dreaming of the *tiger spirit*." Omar stopped pacing again to face him. "Are you dreaming of Nick?"

Bane was, but he decided not to tell Omar that and feed the Indian man's desperate belief that the curse was on the verge of being broken. He then thought of his dirty feet and a corkscrew of unease wound through him. That could have been *more* than a dream last night. If the beast had truly taken control of him outside of the full moon...well, he didn't know what that meant.

I must have been sleepwalking. That's all. The beast is contained.

But despite his attempt to hide the dreams from Omar, the Indian man *knew*. His expression likely had given it away somehow. Omar put his hands flat against the desk and stared directly into Bane's eyes.

"You *have* been dreaming of him," Omar stated. A statement not a fact.

"I...it is a normal thing that I dream of him," Bane said lamely even as he avoided the Indian man's eyes. "He is in the house! He is underfoot! I caught him in my things! He actually looked at the photographs—"

"Did he recognize you?" Omar appeared alarmed.

"He just thinks I'm a throwback. No one ever believes in immortality even when presented with actual proof of it." Bane's waved Omar's concern away.

"Are you *certain*? Nick is *not* like other young men and—"

"I'm sure."

Omar ran a hand through his thick dark hair and began to pace. "How could you not tell me that you were sharing dreams?"

"I did not—and *do not* — know if we are even sharing them! I've dreamed of him. He's dreamed of me." Bane crossed his arms over his chest. He lowered his voice and said, "But it is *nothing*. Truly."

"*Nothing?*"

"Omar, I understand your desire that something occur between Nick and myself in order to break the curse. But the young man is..." His usual adjectives did not leave his lips as he was not certain of them at all any longer. Spoilt? No.

Vacuous? No. Brat? No. Sensitive, artistic and kind? Yes, yes, and yes. He had been wrong about Nick. He could see that now. But it was too late to undo what he'd done. Ruining Nick's family would have stopped anything from happening between them anyways. The only chance he had of keeping the young man near was this deal and that wasn't endearing Nick to him.

So he said, "Nick Fairfax is not for me."

"And who is? It is not the Devon Wainwrights of this world!"

"Why not?" Bane asked even as he already knew the answer.

"Because you will *never* love Devon! You keep him near so that you will avoid knowing a man you *could* love," Omar explained.

"And you think that man is Nick Fairfax? I can hardly stand to be in the same room with him so why—"

"You may lie to yourself about how you feel about Nick, but not to me." Omar put a hand against the center of his chest and thumped it. "At this very moment, you know where he is in this house, do you not? You are eager to have him near you."

Bane reddened. He was attracted to Nick, but it was nothing. Nick might not be a spoilt brat, but he was not someone Bane could have. The dreams were nothing. All of it was nothing.

"He is coming here to phone his father so I am *expecting* him, but I am not *unduly* aware of him." Bane stopped at Omar's second incredulous look of that morning. "You are mistaken, Omar."

"I have known you for over fifty years," Omar said, his voice gently. "Nick *challenges* you. He makes you *remember* your past. He *reaches* you somehow. It is not a comfortable thing, but it will lead to good things in the end if you let it."

Bane thought of his extreme desire to see Nick in his dream. He had never wanted to be with someone so badly that he had dreamed of them. He had never dreamed of anyone at all. Not even Alastair and certainly not Devon.

"I am very surprised that you would want me to *romance* the young man considering the power I have over his family," Bane remarked dryly.

"I would have you *release* him from this deal and romance him outside of it," Omar said, his large brown eyes pleading.

Bane's heart clenched. "If I released him he would surely leave and have nothing to do with me, Omar."

"And that thought bothers you, doesn't it? The thought of him being gone? The thought of him leaving you?" Omar's insightful stare had Bane shuffling his feet like a guilty child.

Bane stopped that guilty movement and instead shrugged and pretended a nonchalance he did not feel. "I am *not* letting him out of the deal so he will *not* be leaving."

"This is folly, Bane." Omar shook his head slowly. "Such folly."

Bane glanced out of the open door. Nick would be coming to his study any moment now to call his father and to take the camera. His palms grew damp. Giving Nick the camera would be an act of complete trust though Nick didn't know that.

But it is just for today. When it is nearer the full moon I will have to keep it locked away. For Nick's sake and mine.

"It is over and done, Omar. I cannot undo this. Nick is here to stay. Now I know that you have duties to attend to before my guests arrive and I—I must finish some work. You are dismissed," Bane said coolly.

"You will be a gentleman to Nick this weekend?" Omar looked at him anxiously.

"Of course. I was last night, was I not?"

Omar's eyebrows rose. "Until you ran away."

The scar burned and he looked away from the Indian man. "I—he seemed to have a better time after I left. He likes *you*."

"So you *were* listening!" Omar looked triumphant.

"I just happened to overhear." A flush of heat ran through him.

"Of course you did."

"Do not look *smug*, Omar. It does not look well upon you," Bane growled.

Omar laughed as he left Bane's study. Bane tapped idly on his computer, not really accomplishing anything. Like Omar had guessed he was *acutely* aware of Nick's location in Moon Shadow. The young man was making sure there were enough fresh towels in all the guest rooms.

Bane was having three guests for the weekend. Devon, Dean Kettering, CEO of Hermitage Pharmaceuticals, and Sloan Wu, a partner in an international law firm that served as outside counsel to Bane's companies. Devon had no connection to the Fairfaxes, but Dean's company had also almost been taken over by them recently and Sloan's legal maneuvering had helped Bane fight off the Fairfaxes' attack. This weekend was partially to celebrate his victory over Nick's family. He frowned as he imagined how Nick would react to people's hatred of the Fairfaxes.

Perhaps I should have Nick serve with Omar, and not have him sit with us. He'll be exposed to less triumph and experience less discomfort that way.

At that moment, his enhanced hearing caught Nick's footsteps approaching the study. His heart beat faster. He stood up and smoothed down the front of his suit coat. Nick knocked and poked his head in.

"Are you ready for me, Bane?" Nick asked. He looked beautiful. His platinum curls gleamed like spun gold. His gray eyes were clear as the sky. His lips were full and plush and kissable. When Bane didn't answer him right away that smile on his lips faded somewhat. "Bane?"

Gentleman. Be a gentleman.

"Yes, of course. Please come in," Bane said with an awkward wave to urge Nick into his office.

The "please" again had that remarkable effect on Nick. The smile returned full force and he stepped inside the room.

"So...how are you?" Nick asked almost shyly.

"Fine. Very well. And you?" Bane gripped his hands before him to stop them from fussing.

"Good. Sleep well?"

Bane remembered his dream and his dirty feet in the morning. "Very... very deeply. What about you? Did you dream of—of anything?"

Did you dream of a tiger coming into your room and climbing onto your bed?

A flush crossed Nick's cheeks and Bane's heart slammed against his chest. The young man looked down at his feet and shuffled. "I've had some really...ah, *vivid* dreams. But I'm sure that will stop once I get used to being here."

A lock of hair fell down on Nick's forehead and Bane moved it back. Nick's head jerked up. His clear gray eyes were wide with surprise. The pink flush on his cheeks turned a deeper rose. Bane's hand was still outstretched though he no longer touched the blond curl.

"Bane..." Nick said uncertainly.

Bane slowly lowered his hand. "I...your hair was..."

Nick put a hand in his locks. "Sticking up? Yeah, that's what happens when I let it air dry. Look okay now?"

"Let me." Bane carefully reached out with both hands and gently rearranged Nick's curls. Nick held very still while he did so. The young man's clean and woodsy scent filled his nostrils and the beast's tail thumped. Bane quickly took a step back and dropped his arms to his sides.

"Everything okay?" Nick asked.

"Yes. Your hair is...it's fine now."

"A little OCD there, Bane?" Nick teased even though he sounded rather breathless.

You have been dreaming of me. I have been dreaming of you. Of tigers and moonlight and forbidden things. Omar is not right. He cannot be right that this means anything. Can he?

"Yes, always," Bane answered calmly. "It is my way."

"Except for your own hair. You should pull it back in a ponytail," Nick suggested. "Show your face."

Bane went rigid. "Show my scar, you mean?"

Nick shocked them both when he brushed the hair off of Bane's face to reveal the scar. "It's not as bad as you think."

Bane moved out of reach. "Polite lies are not necessary, Nick. I am well aware of how disfiguring the scar is."

Nick gave him a sad smile. "You won't believe anything different about it, will you?"

Bane opened his mouth to give some retort, but found himself answering simply, "Yes. It's so ugly. So prominent. How could it not be the first and *only* thing people notice when they see me?"

"It *isn't* the *only* thing. Sure I noticed it, but..." Nick tilted his head to the side. "Now it just seems a part of you. And the whole of you is handsome."

Bane blushed. He didn't blush or not often, but he was blushing hotly now. He lowered his head. "Yes, well...thank you. But you came here for other things."

"My camera." Nick sounded incredibly eager and Bane felt a stab of guilt that he had taken it from him at all.

"Your phone first." Bane pulled out the key to the desk drawer and stuck it into the lock. He turned it and pulled out the phone and handed it to the young man. Nick eagerly took the phone. "Will you call your father now?"

"Do you want me to call here in front of you?" Nick looked wary again.

That had been part of the deal between them. But the truth was that it did not matter if Nick was here or elsewhere in the house. Bane would hear it all. So he could be magnanimous and let Nick take the call in perceived privacy.

"No. You are more than welcome to stay here and call or go anywhere you like so long as you agree to turn over the phone again after you're done," Bane answered.

"I'm surprised you don't want to listen in. Make sure I'm not telling people things I shouldn't." Nick watched Bane's expression carefully.

"You're just calling your father, are you not?" Bane's shoulders tensed ever so slightly.

"And my best friend Jade. I need to assure her that you haven't imprisoned me in some love pit."

"*Love pit*?!" Bane sputtered.

"Yeah. She was pretty convinced that the whole deal was about that," Nick laughed.

A smile twitched on Bane's lips. "Perhaps I *should* listen in then."

"Well, I'm not going to be saying anything that you couldn't hear anyways, especially with my dad, so I'll stay here." Nick made a face that showed his dismay at talking to Charles Fairfax. Bane couldn't blame him.

"And what about your best friend? Jade, right? Aren't you going to gossip about me and the *love pit*?"

"I am going to tell her that there is *no* love pit, Bane." Nick scowled at him, but quickly broke into a grin.

You like to smile, Nick. That is your normal look, I think.

"She will think I'm quite boring then," Bane responded lightly.

"No, Bane, nobody could ever think you were *boring*." Nick shook his head as he started to scroll through his texts and messages. His smile died and he breathed out, "Damn."

"What?" Bane asked.

"Jade's called like seventeen times...uhm, let me rephrase that, seventeen times *this morning* and she's less a morning person than I am. She must be totally freaked out. I've got to call her," Nick said.

"Maybe call your father first and save your friend for later?"

But Nick shook his head. "My father could care less." Seeing something in Bane's face, he added, "My father hasn't called once, because he's sure I'm fine with you, but Jade doesn't know that. I'm calling her first."

"Of course, that makes sense." Bane hid his displeasure at Charles Fairfax. It was yet more proof that Charles was not a worthy person.

Nick turned halfway from him and called Jade. Bane's enhanced hearing kicked in without him even trying. The beast was sitting up, tail wagging happily, tongue lolling out as it watched Nick with complete happiness. The ringing continued on and on, but then finally went to voicemail. Nick cast his voice low and he left a message.

"Jade, I'm *so* sorry that I didn't call or text you back. Everything is fine. Just been really busy," Nick said on the voicemail message. "Everything is good. Bane's having guests this weekend so it's not a good time to visit, but maybe early next week. I might not be able to answer if you call me back, but just know I'm fine." He clicked off.

"Visit?" Bane's eyebrow rose.

"Ah, yeah, she mentioned stopping by to check on me. I was going to ask you if it was okay," Nick said and quickly looked away from him.

"You were going to ask for *permission* or *forgiveness*?" Bane found himself more amused than angry.

"Not sure really. Since you had my phone...well, it wasn't like I couldn't tell her *not* to come until now, right?" Nick looked at him through his lashes.

Bane let out a snort. "True."

"Perhaps I could keep my phone today...in case, she calls back?" Nick asked uncertainly.

"Nick..." Bane broke off.

"You're nervous. You're scared I'll do something you won't like. Here." Nick held out the phone to him. "It's okay. You don't have to let me keep it."

Bane stared down at the cell phone. "You need to call your father first then we'll talk about phone privileges."

Nick let out a soft laugh. "Do I have to? Today's been such a good day so far. You really want to ruin it for me?"

Bane's jaw clenched. "Charles will not hurt you. I will not allow it."

Nick's mouth opened in shock and something else. "You would *protect* me?"

"Yes, of course."

Nick stared at him long and hard. "Even against my father?"

The beast let out an angry growl, ready to rip apart anyone that hurt Nick. Bane swallowed. This was new.

"If he is cruel to you, I will stop it," Bane explained though he doubted that his words made much sense to Nick yet the young man seemed to find a different meaning in them. Or rather a *deeper* meaning than he intended for Nick to know.

"I would love for it to be different between my dad and I, but it isn't. I'll call him though. You'll see," Nick said and dialed his father's phone. He brought it up to his ear. Bane heard a ring and then it was picked up. "Dad? It's me. Nick."

"Oh, Nick! I wasn't expecting to hear from you," Charles said, sounding distracted.

With Bane's enhanced hearing, Charles' voice came in loud and clear to him. Bane also heard the man typing and talking to others even as his son—the son who had given up his freedom for a year—tried to talk to him.

"Yeah, well, Bane thought you might like to know I'm okay." Nick's body was stiff and the line of his back was rigid.

"Yes, well, I'm *sure* you are. After all, he's a good man! What could possibly happen to you?" Charles asked blithely.

Nick's shoulders hunched and Bane wished he could get up and massage them into looseness again.

"Yeah, for sure. Well...how are you, Dad?"

"Brilliant! I am making Bane loads of money. I'll triple his profits in a year," Charles chortled. "You make sure you tell him that, Nick, won't you?"

"I will, Dad," Nick replied, his voice dead.

"I've got to go, Nicky! But you just keep doing a good job for Bane and we'll all come up on top," his father laughed. "You'll see!"

"Bye, Dad."

But before Nick had said those last words his father had already hung up on him. Nick brought the cell phone down by his side. There were long beats before he turned back to Bane and held the phone out again. Bane met Nick's bleak gaze. Instead of taking the phone from him, Bane unlocked the bottom drawer of his desk and took out the camera. He offered that to Nick instead.

Nick blinked. "Are you sure you want to give that to me?"

"Yes, but…"

"But?" Nick looked at him.

"Please be careful," Bane said. He stared into Nick's eyes. "I am trusting you."

"I won't take pictures of your private things," Nick said as he took the camera and cradled it against his chest. "You can see all the pictures I'm taking. I promise, Bane."

"I wish to trust you, Nick."

Before he could say more the doorbell rang and both of them jumped. For a moment, Bane couldn't remember who was coming to Moon Shadow. He just wanted it to be Nick and him. But he had invited guests.

"Your friends have arrived. Shall I get the door?" Nick asked.

"No, I will."

Bane got up walked down the hall to the front doors. Nick followed after him, cradling both his phone and his camera in his arms. Bane flung the doors open and Devon Wainwright smiled back at him. A big, broad smile. He had his suit coat slung over his shoulder. Devon wrapped his arms around Bane and held onto him tight.

"Bane! I've missed you so much! I was so glad you called. It's been too long," Devon murmured against his shoulder. There was a distinct pause and Bane knew that Nick had come into the foyer. Devon drew back. The smile on his handsome face was less *real* as he gestured at Nick and asked, "Now *who* is this?"

CHAPTER NINETEEN
PERFECT

Nick hated Devon Wainwright. Not because Devon was an awful person. In fact, Devon wasn't. Devon was perfect. Perfect hair. Perfect body. Perfect Crest white smile. Perfect pedigree. Perfect job running charities. Nick absolutely hated him.

It made Nick grit his teeth to see Devon hang on Bane like the big man was his own personal jungle gym. Watching them walk down the stairs together arm-in-arm—while Nick finished helping the florist put the final touches on the new magnificent bouquet of yellow roses in the foyer—had Nick groaning internally.

I wouldn't have thought Bane was the touchy-feely type.

Devon's gaze grazed Nick as he and Bane breezed past him. One of his *perfect* hands reached up and tousled Bane's hair. *Tousled it!* To Nick's delight though, Bane drew away from Devon's touch, a slightly puzzled look on his face as if he wasn't sure what Devon was up to. Nick's delight ceased though when Bane quickly covered the scar on his face with that same long fall of hair that Devon had tousled.

He uses his hair as a shield. He thinks the scar is so ugly that he believes he has to hide it. But he's beautiful even with the scar.

Nick could admit that now without any twinge of regret. After last night's dinner where Bane had been actually pleasant and then Omar's revelations about Bane's past, Nick's feelings had softened towards the billionaire. Seeing that movement to hide the scar, which Bane thought of as a massive imperfection made Nick soften even more. He wished he had been able to snatch Devon's hand away before he touched Bane's hair. Didn't that perfect bastard see how self-conscious Bane was?

Of course not. He's too perfect to understand imperfection.

Nick watched their backs as they sauntered down the hall and wondered, just for a moment, how it would feel to have his arm looped through Bane's and to lean against that strong, muscular form. He shook his head. That was ridiculous. He was being ridiculous, because it would never happen.

Nick turned back to the flowers, but the florist had already finished arranging the roses. He thanked the man, walked him out and then headed to the kitchen to see what Omar needed help with. Just then he heard Dean Kettering's laughter roll up the hallway from the porch where Bane and all of his guests had now gathered. He grimaced. The CEO of Hermitage Pharmaceuticals was a creep. He looked like a football quarterback gone to seed. He was one of those men who stood too close, touched too much, and leered all the damned time. As soon as he'd arrived he'd focused in on Nick unerringly like a predator sighting prey. Nick had no intention of being anyone's prey. He would have to make sure not to be alone with Dean.

Bane's third guest was Sloan Wu. She reminded him of a slinky cat, watching everyone with a secret smile. When she'd seen him her eyes had narrowed. He had a feeling that she knew more about him than he would have liked. He didn't recognize her name, but she clearly recognized his. As soon as Bane had introduced him, she'd asked Bane a question with her eyes and he had merely nodded. Confirming something.

Confirming what? Bane likely told her about my family's attempt to take over one of his companies. She's his lawyer. Maybe she was wondering if I was one of those *Fairfaxes.*

With that bleak thought, he stepped into the kitchen and saw Omar standing by the counter. The Indian man was putting together a cheese tray for the guests and making cocktails.

"Quite a varied group," Nick remarked as he leaned a hip on the counter.

"Do you think? They seem all the same to me," Omar said mildly, but the remark surprised Nick because of its inherent negativity.

"The same how?"

"Oh, I do not wish to prejudice you against them. It is only my opinion of them, after all, and it could be wrong," Omar said, still mild.

"I highly doubt that. You seem like you try hard not to judge people unjustly." Nick snagged a piece of the cheese off the tray and popped it in his mouth. Omar scowled at him, but then gave him another slice with a grain. Nick continued, "I admit that this gathering sort of goes against my impression of Bane as a hermit."

"Bane is a man of extremes. He will have these guests for the weekend, but then will want to see no one for weeks after that to recover," Omar explained as he turned from the cheese plate to make a martini. "He expends all his energy being a host and then he must recharge."

"So he *is* an introvert. That makes sense. I admit seeing him so welcoming and *kind* is sort of a shock." Omar started to mix yet another drink, which had Nick remembering that he came here to help not to steal cheese. So he asked, "Can I help with anything?"

"Just take out a few more cheeses from the refrigerator and some crackers out of the cabinet," Omar said and then turned back to the subject of Bane, "You saw a different side of him last night, didn't you?"

"I did though it was clear that he was acting on *your* orders to be a gentleman." Nick grinned, but that grin failed. "It seems with *other* people he doesn't have to be told to be nice, which makes me feel rather bad."

"You shouldn't feel badly!" Omar plinked several olives into an ice-cooled martini glass before turning to a highball glass and setting a lemon peel on the edge.

"I *should* actually." Nick took out a hunk of Irish cheddar and a creamy goat log from the refrigerator and started unwrapping them while he explained, "Because it means that the way he is with me is *particular*. If he was an ornery bastard to *everyone* then I wouldn't feel singled out. So there must really be something about *me* that bothers him so much. Is it just the Fairfax thing or is something about *me* that's even worse than that?"

"He has reacted *differently* with you," Omar answered carefully. "But that is not necessarily a bad thing."

Nick took the crackers out of the cabinet and laughed, "*Really*? How is giving me the *stink eye* a good thing?"

"Stink eye? It seems to me that he quite looks forward to seeing you," Omar contradicted.

"Looks forward? Well ... he did seem almost playful this morning. Teasing and stuff," Nick said as he plonked down the fragrant goat cheese with its crust of spicy pepper on the tray. "But he's in a good mood because of his guests. Because of *Devon*."

"Devon Wainwright does *not* make Bane happy." Omar poured various liquors into a shaker and added a splash of ice.

"He doesn't? I don't know why he wouldn't." Nick twitched cheese around on the bamboo cutting board. "Devon's hot, rich and into good causes. The guy is *perfect*."

"Devon is all of those things," Omar said carefully. "But he is *not* for Bane."

"Bane doesn't deserve a good looking, rich and environmentally-conscious lover?" Nick tried to hide his smile.

"You are missing the *other* adjectives that describe Devon." Omar pressed his lips together.

"What *other* adjectives?"

"Insipid, vain and cruel," Omar said.

Nick blinked. "Those are...wow, not nice."

"He is not nice."

"Well, that's too bad." Nick placed a wedge of gooey brie down as he asked, too casually, "Does Bane not see these things in Devon?"

Omar set a glass down hard, which had Nick turning towards the Indian man in surprise. "That is another of the consequences of his relationship with Alastair."

"I don't understand." Nick wiped his hands clean on a towel.

"Bane is *with* Devon in only the carnal sense. He chose him because he is *pretty*, but he is not anyone that Bane could ever fall in love with," Omar answered as he killed a lime with the juicer.

"And you want Bane to fall in love with someone?"

"It is the only way for him to heal and for..." Omar let out a sigh and shook his head. "The truth is that even if the *only* effect of Bane falling in love would be for Bane to be *happy* that would be enough."

Nick wondered what *other* effect there could be. Omar clearly didn't want to say. Nick just filed it away under one of the other strange things about Bane.

"Are we all set? Should I take the cheese out to them?" Nick asked.

"Yes, I will be out with the drinks in a moment." Omar waved him out of the kitchen cheerily.

Nick picked up the cheese tray and headed out to the back porch. Just as he reached the door, Nick heard the Fairfax name. He froze with his hand on the door knob and his heart in his throat.

"So someone *finally* got one over on the Fairfaxes!" Dean's booming voice rose up. "It would be *you*, Bane, to take out those bottom feeders."

Nick's cheeks burned. So *this* was how his family was seen.

"I heard that they took a swipe at Hermitage last year," Sloan's smooth as honey voice said.

Nick could almost imagine the red-faced Dean shifting angrily in his seat as he gave Sloan a feral smile.

"They *tried*, but they didn't succeed. Hermitage had and *has* a very *healthy* bottomline," Dean responded.

"Bane," it was Devon who said Bane's name as if he were tasting it. He asked archly, "Isn't that young man who is helping Omar a Fairfax?"

Nick's heart beat sickly in his chest as he waited for Bane to tell them about the "internship". The moment they knew about that they would look at him differently. It was one thing to be a servant, but another to be whatever he was.

"He is," Bane said neutrally. "He's working here for me while his father and brothers are working in my companies."

"What? Seriously?" Dean let out a disbelieving chortle. "You made the youngest Fairfax into your *slave*?"

Bane began, "He is merely working—"

"Are you paying him?" Devon interrupted him.

"In a way," Bane said tightly. "I'm giving his family a chance to get back what they lost. They work for my companies. Nick works here."

"By having him be your cabana boy? Can't you put him in a mailroom somewhere if he's incapable of doing anything else?" Devon's voice held a touch of acid. Though he seemed against the deal, his anger seemed to stem from the fact that Nick was *here* not because of the deal itself.

"He's needed *here*," Bane's voice went tighter. "He helps Omar. There's nothing untoward going on."

"Bane, you are just *full* of surprises," Sloan murmured after long moments of silence fell.

Nick heard the tinkle of glassware behind him and spun around to see Omar. The Indian man had a tray full of drinks. He wondered how long Omar had been standing before he made a sound. Their gazes locked and Omar gave him a empathetic smile. He'd been there long enough.

The last thing that Nick wanted to do was to go out that door and see those people. What expressions would be on their faces? The lascivious Dean would likely be laughing at him. Devon seemed only to care about how the deal *looked* not how it *was*. Sloan found it amusing. And Bane? Bane seemed more concerned about how his friends viewed *him*. Not how Nick was seen. After all, he was one of the bottom feeders Fairfaxes! He didn't have feelings! He wasn't a separate person from his family! He didn't matter at all.

"You can leave that tray here," Omar said quietly. "I will take it out. You don't need to help with this."

"No, no, Omar, I can take this out, but…would it be okay if maybe I worked outside today? Clearing the garden or something?" Nick asked, his voice brittle as old glass.

"Yes, of course," Omar murmured.

Nick held his head up high as he went outside. He did not look at any of their faces. He decided that he didn't need to see what they thought. He placed the cheese tray down. Everyone was silent and sweat broke out on his upper lip. Omar's cheery voice, higher and louder than usual announced the drinks, taking the focus off of him. Just as he straightened up and was about to go inside again, his eyes met Bane's. The big man's cheeks were flushed from anger or embarrassment, Nick didn't know. But Bane's gaze was flinty as if *Nick* were the one responsible for what had been said.

Nick gave Bane a hard, tight smile that felt more like a slash across his face.

So much for thinking Bane was anything other than a bastard.

Nick turned on his heel and headed back inside without a backwards glance. He ran up to his room and grabbed his camera before going back outside. He exited through the front door though and *not* the back. He didn't take the time to put on any sunblock. He immediately headed to the fountain. He would photograph the transformation of this small part of Moon Shadow. He wouldn't think about anything. He certainly wouldn't think about Bane. He would just lose himself in the work and the sun.

CHAPTER TWENTY
ONE MISTAKE AFTER ANOTHER

Several hours later ...
"Walk with me, Bane?" Devon asked.

He extended a hand to Bane as if his slender frame could actually lift Bane's weight from the couch. But Bane had noticed that Devon had been quite *intent* on touching him as often as possible this visit.

Bane had a feeling he knew what this walk was going to be about: Nick. It surprised him on one level. He and Devon had never had any claim upon one another. It was purely friendship with sexual benefits and nothing else. It was how they both had liked it. But Devon's reaction to Nick's presence and the "internship" almost seemed like jealousy. Or perhaps Devon was just horrified by the whole deal. Maybe Bane was trying to read into his reaction something petty so he could avoid the guilt of having, essentially, an indentured servant.

A beautiful, passionate, artistic indentured servant under my roof.

"Of course, Devon."

Bane did not take his hand but rose with his tigerish grace on his own. He nodded to Sloan and Dean, excusing himself.

Dean was quite red in the face, already having drunk too many cocktails and it wasn't even dinner. Sloan looked cool and unconcerned with her long legs tucked beneath her as she responded to the unending emails on her iPhone. The life of a lawyer meant she was never off the clock.

Bane joined Devon on the stairs. He slid his hands into his pockets as the two of them sauntered into the overgrown rose garden. The beguiling scent of roses embraced them. Bane couldn't resist dipping his head down periodically to smell the blooms. He heard the shush-shush-shush of their feet in the grass. Green juice stained his shoes, but he didn't care. Eventually, he'd have the gravel paths redone, but he rather liked the wildness of it. The untamed nature of it. He wondered if Nick would be able to capture it with his camera. If the photographs were good then even when he redid the garden they would have the memory of this untamed landscape. The beast kneaded the interior of his chest, wanting him to turn his feet towards where Nick was now, out in front. It had been urging him to go to Nick all afternoon.

He won't want to see us with Devon, Bane reminded the beast.

It snorted and kneaded his chest again. It wanted Nick. It wanted Nick *now*.

"It's beautiful here," Devon remarked as he linked his arm with Bane's again.

Bane was tempted to shake free of it, but that would be ungentleman-like. He made a grunt of agreement in response to Devon, but said nothing. His thoughts were full of Nick.

"Moon Shadow is really *you*, you know, Bane?"

Devon looked up at him with a teasing smile. His smile showed a flash of brilliant white teeth, which glowed against his tanned skin. He was handsome. Bane had always thought so, but this time when he saw Devon, he felt no desire for him. None whatsoever. The beast kneaded his chest. Nick. Nick. Nick.

"Ancient and ruined?" Bane gave him a half smile.

Devon laughed and slapped his arm. "Of course not! You are *neither* of those things."

You have no idea, Devon.

"So what it is about this magnificent pile that reminds you of me then?" Bane gestured to the back of Moon Shadow. The mullioned windows reflected the garden at him. It's dark stone made it look like it had been in this spot for centuries.

It's a family home. A place where one can put down roots.

As he thought that, he imagined seeing Nick sitting on the porch. His elegant bare feet, crossed at the ankle, resting on the coffee table. A book in his hands and a peaceful expression on his face. Bane imagined walking onto that porch with an armful of roses. Nick would look at him with a beaming smile on his face. Bane drew in a deep breath at the power of that vision.

"Well." Devon tapped his chin as if in deep thought, which brought Bane out of his own. "Moon Shadow is *mysterious*."

"You find me mysterious?" Bane's brows drew together. Could it be that Devon saw beyond his facade?

"Yes. A little. You do the most *surprising* things," Devon responded.

Ah, here we go. Nick.

"Such as?" Bane gave him the opening. Best to get this over with.

Devon let out a soft laugh. "You already know what I'm going to say."

" You have *concerns* about the internship and Nick."

"*Concerns*? That's a *mild* way of putting it," Devon's tone was cool, but his words were hot. "You have a nubile young man in your house, in your control, whose very family's existence depends upon him *pleasing* you. I am *more* than concerned."

"*Nubile?*"

"Did you see those shorts? I could practically see every contour of his ass."

Bane *had* actually noticed the shorts, but he had thought Nick looked rather nice not slutty like Devon was intimating.

"Let me put your concerns to rest. Nick would *never* sleep with me. Not even to save his family," Bane laughed. "He made that clear in no uncertain terms. So his *shorts* are not to attract me, but what he feels comfortable in."

Yet even as he said it, he still imagined Nick sitting on the porch, waiting for him, face wreathed in a welcoming smile. The beast's tail wagged eagerly.

"So you *asked* him to sleep with you?" Devon's voice rose up.

"What? No! I told him that this arrangement had *nothing* to do with sex. Only in his *fevered* imagination was I going to take him under the moonlight in the garden." And as he said that, he thought of how the moonlight had caressed Nick's skin at dinner the night before.

"Oh, what a relief, I suppose." But Devon did not sound exactly relieved.

They were rounding the far edge of the formal rose garden. There was a field of long grass beyond that. In the far distance were corn fields. Moon Shadow was beautifully isolated, which was necessary when the beast managed to get loose from the basement prison he had constructed for it. As if sensing he was thinking of it, the beast once more urged him again to go to Nick. It was more than just a desire to see the young man. The beast was worried about him, but Bane had no idea why. He continued to guide Devon along the back of the roses.

"What are your objections to the internship, Devon, even if there is a sexual agreement between Nick and I?" Bane asked.

Devon's arm tightened around his. "Outside of the *crudity* of the whole thing?"

Bane's lips flattened. "Yes, other than *that*."

"Why would you do this? Keep that boy in your house for—"

"For a year. He's to stay with me for a year. And Nick is not a boy," Bane corrected him.

"A year?!" Devon stopped and turned to face him. "You barely tolerate Omar around you, but now you'll have some stranger in your home for a year?"

"Omar needs help and I wanted to have someone...someone that I *chose* here."

"And you *chose* Nick Fairfax?" Devon's eyebrows rose up into his hairline.

"Yes." He said nothing more. What could he say that Devon would not find strange if not downright objectionable?

"I see...or rather, I don't."

They began walking again. Devon's hands rubbed together in front of him.

"What else is bothering you?" Bane asked, noticing the nervous gesture.

"I haven't heard from you in some time. You've said you're so busy and—"

"I did not just *say* I was busy. I *was* busy," Bane corrected. The truth was a little different than that. He had wanted time alone. Devon was a distraction that he only desired some of the time. And after he had seen Nick that first time in the street he had no interest in anyone else. "I had to deal with the Fairfax takeover."

"And then you called and asked me to come for the weekend and I thought ..." Devon stopped again and looked up at him out of doe brown eyes.

Bane stiffened. "You *thought* what?"

Devon touched his forearms, his expression earnest. "We're friends, aren't we?"

"Yes," Bane said uncertain as to where this was going.

"And we get along?"

"Yes."

"We are compatible. Not just sexually, but emotionally and financially even," Devon said.

Bane recoiled at the financial comment. It reminded him of Alastair. "What do you mean by that?"

"Neither of us needs the other for money, Bane," Devon explained quickly.

"I suppose not," Bane admitted.

"I've had *issues* before with people after my money. I'm sure that you have, too. Even Nick is only here because of *money*," he pointed out.

Bane flinched, but then he smoothed a hand down his chest to hide it. "He's here to save his family."

"From poverty, right? What I'm trying to say is that this isn't a concern we ever have to worry about with one another," Devon explained.

The beast bared its teeth silently at Devon. It wanted to go to Nick. It didn't like this pointless conversation. It wanted Bane to move. Now. Nick. Nick. Nick.

"As we are not getting married, it hardly matters even if you *were* after my money," Bane snorted softly.

Devon caught his arm. "Have you never wanted to?"

"Get *married*?" Bane stared at Devon as if he had a second head. Again, that image of Nick waited for him on the porch presented itself. "Ah... *no*. Have you?"

Devon smiled at him, but said nothing. They had reached the end of the line of roses. The beast's need to see Nick crested over him again and he didn't want to resist it any longer. He desperately needed to see Nick right then.

"Dinner is soon. You should go shower and change," Bane suggested.

Devon's expression went blank for a moment, but then he smiled. "Of course. I'm looking forward to it. You coming in, too?"

"In a minute," Bane lied. He was going to see Nick. That would take longer than a minute. Much longer, he hoped. He would be able to escape everyone. Now he wished it were just him, Nick and Omar that weekend. But he had planned this instead.

"All right. I'll see you later." Devon got up on his tiptoes and tried to kiss Bane's mouth, but Bane turned his cheek at the last moment and Devon's lips brushed across his jaw.

Bane gave him a smile that he knew didn't reach his eyes. Yet Devon beamed at him before he loped off towards the house. Bane waited until he was out of sight before moving. Bane strode swiftly, a touch of animal speed and grace in his movements, towards the front of the house. He could hear Nick's heartbeat.

Nick's shirt was off and sweat gleamed on his shoulders and down the length of his spine. His fair skin looked alarmingly pink. He was on his knees in front of the fountain that was now clear of the runaway foliage and flowers that had engulfed it. Nick was busy trying to clean out the remaining dirt and weeds that were clogging the broad basin that would catch the water once it was working again. Beside him was a large bag filled with the detritus that had been in the well and beside that was Nick's camera. Bane's heart sped up a little at that even though there was absolutely no harm in Nick taking pictures here and now. If he had taken any it would give Bane a chance to see if he had any skill.

The beast's kneading in his chest grew frantic as Nick turned his head to the side and wiped one forearm over his sweaty brow. If his back and shoulders had looked pink, his face was *red*. Bane winced in empathetic pain. The young man was sunburned and the color he was sporting now would be *nothing* compared to what would come in the next day or two.

Nick spun around to face him when Bane's shoes made a crunching sound on the gravel. His bare front was not as sunburnt as his back or face, but constellations of freckles had appeared across his pecs. Nick's flat, muscular stomach was only a pale pink. That brought another wince as Bane mentally compared the color of his shoulders to his stomach. The beast groaned. This was what it had wanted Bane to see. Nick was burned and the beast didn't like it. The beast sensed the pain that Nick would likely be in later and it had wanted him to do something about it. But it was too late. He had not sought out Nick early enough.

Why do you care? You've never cared about anyone. Yet here you are all up in arms about a sunburn, why? He asked the beast.

Its blue eyes narrowed at him as if he were a fool. After that conversation with Devon he was feeling like one.

"Oh, Bane, it's you," Nick said, his voice oddly colorless.

Bane noticed that Nick's gaze slid past him, looking to see if he was alone or with one of his guests. He knew that Nick had heard what Dean and the others had said out on the porch. Nick's expression had been carefully shuttered, but the spark of hurt and anger in those sensitive gray eyes when their gazes met had told him as much. Bane had hated himself at that moment. Hearing Dean's crude comments had gotten his back up. And if he was honest with himself, they had plucked at his conscience. He was not keeping Nick here for sexual favors, but people would *think* he was and they would, more importantly, think that *Nick* was giving them to him. Devon's remarks were further evidence of that.

"Do you need something?" Nick's voice was flat.

Bane realized that he had been staring at Nick's sunburn silently for a long time. "I wanted..." *to see you. The beast wanted to see you, too.* But those things could not be said. "I wanted to let you know that you don't have to attend dinner tonight. You can eat with Omar or by yourself, if you so choose."

Nick stared at him, gray eyes unreadable. "Of course, if that's what you want. I'm sure you wish to enjoy your guests."

Bane didn't want to be alone with his guests. He wanted Nick there. He wanted Nick there more than any of them. But then he flashed back on Dean's red face and he knew that the man would say unfortunate things. He had to protect Nick from that.

"I just think that you would be more comfortable not having to...well, if you would help Omar in the kitchen that would be quite useful," he said lamely. Internally, he winced. It sounded like he was categorizing Omar and Nick as the "help" who weren't worthy of sitting at the table with the rest of them. His father *would* have thought that.

Nick's bland expression confirmed the young man was thinking just that. His voice was dry as he answered, "I'd be happy to help Omar."

He knew he should explain that he just didn't want Nick exposed to Dean, but the words didn't come. He was having a hard time expressing himself. So all he said was a clipped and formal, "Thank you."

After a few more awkward moments, Nick asked, "Was there anything else you needed?"

"You should put a shirt on," Bane blurted out. He swore he could see Nick's skin burning as he watched it.

Nick looked down at his bare chest. "It was really hot so I—well, I'm not like you. All *formal* and stuff all the time."

Bane looked down at his own summer suit. It was a light gray-green and his tie was yellow. He was not dressed extravagantly, but clearly more formally than Nick was in his shorts. "I do not care if you dress the way you do when you're working. I'm just concerned..." Hearing the utter ridiculousness of what he was saying, Bane got out, "You're burning. You're sunburnt already. I hurt just looking at you."

Nick blinked and then raised one of his red arms. "Oh, yeah, I sort of forgot to put on any sunscreen when I came out here. I didn't think the sun was going to be this strong."

"You should *always* put some on. You're very fair." Bane touched Nick's forearm without thought. It was only when Nick glanced up at him, surprised, that he removed his fingers from that hot skin. "So...you should put your shirt on. Stop the damage."

Nick picked up the t-shirt that he had left hanging over the side of the fountain's basin and shrugged it on. The beast tensed as Nick let out a soft sound of pain as he drew it down.

"Damn, I guess I really got more sun than I thought." Nick grimaced.

"Yes, well..."

He felt the beast looking at him with disgust. It had wanted to see Nick for *hours* but Bane had resisted going and now look what happened! He should have gone out. He should now take Nick in. But he stood there stupidly.

"You seem to have been working quite hard here," Bane said awkwardly.

Nick shrugged but there was a momentary brightening in his eyes with pride. "I've cleaned out the fountain. I think you'll need to get a plumber or whoever services fountains to come out and get it working. That's beyond me. But it's clean now."

Bane went over to the fountain and pretended to look it over, but his gaze went to Nick again. When Nick glanced over at him, he returned to staring into the now empty basin. He could almost imagine water arcing out of nymph's horn at the top and then splashing into the seashell below. The stonework was lovely. It would be beautiful when fully restored. For a moment, he had this fantasy of standing beside Nick, his arm around the young man's waist as it was turned on the first time in twenty years. They would let out cries of delight and clap and then he would look into Nick's smiling face, lean down and kiss him. He could *feel* Nick's lips beneath his. He swore he could even taste the young man again. He cleared his throat and forced the image from his mind.

"It looks ready to use," Bane remarked. "You did a...a good job."

He saw Nick's lips curl into a half smile of pride again but then he flattened them into a tight, white line. "Yeah, well, you need to get your money's worth out of me."

The young man turned to the bag filled with all the weeds and garbage from the fountain and began to tie the top of it. Bane felt he had to say something. It was more than a feeling. It was *knowledge*. He took in a deep breath.

"Nick, I know you overheard what was said on the porch earlier," he began.

Nick didn't look at him, but said, "You don't need to explain. I get how people view my family and how they must view me."

"But they would be wrong!" Bane was surprised at his own vehemence.

Nick seemed to be, too, because he stood up and looked at Bane. "You've told me what you think of me many times, Bane. That your friends feel the same way is really not a surprise."

"But I don't think bad things about you," Bane protested. "You're not here to—to service me like a boy toy or something. You're here to do honest work."

Nick was still for long moments. "So *that's* what you're concerned about. How they're viewing *you*."

Bane stared at him, confused for a moment at where Nick's absolutely icy anger was coming from. He was trying to explain how he did not agree with Dean, but somehow he was making this worse. "No, I...I mean yes, to an extent, but I also was concerned about their impressions of you."

"That's the funny thing, Bane, people make *assumptions* about us all the time. Sometimes it's based on who our *family* is. Sometimes it's based on the *job* we do. And sometimes it's based off of *misreading* circumstances," Nick listed out and Bane flinched as these were things he had based his judgment of Nick on. They seemed very *thin* indeed now. "So the fact that these people who don't know me assume I'd *whore* myself out to save my family...well, I don't really care. They don't know me."

"No, they don't. I—"

"But they *do* know you," Nick interrupted. His eyes were steely. His back was stiff. He was rigid and angry and staring at Bane with this arctic smile. "And if I were you, the thing I would actually be upset about is the fact that none of them seemed to have *any* doubt that you *would* take advantage of me like that. They're your friends and *that's* what they think of *you*. That's what they think you're capable of."

"I would never do that. I would never hurt you," Bane whispered.

"Yeah, well, it sucks when people make the wrong assumptions about you, doesn't it? Kind of really blows when the person they imagine you to be is really pretty awful," Nick retorted.

"Yes, it does," Bane answered faintly.

They stared at one another. The beast let out a low whine. Nick looked away from him.

"I better get in and get changed. I'll be serving dinner tonight. Don't want to keep you waiting," Nick said tightly.

The young man grabbed his camera and the bag of garbage off the ground and walked away from Bane. Bane felt strangely cold in the hot summer sun as he watched Nick leave and realized what a mess he'd made of things.

CHAPTER TWENTY-ONE
FALLING

Nick slowly drew the beautifully tailored pale blue shirt up his very sunburned arms. He winced at the lightest brush of the fine cotton against his tender skin. He wasn't sure how long it was going to take for him to get this stupid shirt on and he had to get downstairs to help Omar.

If I'm going to be a servant at this party I'm going to be a damned good one!

Bane's apologetic expression at the fountain earlier flashed before his mind's eye. For a moment, Nick actually had felt bad for him. It was as if Bane had been *trying* to be nice but it had come out all wrong. Nick shook that thought away though as he remembered Dean's chortling about him and his family. Bane had just defended his own honor. Not Nick's. Bane wasn't worth feeling sorry about.

He looked over with longing at the cell phone on the nightstand. He'd been so tempted to phone Jade and tell her everything that had happened so far, but he'd restricted himself to a few funny texts and assured her he was not chained up in a dungeon. But right now he wanted to vent to her about the unfairness of it all, about Bane's assholery, about Dean's lechery, about Devon's perfection and Sloan's slow, knowing smiles. Jade would not only listen but would want to come over right away and give Bane and all the rest of them a piece of her mind. She would be in full best friend defense mode.

And that's why I can't call her and tell her any of this. I've got to keep a cool head and not blow it.

The thing was that he'd allowed himself to start to *feel* things for Bane that were something other than: bastard, jerk, snob, and controller of his family's fortunes. He'd started to think: beautiful, intelligent, intriguing, intense and worthwhile. That had been his mistake. He'd allowed himself to be disappointed by Bane's behavior. If he had reminded himself that the man was a bastard he wouldn't have been so knocked off kilter that he'd done something as stupid as working outside all afternoon with his shirt off and no sunscreen.

He let out a groan as he finally got the shirt all the way on. There was a soft knock at his bedroom door and Omar's voice asked to come in.

"It's open, Omar!" Nick winced as it seemed that even the vibrations of his voice hurt his burned flesh.

Omar bustled in, carrying the light charcoal gray suit coat that Mr. Fioretti had dropped off. Omar had insisted on pressing it one last time. The smile on his round face died instantly as he caught sight of Nick's flaming red chest. "Oh, you are burned! I did not notice before. The front hall was so dark."

Still grimacing as he started to button the shirt, Nick said, "It's my curse. I rarely tan. I burn. My damned fault for not putting sunscreen on."

"Oh! Oh! Let me help you." Omar gently placed the exquisite suit coat that matched Nick's pants on the bed before coming over and buttoning the shirt for him. "You did a beautiful job on the fountain. Bane stayed out there for some time just admiring it."

"He was probably just avoiding going into the house and his guests," Nick said. "Is he really friends with those people?"

"They are business associates." Omar tenderly buttoned up Nick's shirt. "And Devon is his...friend, I suppose."

"Well, Devon can have Bane for all I care," Nick muttered.

Omar's motions slowed and he asked carefully, "Did something happen when you spoke to Bane by the fountain?"

"He told me that I wasn't to eat at the table with his guests. That he would prefer me to *serve*, which is totally fine. I'd rather be with you than them." Nick sucked in a breath as he tucked the tails of his shirt into his pants.

"I do not think he meant that in a bad way. Sometimes he is not good expressing himself. I know he *likes* you and I am certain that he prefers you to Devon and—"

"Omar, Bane is probably my *least* favorite person right now. I don't want him to *like* me." Yet Nick couldn't help but feel a slight satisfaction at the thought of Bane preferring him to Devon. It was unlikely, but he wanted it nonetheless.

The Indian man held out the jacket, which Nick shrugged on. He let out a slow breath and relaxed his shoulders. His skin was so tight and painful. He felt something wet pop and realized he had blisters on his back. He really wasn't going to win any beauty contests tonight.

"You are rightly angry, but do not judge Bane by Mr. Kettering and the others. You have seen the other side to Bane. He is so much more than they are." Omar smoothed down the front of Nick's suit. "You look very handsome."

"You mean I look very red." Nick grimaced.

Omar opened his mouth to contradict him, but then said apologetically, "Yes, you do. But you are still handsome."

"Let's get downstairs and start this dinner," Nick said and opened the door for Omar.

"It will be quite the evening."

Serving Bane and his odious guests while feverish was like swimming into a shark tank with a bleeding wound, but Nick was determined to do it without showing anything of his discomfort. He would glide through the experience as his brain cooked and the blisters on his back wept. He shuddered at what they were doing to the beautiful suit that Mr. Fioretti had created for him, but he couldn't wear a t-shirt and shorts or better just shorts to serve them. He wondered how *that* would go over with Bane's friends.

Nick Fairfax! Boy toy extraordinaire! Except for when he forgets to wear sunscreen and then he plays his second role as a giant tomato!

Nick suppressed the inappropriate grin and smoothed his expression into blandness. He had to soldier on for his family. Not to mention that he couldn't leave Omar with all this work. He picked up the tureen of gazpacho—a soup made with fresh tomatoes, cucumber, bell pepper, onion, garlic, bread, olive oil and wine—and headed into the dining room. Like in the foyer, the table was set with a spectacular arrangement of yellow roses. Nick remembered somewhere that yellow was the color of friendship in the language of flowers.

Maybe business associates and Devon are the closest things to friends Bane has.

One look at Bane's face though as he caught sight of the billionaire sitting at the end of the long mahogany table told him that Bane was *not* happy to be there. He wasn't scowling exactly, but he had this closed off expression that clearly was stifling conversation among the others. Nick had a sudden wish that he was eating with them instead of serving. He could have drawn Bane out. He could have made the man smile or, at least, have him take an interest in the people around him. But as soon as he had that thought he quashed it.

Bane's the one who wants me to serve! He made it seem like he was doing it for MY comfort, but I'm sure he just didn't want the boy toy at the table. Though looking at the rest of these people, a boy toy would class it up.

Dean was taking large swallows of white wine. His face was almost as red as Nick's, but from alcohol instead of sun. The ex-footballer had already started tugging at the blue silk tie he wore so that it was askew. In contrast, Sloan looked elegant in a long black evening gown and a simple silver necklace with a large ruby that dipped between her small breasts. Devon was, of course, *perfect*. He had a linen suit that didn't dare wrinkle and a striped blue and green tie. He wasn't *smiling* though as he had been every other moment that Nick had seen him with Bane. Instead, he kept stealing glances at Bane and then pressing his lips together in dismay as Bane's expression remained dire.

Bane looked beautiful as always. His hair was glossy. He wore an expertly tailored slate gray suit, lighter gray tie and an icy white shirt. Mr. Fioretti had worked his magic and created yet another outfit that flattered Bane's massive frame. The only thing about him that did not look well was the scar. The few edges that Nick could see of it looked as red and raw as his own back was.

It looks so painful and fresh like it just happened, but I'm pretty sure that Bane's been scarred for a long time.

As if sensing Nick thinking about him, Bane's Siberian blue eyes flickered to him and tracked Nick's progress as he started dishing the soup into the delicate white porcelain bowls. Bane wasn't the only one watching him.

Dean's eyes were narrowed as he stalked Nick's very careful movements. When he served Dean, the letcher, touched his ass. Nick jumped and Dean gave him a muted, "Sorry. Didn't realize that was you."

"Of course," Nick answered stiffly.

After that, he kept his ass out of Dean's reach. He noted that Bane was scowling at his alleged friend. He renewed his vow never to be in Dean's presence alone. Nick continued to serve. He had to be careful not to move too quickly or searing pain would race through him as another blister on his back broke. He hoped that the wetness hadn't soaked through his suit coat.

Devon's gaze flickered from Bane's face to Nick and back again as Nick approached. Devon's lips were white as he pressed them together in a tight line. He took a large sip of his wine. Only Sloan seemed disinterested as she stared at the roses instead of Nick or anyone else.

The room was completely silent except for the tap of Nick's shoes and the splash of the soup into the bowls. In Nick's feverish state the red gazpacho started to remind him of blood, especially against the stark white of the bowls. His stomach did a nauseating flip, but he swallowed down the bile that rose up. He would not puke. It was just the fever that was making him see things like this.

He filled Bane's bowl last. As he stood beside the big man, he saw Bane *sniff*. Was Bane smelling him? Did he smell bad? Were the water blisters giving off a terrible scent? Sweat started to bead on Nick's upper lip and the hand holding the ladle trembled. He nearly dropped it, but lightning quick, Bane caught his wrist to steady it. His heart raced as they both remained utterly still.

"Are you all right?" Bane asked, his voice pitched low.

"Just a little sunburned," Nick got out as his vision swam a little bit. He was far worse off than he thought. A bird of panic started fluttering in his chest that he would pass out in the dining room, his face ending up in Bane's soup bowl as he fell forward. "I'm okay. Everybody good with the soup?"

There were nods all around. Nick made to leave but Bane still had his wrist. The grip was not painful. It was simply firm and unyielding.

Devon noticed that, too, as he said, "Bane, you need to let the *boy* go. He's got to get back to the kitchen."

Nick ground his teeth at being called a "boy" and the assumption that he belonged in the kitchen. Devon's brown eyes flickered up to his as he gave Nick an unfriendly smile. Nick ignored it. Bane didn't immediately release him so if Devon thought he'd won any victory by calling Nick a "boy" instead of a "man" that was quickly quashed.

"Are you *certain*, Nick?" Bane asked, acting as if Devon had not spoken.

"I'm good. It's just a sunburn and Omar needs me," Nick said even as his legs felt weak beneath him. He firmed them with a force of will.

Finally, Bane let go, but Nick felt his reluctance to do so. He clearly didn't believe that Nick was okay. He was *concerned*. Very concerned. Bane seemed to sense everything that Nick was trying to hide.

"So, Nick, how are you enjoying the *internship?*' Dean asked.

Nick's shoulders tensed, which caused his skin to bunch and pain to flare white-hot behind his eyes.

"I don't think that is a good topic of conversation, Dean," Bane began.

"It's fine," Nick got out as the pain eased.

"Must be a bit of a change from what you're used to." Dean leaned back in his chair.

Dealing with assholes like you? No, not really.

"I like helping Omar," Nick said, keeping his voice even.

Dean's wine glass dangled in his hand. He waggled it. "Could you refill my glass?"

"Of course."

Nick gritted his teeth but he set the tureen down on the sideboard and moved over to the wine bucket in the corner of the room where a bottle of white wine sat cooling on ice. Nick was tempted to grab a handful of the cold cubes and run them over his skin, but he didn't. Instead he pulled the bottle out of the bucket, cleared the perspiration from it with a towel and refilled Dean's glass.

"Cleaning toilets and serving canapes is a far cry from raiding companies." Dean took the glass from his hand.

"Wouldn't know. I've never raided a company," Nick answered stiffly.

"Nick's not a part of that," Bane broke in. "He's an artist. A photographer."

Nick stared at him in shock. *He's defending me. He...he called me an artist.*

"Truly?" Sloan lifted her head. Suddenly, she was regarding Nick and not the flowers. "Have you had any shows?"

"No, nothing like that," Nick answered quickly. His skin was already so red that they wouldn't be able to see him blush. "I'm just an amateur. Going to school for it."

"Nick is going to take pictures of the transformation of Moon Shadow," Bane said. He wasn't looking at Nick. He was staring into the soup bowl, but Nick felt his regard nonetheless.

What are you doing, Bane? Why are you being kind?

"You're going to let me—I mean, yes, of course, I'm taking pictures of Moon Shadow," Nick quickly recovered, but he saw that Devon had caught the slip.

"You're so private, Bane, and yet now you're letting Nick live here with you and take photographs," Devon said. He took a large swallow of wine and met Nick's eyes. "You must be quite the *artist*, Nick. You've had an incredible *effect* on Bane."

Nick's gaze slid to Bane. The big man was still staring down at the soup bowl. One of his large hands was curled halfway into a fist. The other was hidden beneath the table.

"An artist who makes beds and keeps your glass full of wine," Dean chortled. "I wouldn't mind having one of my own."

"There's only one Nick," Bane said. His head lifted then and he met Nick's gaze. "Only one and he's...well, he's taken. Go back to the kitchen, Nick. Omar needs you."

I'm taken? Yes, I suppose I am.

Nick nodded, feeling strangely grateful to Bane. He moved as quickly to the door out of the dining room as possible. When he got to the kitchen he sagged against the counter after he set down the tureen.

"How is it going out there?" Omar asked as he took out a beautiful roast from one of the double ovens.

Nick quickly straightened and nearly screamed as the cotton—which normally would have felt soft and smooth against his skin—felt like sandpaper instead and more blisters popped. He bit his inner cheek to stop from whimpering. When he was certain he had his voice under control, he said,

"I think they're going to need some more wine, Omar, especially with the way Mr. Kettering is downing it."

"I think Mr. Kettering has had *enough* alcohol for the whole weekend today," Omar said primly.

"Yeah, the guy's drinking like a fish. I wonder why," Nick said and then shook himself. "What am I saying, I don't want to know anything about that guy."

"Why? Has he done anything? Said anything more to you or about you?" Omar asked alarmed.

Other than the jerky things he said on the porch earlier and then patting my ass in the dining room? No. But my creep alert is going off.

"No, no, just…I don't like him," Nick said. He looked yearningly at the chairs around the island. He wanted to sink into one. But he couldn't just sit while Omar worked. Instead, he picked up the tureen again and went over to the sink to wash it out.

"Oh, Nick, do not worry about that. I will do it later. You sit down," Omar ordered.

"But you shouldn't be doing everything. I want to help."

"You are helping by serving. That allows me to concentrate on the cooking. Besides washing up risks soiling your beautiful suit and I do not think Bane would like that," Omar said gently.

Nick thought of the water blisters that were currently soaking his shirt. He had a feeling that this suit was likely toast, but said nothing to Omar.

"So sit down for ten minutes and then go out and collect the bowls and refresh the wine glasses then the next course will be ready," Omar said.

Nick gratefully sank onto one of the bar stools. He was careful not to let his back touch the back of it. He let his head fall forward and rested his forearms on the cool marble of the island. He was so hot that even through his shirt and suit coat he could feel the coolness of the stone.

"Do you think they're right?" Nick asked. His feverish thoughts had plucked one out of the things that had been bothering him all day. Underneath the layer of self-defensive anger he'd brought up, the hurt was as raw as his skin.

"Who is right about what?" Omar's back was to him as he took sizzling potatoes out of the oven. They were drizzled with olive oil, speckled with fresh rosemary and dusted liberally with sea salt and pepper.

"Sloan, Dean and—and Bane. Are they right about my family?" Nick asked.

"I don't think people can be so easily placed into categories," Omar finally answered as he slid the potatoes off the baking sheet and into an elegant white bowl.

"I knew that my family were considered sharks in the business world. I knew that people hated them. But it was sort of just a *concept*, you know? I'd never *seen* the hate." Nick shivered and he wasn't sure if it was from the emotion or the sunburn.

"I think one of the reasons why Bane became so angry about your family trying to take over his company was because he was afraid it would work," Omar said as he next plated miso-glazed carrots.

"Bane? *Afraid*?" Nick snorted.

"Yes. Your father and brothers are *very* good at what they do. Better than that. Quite excellent. It took a lot of effort to stop them," Omar explained. "Many late nights with Sloan and others. It took nearly everything Bane had to put a stop to the takeover."

"Well, he definitely put a stop to the Fairfaxes all right." Nick ran a hand through his hair and quickly removed it as his scalp was burned, too.

"He also offered them jobs," Omar pointed out. He was tossing fresh green beans with caramelized shallots and almond slivers.

"They'll make him a lot of money for sure, but Bane...Bane seems to have enough money," Nick pointed out. Though really it seemed most rich people he knew *never* had enough.

"I do not know if he wants them to do something so much for *him* as for *themselves*. Have you never thought about what would happen if all that intellect and power were turned towards doing good? Think of all the marvelous things that could come out of it!" Omar scooped green beans on a long, white rectangular platter.

Nick's brows drew together. "I—I guess, yeah, I have thought of that, but without direction they'll just do what they do best, which is be vicious. If Bane expects them to do things his way he's got to tell them so. I mean *bluntly* and correct them if they go back to their old ways."

Nick felt a touch of unease at this. Hadn't Bane said something about the Fairfaxes having to run the companies like *he* wanted, with his ethos? Did his father and brothers realize that doing things their way might end up *failing* to uphold their end of the bargain? But Nick's feverish brain couldn't keep hold of these thoughts and he found himself asking an even more personal question.

"Do you think I'm right to do this? Serve Bane for a year to help my family?" he asked.

Omar paused in his movements. "I think that you are doing a very good thing for *them*."

"But a bad thing for *me*?" Nick asked.

"It depends on *why* you are doing it," Omar answered, still without turning around. "I just hope that you are not disappointed in how things turn out with them."

Nick thought of his father's disinterest in him from the way he'd packed the suitcase to the phone call that morning. Depression settled down on him like a thick, coarse blanket. He couldn't just sit there and think any longer. If he did, he'd really go into a funk. Besides it was time to go back into the shark tank. He got up from the island with a clenched hiss as the shirt pulled away from his skin. Fever flooded him and the room spun. He caught hold of the island and clenched his jaw.

I can do this. I can. I'll be fine. Just fill the wine glasses then take away the soup bowls. I'm not going to mess this up.

"Nick? Are you all right?" Omar asked.

"I—I'm fine. Don't worry. I'll just get the soup bowls," Nick said as he wobbled out of the kitchen.

When he went into the dining room this time there was some desultory talk going on though Bane was giving out only one word answers while Devon prattled on about some charity he was running.

"We actually raised twice our goal at Mrs. Delaster's tea service! I swear that woman works a room like no other and she's 93," Devon laughed.

"She knows everyone," Sloan was saying. "The woman just needs to raise her little finger and the money pours in. So I'm not surprised you did so well."

"You should be counting your lucky stars that she agreed to work with you at all, Devon." Wine sloshed in Dean's glass. It came dangerously close to spilling onto the ground as he waved his hand around. "She turned me down flat on the charity I was chairing a few years ago. Claimed that too much money was going into the hands of the people running the charity and not enough towards the subjects of the charity itself. Judgmental bat."

Nick scanned the wine glasses and everyone but Bane needed a refill. He took out the white wine from the ice bucket and the world blurred. He bit his inner cheek. The pain and blood cleared his head and he was able to go back to the table and pour wine into the glasses without splashing it everywhere. He wasn't, however, swift enough to avoid Dean's arm around his waist.

"You're a sweet handful, Nick!" Dean laughed.

"Let me go, Mr. Kettering." Nick tried to twist out of his grasp, but the fever was making him weak and stupid.

"Oh, don't be so mean! Let me just - AH!"

Bane was on his feet so fast that to Nick he seemed to dematerialize from his seat and the table and rematerialize by Dean's chair. Dean's hand was pried off of Nick's waist. Dean let out a howl as Bane bent his wrist back.

"Don't *touch* him!" Bane hissed.

"You're breaking my wrist!" Dean gasped.

"Bane, what are you doing?" Devon cried.

"Bane, it's okay," Nick tried to say, but his vision went all blurry. "Please don't—don't—"

The big man growled, "He has no right to touch you. He has —NICK!"

Nick heard Bane's cry as if it were coming from very far away. Because Nick was falling. The fever crested and was taking him down, down, down to the bottom of a boiling ocean. Bane caught him before he hit the floor. The wine bottle though shattered and that was all Nick knew.

CHAPTER TWENTY-TWO
START OVER

Bane lifted Nick up into his arms. The young man radiated heat and let out a low moan of pain as Bane cradled him. The beast was frantic as it regarded the young man's prone body, but Bane was holding both of their emotions in check. Nick's eyelids fluttered open and feverish gray eyes looked up at him in confusion.

"W-what happened?" Nick mumbled. "Did I—did I drop the wine?"

"You were the one who dropped, Nick," Devon said, his forehead creased with concern.

"Do not worry about anything. I am taking you upstairs, Nick." Bane turned to Devon. "Tell Omar to call Dr. Trevelyan."

And with that, he carried the young man out of the dining room and up to Nick's bedroom. Nick struggled weakly to get down.

"I can walk. You don't have to carry me!" Nick protested.

"Forgive me if I don't believe you," Bane said.

"It's just a sunburn," Nick said and a flash of frustrated tears were in his eyes as he mumbled against Bane's shoulder, "Why can't I do anything right?"

Bane's heart lurched at that. "You've done *nothing* wrong."

"You should be with your guests. I should be helping Omar."

Bane could feel wetness against his hands from Nick's back. The wetness likely came from bursting water blisters.

His back must be a mess.

"This isn't a *little* sunburn, Nick. You're very ill. Dr. Trevelyan is an excellent physician. He'll be able to help you," Bane said.

Nick pulled his face from Bane's shoulder, alarm written across it. "I don't need a doctor. I'll be fine in the morning."

"This is not a democracy, Nick. You need a doctor. You are getting one. No more discussion," Bane answered tightly even as he saw that small blisters were forming on Nick's cheeks and in his hairline, too.

Why didn't I send him to bed earlier? Why did I let him keep serving? And that bloody fool Dean! I should have broken his damned wrist for touching Nick!

Bane shouldered Nick's bedroom door open and then carried the young man into the bathroom. He flipped on the light with the tips of his fingers. He gently sat Nick down on the wide edge of the tub. He kept his hands lightly on Nick's shoulders to make sure he was steady before he reluctantly removed them. He then stripped off his own suit coat and tie laying both across the sink. He undid his cufflinks, laying them on the sink, and rolled up his shirt sleeves. He watched Nick in the mirror.

The young man's eyelids had closed and he was swaying slightly. His face was beet red. His expression was tight with pain. He gripped the edge of the tub so hard that his knuckles were white. Bane's every instinct was to comfort. It had been so long since that need had been triggered, but there it was big and bold and neon-colored. The only problem was that Nick might not want his comfort.

There was a knock on the bathroom door and Omar poked his head in. Bane turned around and leaned against the sink as Omar bustled over to the young man.

"Nick! Oh, Nick! Are you all right? What am I saying? I can see you are not," Omar twittered. He looked the young man over with his incisive gaze, but did not dare to touch him.

"It's okay, Omar. Just a sunburn, remember?" Nick gave him a weak smile.

"Dr. Trevelyan says that a sunburn like yours is very bad. He is coming right away. But in the meantime he advised that your back should be washed with this." He held up the brown bottle he was carrying, which he then promptly thrust at Bane. "There are clean towels right there you can use, Bane. Also, he advised aspirin." He thrust the bottle of aspirin at Bane, too. "And aloe." That was pushed into Bane's hands as well.

Nick blinked and asked, "Aren't you going to help—"

"No, no, I must handle the guests. Bane will help you," Omar said and he lightly patted Nick's arm.

"Please bring Trevelyan up as soon as he gets here, Omar," Bane said as he placed the brown bottle, which was hydrogen peroxide, on the sink's ledge.

"Of course." Omar cast one look back at the two of them before he bustled out again.

Silence fell between Nick and Bane. Bane studied the young man. He looked so small huddled on the edge of the tub. The beast felt the great need to touch him. It urged Bane to go over and strip off Nick's clothes and see his hurts. Nick might not want his comfort or his help, but Bane could not resist the urge to offer both any longer.

"Now let's get that coat and shirt off. I want to see how bad the burn is," Bane ordered.

Nick looked up at him mulishly. "It's fine."

"Really? Because my hands are *wet* from just carrying you," Bane remarked with a coolness he did not feel. The beast was pacing in his chest. It wanted to see the young man's wounds. It wanted to lick them clean. It wanted to curl around Nick until he was recovered.

Nick managed to blanch, which only took him down to his semi-natural color. "I'm sorry about the clothes. I know they must have cost a lot of money. I'll find a way to pay you back if they're ruined."

"I don't give a damn about the clothes." Bane pushed off of the sink and got down on his haunches in front of Nick so that he could see Nick's eyes. The young man had dropped his gaze to the tile floor. He glanced up at Bane and then back down again. Bane modulated his voice, softening it, as he said, "I'm worried about *you*. Please let me help you."

Nick let out a shuddery breath and finally nodded. "Okay. Okay. I don't think I can take them off myself anyways."

Bane felt a flutter of something go through him. The beast let out a low purr. "Let's remove the suit coat first."

Nick tried to shrug the coat off himself, but didn't succeed. He let out a hiss of pain and dropped his arms down again.

"I'll do it, Nick. Just sit still."

He hooked his thumbs under the jacket's lapels and slowly slipped it off of Nick's shoulders and down his arms. Nick's jaw was clenched the entire time. The young man let out a relieved breath only when it was off. Bane set the coat to the side. He turned back to Nick and felt another stab of guilt.

"You're trembling," Bane said.

"C-cold," Nick admitted.

Bane leaned over and turned on the hot water for the tub. Soon steam would rise up and warm the bathroom. Some of Nick's shivering eased almost immediately. The gush of water was comforting. It reminded the beast of a waterfall. Bane's hands went to the buttons of Nick's shirt. He imagined doing this in very different circumstances. But this was not a sexual encounter. Nick was so very hurt. He undid the first button.

"I am sorry about Dean. He should *never* have touched you." Bane felt the rage build inside of him again. The beast bared its teeth. He undid another button and then another, revealing Nick's chest. Nick's beautiful, muscular chest was a painful, bright, cherry red.

"It's not your fault," Nick said, his words blurry with fever and pain.

"Anything that happens to you while you are in my house and under my protection *is* my fault."

Nick's expression was strange as Bane finished that sentence. "Well...he was drunk. People do stupid things when they're drunk."

"Not to you. Not with me there." Bane pressed his lips together after the words spilled out.

Nick looked down and played with the cuffs of his shirt, saying nothing. Bane finished unbuttoning the shirt. He spread it wide and saw red, red everywhere. The beast let out a whine in empathy.

"Oh, Nick..."

Nick looked down at his chest and gave out a pained laugh. "I think my back is worse...if that's possible."

"Let us get the shirt off now."

Nick drew in a deep breath. "It's going to hurt, isn't it?"

Bane met Nick's gaze. "Yes, but I will be quick. One moment of pain and then it will be over."

"I—I trust you." Nick quickly looked away from him.

He grasped the sides of the shirt. "Ready?"

"Do it."

In one fluid movement Bane peeled the shirt off of Nick. There was a wet ripping sound as the shirt had already adhered to places on Nick's back. The young man let out a yelp and Bane saw him bite his lower lip to stifle any more cries. He dropped the shirt by the suit coat. The entire back was soaked with pus and blood. He tenderly turned Nick so that he could see his back.

"How does it look? Because it feels like raw hamburger," Nick got out through trembling lips.

Nick's back was a solid sheet of red. The skin had bubbled up in places. Bane knew the pain of burns. His own skin throbbed in sympathy. Nick's back looked so painful that Bane had to dig his fingernails into his palms from letting out a cry of agony himself.

"We should clean it up a bit," Bane said simply. He picked up the hydrogen peroxide and the clean towels that Omar had pointed out.

"You really don't have to do this. The doctor will be here soon. I don't want you to miss out on time with your friends."

Bane looked back at Nick. The young man's slender neck was bent like a flower's in the wind.

"I'd rather be here," Bane answered truthfully. "But if you would like me to go…" He left the sentence hang.

Nick shook his head. "I don't *want* you to go. I just don't want you to be angry with me later."

"You think I would be *angry* with you for this? What you must think of me?" Bane whispered. But then he shook himself as he realized his questions were self-indulgent. "I'm not angry with you and I won't be. I'm angry at myself." He softened his voice even more as he said, "I want to clean your back. Your blisters are weeping. May I?"

He picked up the washcloth and showed it to Nick as if to demonstrate he meant only what he said and no harm.

"I—I—sure, okay."

Bane had a feeling that Nick was disconcerted to hear Bane be polite instead of demanding and rude.

Nick turned slightly so that his back was fully towards Bane. Bane doused the washcloth with the hydrogen peroxide. Bane dabbed the washcloth against Nick's skin starting on his right shoulder. Nick hissed likely at the coolness and sting of the antiseptic. Bane made an empathetic sound.

"I'm sorry. But this must be done and you will feel better after I'm finished."

"Right." Nick fisted his hands on top of his thighs. He fought to remain still as Bane continued to dab at his skin and clean the open blisters.

"You said you were angry with yourself. Why?" Nick asked.

A flash of self-loathing crossed Bane's features. "I knew you were ill at dinner, but I didn't say anything. I let you keep working."

"Oh," Nick said softly. "Well, who knew I would cock up my first day? You probably knew."

"Why would I think that?"

"I mean who else could make such an idiot of themselves to not wear sunscreen when weeding. I got injured *weeding*!" Nick slammed his hands down on his thighs. "I wanted to show you and them that I could do *work*. Instead, I managed to pass out at dinner."

Bane thought of what he had said to Nick over and over. That he was spoilt. That he was useless. That he was lazy. Of course Nick had wanted to prove him wrong even at the expense of his health.

"I promise that tomorrow I'll do better. If I could just work inside tomorrow that would be—"

"You will not be working tomorrow or any time soon. We will have to see how you are day to day."

"Oh," Nick said. "I—I—that's—thank you."

Bane washed the towel in the tub. The water was burning hot. He then put more hydrogen peroxide on the towel. His movements were jerky and his lips were trembling. He firmed his mouth to stop it.

"Bane, what's wrong?"

Bane leaned forward and his hair shaded his face. "You honestly thought I would make you work tomorrow when you are—are *like this*?"

"I—I guess so. I just want to keep up my part of the bargain and I know you think I'm lazy—"

"I don't! I mean I...I *know* what I said, but...I'm *not* a monster, Nick. I'm *not*." Silence fell between them for a long moment.

And then Nick said something extraordinary, "We could...*start over*."

Bane's head lifted. "How do you mean?"

"I don't want to hate you," Nick said. "It's exhausting." His head drooped slightly. "I don't hate people. I don't want to start."

"You hate me?" Bane's voice was low. "Because of what I've done to your family—"

"No, not for that. Not really." Nick let out a weak laugh. "I hate you—or *dislike* you—for a far less noble reason."

"And what reason would that be?"

"Because you don't seem to like me all that much." Bane was shocked into silence, and Nick evidently took that as agreement as he quickly went on with, "I'm not asking you to *like* me or even saying that I would like you in return. Just..." Nick's hands were shaking in front of him and he quickly fisted them again in his lap again. "I can't live with you always *cutting* into me all the time. Not for a *year*."

But then Bane spoke, "I am not a nice person, Nick."

Nick laughed. "No, I know you're not. I'm not terribly *nice* either. But that doesn't mean we have to be cruel to each other all the time either."

"No, it doesn't," Bane agreed.

He put the cloth down and picked up the tube of aloe. Nick stiffened slightly as he heard the snick of the tube opening. Bane's hands were going to be directly touching Nick now. Skin against skin. There would be no washcloth between them. The beast's tail thumped.

Bane smoothed the cool gel over his sun ravaged flesh as if Nick was the most delicate crystal. Nick's eyelids fluttered half shut as Bane continued to caringly rub the aloe into his skin. Bane's fingertips fluttered over the base of his neck and slid up into his hair. Nick's shoulders relaxed and his hands unfisted in his lap. Bane's hands slid over the tops of his shoulders and down to his biceps. He slowly massaged Nick's arms.

"I wish," Bane's voice was low. His breath ghosted over Nick's throat. Nick's eyes completely shut. "*I wish to start over.*"

Nick let out a soft exhale.

"There will still be *rules* about the phone and the camera. I will not be *easy* on you," Bane said, which had Nick still smiling though shaking his head. "But I will be a gentleman."

"Sounds like a start," Nick said.

Bane's hands were still on his biceps. His chest was nearly touching Nick's back. He was almost holding Nick.

"You are shaking again. The fever is building," Bane said suddenly.

His hands moved from Nick's arms. Nick's eyelids fluttered open and he nearly pitched off the side of the tub. Bane caught him easily and held him. Nick curled forward as another round of trembling go through him.

"We need to get you in bed," Bane said.

He stood and offered Nick his hand. The young man took it. Bane helped Nick to his feet. The young man's legs appeared weak as water beneath him. Bane wrapped his other arm around Nick's waist, holding him upright.

"It's not far. I could carry you again," Bane said, worry threading his words.

"No, it would hurt," Nick confessed. "Just if you could get me to the bed."

Nick's body radiated massive amounts of heat yet his teeth were chattering. They slowly walked to the four poster bed together. Omar had lit a fire. The only other lighting on in the room was the lamp by the bed. The dark blue duvet was already pulled down, revealing crisp white sheets. Nick stumbled slightly and Bane held him more tightly.

"The sheets. The bedding," Nick murmured.

"What about them? If you lay on your side, the material shouldn't hurt you," Bane soothed.

"Not that. The gel, I'll mess everything up," Nick said.

"Sheets and blankets can be washed or replaced. Come now. No more stalling. You need to get in bed," Bane chided.

Nick let out a soft laugh as he sank down onto the edge of the bed. When Bane looked at him curiously, he explained the laugh, "You just sounded like my mother there for a second. Not exactly what I expected."

Nick attempted to undo the laces of his shoes, but he swayed perilously forward and missed his laces by a mile.

"Let me do that." Bane knelt before Nick.

He undid the laces and slipped the shoes off of Nick's feet and then took off his socks. Bane's touches were gentle, but evidently still tickled as Nick laughed. He looked up into Nick's eyes.

Looking someone in the eye when they are so close is dangerous, Bane realized. *Because when you are this close it's as if there is a physical tether between you, reeling you into that other person. You either wrench yourself away or you...fall forward.*

Nick was suddenly leaning forward and Bane was moving towards him. But then he caught the flare of fever in Nick's eyes and *knew* that he needed to *not* let anything happen between them. Not at that moment.

"Lay back," Bane commanded softly.

"W-what?" Nick's feverish eyes were bewildered.

"You must lie back," Bane explained. His gaze slid down from Nick's face to his chest and then to the belt of Nick's pants. "We must get you fully undressed."

Nick slowly lowered himself down onto the bed. He reached for his belt buckle, but Bane's hands were already there.

I can control myself. I can protect him not ravish him.

"May I?" Bane's voice was barely above a whisper.

"Yes," Nick answered, his voice lower than Bane's.

Bane's fingers unhooked the buckle and then tug the tongue of the belt through it. His fingertips brushed Nick's stomach as he undid the button. Nick sucked in his belly. Bane rested one knee between Nick's thighs as his hands slipped over to Nick's hips and he pulled the pants off of him, leaving only the boxer briefs in place. Bane then stood there at the edge of the bed with Nick's pants in his hands for long moments, just staring at Nick sprawled out on the bed.

So beautiful...if only ...

"What do you see when you look at me?" Nick asked.

Bane's eyes snapped up to his face. "I was just looking to see how burned you are. We should get you on your side so that the doctor can see all of you."

That's not what I was thinking. I was thinking of how I wished I were doing this in preparation to make love to you.

Bane folded Nick's pants and placed them over the arm of a chair. Nick was already rolling slowly onto his side and drawing his legs up and under the covers. Bane grasped the thick duvet and brought it up to Nick's chin. He stood there for another moment, looking down at Nick. Unable to take his eyes off of him.

There was a knock on the door then. It was Omar with Dr. Trevelyan. Bane didn't know whether Omar had the best or worst timing in the world at that moment. He just knew that he was already missing being alone with Nick.

CHAPTER TWENTY-THREE
WORTH

"You're much improved since when I saw you last night, Nick. Bane, Omar, you've done a wonderful job taking care of his sunburn. Don't let the word 'sun' in front of 'burn' minimize what it is, which is a very nasty burn," Dr. Trevelyan said as he continued to examine Nick's back. "These early summer days are responsible for more sunburns than later in the season as the cooler air hides the danger."

The doctor was sitting on the edge of Nick's bed. Nick was lying on his stomach. He wore only the boxers that Bane had left on him the night before. Out of the corner of his eye, Nick saw Bane stiffen and straighten up from his spot by the door as the doctor's hands slowly moved over Nick's wounded back. It was a possessive, protective reaction that had a thrill going up Nick's spine. Since last night he had felt so different about Bane. Maybe because Bane was acting so differently towards him.

"I got a burn almost this bad once before when I was a kid. You would think I'd have learned, but evidently not," Nick confessed. He could feel that his cheeks were still a hectic red and his eyelids were nearly puffed shut. "I didn't feel myself burning at all. It was just so warm and pleasant."

Dr. Trevelyan's wrinkled, handsome face broke into a smile. He lightly touched Nick's forearm that was only pink instead of completely scalded. "That's the sun's charm. But it has a very high price if you are not careful."

"Yeah, yeah, I'm paying for it now," Nick groaned. He thumped his head against the pillow and grimaced as his burned face stung from the blow. "I so should not have done that."

"Nick, you must lay still so the doctor can examine you!" Omar tutted from his place at the bottom of the bed. He stood there with a small notepad in one hand taking detailed notes of all the things that Dr. Trevelyan wanted them to do for Nick.

"Considering every time I move it hurts, I shall endeavor to remain absolutely still," Nick mumbled even as he felt absolutely touched by Omar's evident concern for him.

"You are in pain?" Bane asked. He took a step towards Nick as if he would physically do something to stop it.

The blisters that had broken the night before had reformed worse than before. They were larger now and his pain was larger, too. But Bane couldn't do anything about that and he didn't want to worry the big man any more than he already had.

"Just a little," Nick downplayed even as the pleasure tripled at the fact that *Bane* was clearly intent on doing whatever it took to help him.

My family wouldn't do this much. Not half this much. Bane cares for me more than my family does. Nick didn't know how to think about that.

"A little?" Dr. Trevelyan's gentle gaze was upon him.

"Maybe more than a little. I could use another aspirin," Nick suggested.

Omar jumped to get Nick a glass of water and some more tablets from the bathroom.

Dr. Trevelyan leaned over and studied those blisters. "I do not think that these will scar—"

"Scar?" Bane said sharply One of his hands rose up to the scar on his own face.

Everyone froze and looked at Bane in surprise. Omar had even stilled in the doorway of the bathroom and his expression was so sad. One of his hands half rose up towards Bane as if to calm him, but he quickly dropped it to his side.

"They should *not* scar so long as my orders are followed," Dr. Trevelyan said gently. "Be at ease, my friend."

Bane's shoulders relaxed only slightly. He glanced at Nick's face. Nick couldn't help but gaze back at him curiously. Bane smoothed those large hands down the front of his rumpled button down shirt. That shirt had been crisp and clean last night, but now it needed washing and pressing after a night of taking care of Nick. Yet Bane still looked stunning.

"I—I am relieved to hear it," Bane said finally, but he didn't sound like he quite believed it.

"It's going to be okay, Bane," Nick assured him. "Seriously, even if it does scar a little it will add character—"

"No!" Again, the sharpness of Bane's voice caused silence to fall. He took in a deep, calming breath, but he was still shaking slightly. "No, we will do whatever it takes to ensure that you do *not* scar."

There was silence for a long time. A stab of sympathy ran through Nick. It was clear that Bane believed he was defined by the burn scar on his face.

No wonder he doesn't want me to have any scars. To him being scarred must seem like the worst thing in the world.

"How should we continue to take care of him, doctor?" Omar asked as he hustled over to Nick with a glass of cool water and the tablets. He immediately took out the pad and paper again to take notes after Nick had taken the tablets from him.

Nick got up on his forearms and slowly turned onto his side. He put the tablets on his tongue and swallowed them down with a gulp of water. He felt Bane watching his throat as his adam's apple bobbed up and down. The big man's gaze slid down to Nick's chest. Nick knew that the sun had burned him all over. Even his nipples were scorched. Nick had no illusions that Bane was checking him out. Any beauty he might have was well hidden under the redness, the blisters, and the scent of aloe.

"The blisters will burst on their own, but they can become infected so I've brought some antibiotic ointment to be applied along with the aloe." Dr. Trevelyan took out the sterile white tube from his black doctor's bag. He handed it to Omar.

"I will be the one to apply it." Bane's hand thrust out to the Indian man. Omar placed the tube in that massive palm and Bane quickly slid the medicine into his pants.

"Ah, well, yes, Nick cannot apply it properly by himself so your assistance will be beneficial," Dr. Trevelyan said, blinking at Bane with blue eyes that were just starting to show cataracts. "Apply this two times a day with clean hands. Continue to use cool cloths on the affected areas as well."

"That seems simple enough," Bane said. "I will certainly see that it is applied thoroughly."

Nick let out a self-conscious laugh. Bane tilted his head at him to ask for an explanation of *why* that was funny. Nick just waved it away even as his cheeks burned with amusement more than sunburn.

Dr. Trevelyan cleared his throat. "Quite. Well, in addition, Nick should take frequent showers. Also, afterward, aloe should be liberally applied. I assume that you, Bane, can do that, too."

"Of course," Bane answered neutrally.

Nick swallowed. Those bigs hands had been on him the night before and they had felt heavenly even with the terrible burns. But he had been feverish and not quite in his right mind when that had all happened. Now he would be awake and aware while Bane smoothed creams and ointments onto his skin. He would be acutely aware of every single touch. Heat bloomed between his thighs and he grimaced. Being "friendly" with Bane didn't mean he was going to sleep with the man!

Besides he has Devon, the most "perfect" man in the world. So he wouldn't want me anyways even if I was willing. Speaking of which, where is Devon? He came in every hour this morning. He's overdue to 'drop in'.

Dr. Trevelyan cleared his throat again. "Also, Nick, you need to drink plenty of water and take aspirin."

"Yes, doctor, he will be overflowing!" Omar promised brightly.

Nick chuckled at Omar's enthusiasm. He wondered what the Indian man meant by "overflowing". He suddenly pictured himself like the fountain out front, full of so much water, that he was constantly spitting out a stream of it.

"And finally," Dr. Trevelyan said.

"What?" Nick asked.

"You need to rest," the doctor said and very gently squeezed Nick's left shoulder. "Bane tells me that you're quite the little workaholic, always wanting to make things just so. But you need to take care of yourself. That will ensure that you are back to your old self in no time."

Bane said that?! Nick's gaze swung back to the big man. Bane's expression remained elusive and unreadable. *He didn't have to say that to Dr. Trevelyan. He must have actually meant it.*

"We will ensure that all those instructions are followed to the letter," Omar said as he tapped his pencil smartly against the pad.

"I'm sure you will. And will you, young man, be more respectful of the sun?" Dr. Trevelyan asked, waggling his bushy white eyebrows at Nick.

Nick nodded and then winced.

"Nick will be completely taken care of. He will make a full recovery," Bane promised and there was a tone in his voice that brooked no argument.

And who would disobey that masterful tone of that voice?

Dr. Trevelyan rose from the bed. He moved a little creakily. Bane pushed off the wall and went to his side, offering his arm so that the doctor could fully straighten. "Thank you, Bane, but I'm all right. Not as spry as I used to be."

"Your mind is sharper than ever," Bane said.

Dr. Trevelyan patted his shoulder. "You are too kind. I will come tomorrow to check on the patient."

"Thank you for all your assistance, doctor," Bane said.

"Yeah, thank you," Nick called.

"Let me take Dr. Trevelyan downstairs. Bane, I'm certain that you will want to start with Nick's treatment. With the ointment," Omar said, too innocently.

Nick made a muffled laugh into the pillows.

"Yes, well..."

But before Bane could say anything more Omar had already led Dr. Trevelyan out of the room. The door closed behind them leaving Nick and Bane alone again. Silence fell. It had been so much easier when he had been blurred by fever to talk to Bane. Now they both were aware and awake. It was time to see whether their joint promises to start over would actually hold. Nick really didn't want to start the sniping again. From the silence, it was apparent that Bane didn't want to either.

Nick studied the dust motes that drifted in the small blade of sunlight that snuck between the still closed curtains. Bane walked over to the window and pulled the curtains fully shut and then turned up the lamps on the bedside tables. Nick sighed. He had absolutely no need to be exposed to more sunlight.

"Another bright, beautiful sunny day," Nick said.

"Yes, it is. But there will be plenty more of those for you to enjoy, Nick. So do not worry about missing one of them or even a *few* of them," Bane assured him as he continued to fuss with the curtains so that every inch of daylight was blocked out.

"I'm not worried. I was more thinking about the fact that it would have been a good day to work in the garden," Nick said.

Bane stilled his movements. "There will be plenty more days for you to work, too."

"You shouldn't miss this day as well," Nick said quickly. "You should go out. Be with your friends. I mean you don't have to be the one to put the ointments and stuff on me either. I think Omar—"

"I wish to."

"Oh," was all Nick found himself able to say in response.

Bane went into the bathroom and there was the soft shush of water as he washed his hands. When he came out he had a towel that was wetted down, ready to clean Nick's back. Nick tracked his progress across the room, noting how silently Bane moved for a man of *any* size, let alone for how big he was. Bane's tigerish grace seemed more accentuated today.

When Bane sat on the edge of the bed, Nick sucked in a sharp breath. He and Bane on the same bed was going to get some getting used to. Bane then took out the tube of ointment from his pocket and Nick's heart thudded heavily in his chest. They weren't just going to be on the same bed. Bane was going to be massaging him. Nick bit his lower lip to stop the nervous laughter that wanted to bubble out of him.

Bane had been studying Nick's back, but finally, he looked into Nick's eyes and said, "I never meant for you to be hurt."

Nick's forehead furrowed. "This totally wasn't your fault. It was mine and—"

"You did it to prove to me that you weren't lazy. You pushed yourself beyond your limit, because of me," Bane interrupted.

Nick caught his lower lip between his teeth. "I didn't want you to have any complaints. I didn't want your friends to think that I was useless."

"My friends!" Bane let out a bitter laugh. "I have no friends. Well, other than Omar."

"But what about Devon?" Nick wondered if the "perfect" man was hovering outside his bedroom door right now, hearing this.

Bane's expression grew chastened. "He does not want my friendship. He wants something more."

Nick found his heart starting to beat sickly in his chest. "And what do *you* want?"

Bane's Siberian blue eyes met his for long moments. "I want him to go away."

Nick was stunned into silence. That was *not* what he had ever thought to hear Bane say.

Bane let out a self-conscious laugh. "Omar would be so *pleased* if he heard me say that."

"Omar doesn't like Devon," Nick agreed faintly.

Bane gave a rueful smile. "He has made me quite aware of his feelings."

"What's changed your mind about Devon?"

Bane's Siberian blue eyes flickered up to his face and lingered there for one long moment before they dropped away and he shrugged. "I do not believe in—"

"In love? Yeah, I remember."

"You think that very foolish. I can tell from your tone," Bane said as his fingers played with the tube of ointment.

"Foolish? No. It's just I think you *do* believe in love. I'm pretty sure you believe in it a lot. But people have let you down, make you *feel* foolish for believing in it," Nick said carefully.

"I know that Omar told you about—about Alastair," he said, determinedly looking away from Nick.

"Do you want to talk about—"

"No." Firm. Certain.

"Okay, we won't. What about—what about Devon though? What does this all have to do with him?"

"Devon wants more than friendship and I want him to go away. I think it is pretty clear that things are over for him and me." He twisted the cap off of the ointment. "I wish it was just you and I here. Having dinner together. Reading on the back porch. Picnicking in the forest. Listening to the night breeze. Long, lazy days and beautiful nights." There was a beat and then Bane added, "And Omar would be here, too, of course. The three of us...I mean...I...well, that will happen soon enough once the guests are gone."

Nick's lips were parted. The description Bane gave of what they would be doing together sounded...*perfect*. He could almost picture them together. Curled on the sofa on the porch. Rolling in the grass after a picnic. Looking at the stars from the tower. Nick was so caught up in his imaginings that he failed to answer Bane.

"You don't have to say anything, Nick. I like my privacy. Somehow you do not disturb that unpleasantly. But I am certain that *you* would like to be somewhere else perhaps with your friend, Jade. Far away from me."

"I'd like to see Jade for sure, but..." Nick stopped. He would like to see Jade, but he really wanted the life that Bane had painted for him. To be at Moon Shadow. To be with Bane.

It would be wonderful. God...it would be...

"I'm looking forward to it just being the three of us, too," Nick responded firmly.

Bane paused in what he was doing and looked up at Nick through his fall of dark hair. There was this timeless moment where they just stared at one another and then Bane said, "Well, we shall have that soon enough." There was another beat and then Bane commanded, "Lay down on your front."

Bane lowered his head so that Nick couldn't see his face at all. Nick shifted over onto his stomach so Bane could put the ointment on him. He felt the washcloth on his right, upper shoulder. Bane drew it down until it reached his waist. Bane didn't use much pressure, but Nick felt one of the blisters burst.

"I'm sorry, Nick," Bane said, frantically dabbing at the skin.

"No, that felt good. I would scratch all the blisters off if I could," he confessed.

"Absolutely not, that will ensure that they scar," Bane said firmly. "We will not have that."

Nick bit his lower lip but then said, "You know that scars aren't terrible."

"Meaning that *my* scars are not terrible?" Bane tenderly wiped his back again. He was moving the washcloth down the very center of Nick's spine and Nick couldn't help but let out a pleased sigh.

"They aren't. I notice that you hide yours a lot of the time and I thought you should know that you don't need to," Nick answered honestly.

Bane let out a grunt of amusement. "Are you worried that I have low self-esteem about my looks?"

"No, that makes it far more simple than it is." Nick's eyes were sliding closed as Bane washed him. Exhaustion was plucking at him again.

"I'm surprised that you worry about anything at all about me." Bane ran the washcloth along Nick's shoulders.

"God, that feels so good," Nick moaned.

"It doesn't hurt?" Bane must have leaned in. Nick could feel the light heat of his breath against his left cheek.

"No, no, it's—it's perfect."

"Good. I'm going to put the ointment on you now."

Skin on skin. Bane's movements were so careful and slow so as not to hurt him. The big man smoothed his hands slowly down Nick's ribcage and lingered at his waist. Then he started again at the very top of Nick's spine and slowly, oh so slowly, drifted down to the swell of his ass. The ointment was light and not greasy.

Nick groaned. He wasn't even trying to hide the pleasure he felt. "Magic hands."

"Would you—would you like to speak to your father?" Bane asked.

"My *father*?" Nick's eyelids flew open in shock at the change of subject. The last thing he wanted to think or talk about was his father when Bane was massaging him. He could almost *hear* Charles' disgusted reaction if he told him he had gotten sunburnt and caused Bane trouble. His heart beat sickly just thinking about his father's disdainful words.

How could you be so foolish, Nick?

You've put our entire family in jeopardy by doing something unutterably stupid!

I think you must have done it on purpose! You don't love us. You want to see us out on the street!

How could I have such a useless son?

Bane must have felt his tension as he gentled his touch, easing Nick back down onto the bed. He hadn't realized he'd half risen up.

"Your father deserves to know what happened." Bane's voice was tight as he added, "I promised you would be well taken care of. That nothing bad would happen to you. I *failed* in this."

"Nothing bad has happened," Nick mumbled into the pillow. His chest felt tight with worry.

"Your father would be concerned about your burns," Bane said awkwardly. "He would want to know about your condition."

"It's a sunburn," Nick said, thinking just how much he *didn't* want his father to hear of his stupidity. "That's all."

"If you could see what I'm seeing you would not think that," Bane murmured. "He would be very concerned."

"No, he wouldn't, Bane. And even if he was, I would rather *not* talk to him," Nick answered. His own voice was tight with stress.

"If it would upset you to speak to him then you don't have to," Bane said after a long moment.

"It wouldn't be comforting. Let's just put it that way." Nick gripped the pillow.

"I see."

"I don't think you do," Nick sighed.

"I suppose I shall have to learn more about you then to understand your relationship with Charles," Bane said.

"There's no relationship with my father." Nick's breathing was coming in high and fast. "If he knew I messed up, Bane—"

"You haven't—"

"He would think so! Please don't tell him about this. Please don't make me tell him." Nick went very still while he waited for Bane to respond.

Bane smoothed more ointment on his shoulders. "I will not if that is what you wish."

"I do wish it." Nick paused then added, "Thank you."

"Of course."

Another silence that fell between them. Even though Bane had covered his back twice with ointment, his hands did not leave Nick's skin. He was massaging Nick everywhere that could be touched now. Nick's muscles were relaxing under that surprisingly gentle touch.

"My father..." Bane began and then stopped.

Nick held his breath. He doubted that Bane would speak of his father lightly and from what Omar had said, Bane's father was a more sensitive subject than his own.

"My father," Bane began again, his voice deepening. "Was a hard man, too. I could not please him no matter what I did. When I tried to do the things that I felt I was skilled at he scoffed. When I tried to do the things that he seemed to value, he scoffed even *more*."

Nick winced, hearing the pain in those simple statements. "I'm sorry."

"The fact that I could not please him or make him proud caused me great pain for a long time, but then I realized that it was not *me* that was the problem," Bane explained. "It was *him*. There was nothing *I* could do. All that was wrong was inside of *him*. Do you understand what I'm saying, Nick?"

Nick was surprised by the tears that welled up in his eyes and dripped onto the pillow. "I think I do, but your father must have been *blind* not to have seen value in you. My dad...well, he might be — be ruthless and cruel at times, but he's smart. He sees the value in things very clearly. He can look at a person and *know* what they're worth. But when he looks at me..."

Nick found that he could not say the rest. But he didn't have to. Bane knew.

"We cannot often see what is right before us, Nick. We think we do, but we don't always," Bane answered.

"You asked if I was here because I wanted my family to love me. Jade asked me that, too. I said no to both of you but...but I think that's a lie. I think I've been hoping that they would realize my worth because I was willing to do this for them. God, that sounds so stupid! I can't even weed a flower garden right. I'm—"

"Gentle, kind, intelligent, artistic and *beautiful*," Bane cut him off. "Those are all the things you are. I know the value of a man, too, Nick, I see yours."

"But you didn't before."

"Because I would not let myself see you."

Nick twisted his head around to look at Bane. That long curtain of hair covered half of his face. "Why not?"

Bane pulled his hair away from his scar. It was not so red and raw looking in the golden light of the lamps. "I did not get this because I've seen the worth of things clearly all the time. I received this because when I am blind, I am *truly* blind. I think...I think I was like that with you."

Nick didn't know what to say at first. There were so many questions he wanted to ask, but they wouldn't come out. This scar defined Bane. It represented some terrible tragedy that had befallen him.

"How did it happen?" Nick heard the words leave his mouth before he could stop them.

A mirthless smile curled Bane's lips. "*Arrogance*."

When he said nothing more, Nick laid back down and Bane's hands were on his back again. Bane dug into the unmarred skin along Nick's shoulders. There was another moan dragged out of Nick. Bane lightened the pressure and slowly drew his fingers along Nick's sides again. Nick's muscles bunched and released under his fingers. Sleep approached again on tiger's paws.

"Did you ever do this for Devon?" Nick asked, his voice blurring slightly.

"You wish to talk about Devon at a time like this? I thought we were *done* talking of him." Bane's fingers trailed along the waistband of Nick's boxer briefs.

"You brought up my father." Nick didn't open his eyes.

"You appear to be able to pout even though your features are very puffy," Bane said, but he immediately began to massage in more of the ointment into Nick's back.

Nick chuckled softly. "You seriously know how to give a guy a compliment."

"I do try."

"Yeah, well, you need to try harder. Oh, yeah, that's nice and hard." Nick was referring to Bane's hands that continued to smooth over Nick's skin.

"Not hard. Soft. Gentle. You've had enough hard for some time," Bane whispered.

"I'm falling asleep," Nick murmured. The fever was rising again, too, and pulling him down, down, down.

"I can see that," Bane said as he slowly drew his fingers along the gentle rise of Nick's ass.

"I have a favor to ask," Nick's voice was hardly a whisper now. "When I wake up will you still be here?"

"If you wish," Bane said.

"I want you to be. I want us to get to know one another. You seem so—so approachable right now. Not so wild. So will you?" Nick found himself asking without shyness. "Will you be here?"

Bane paused and then said, "I will."

CHAPTER TWENTY-FOUR

CATCH

Bane took in a deep shuddering breath himself as Nick's breathing slowed with sleep. The beast inside of him whined, annoyed it had to be contained. It really wished to nose Nick's wounds and lick them clean. For one moment, Bane imagined being on top of Nick, leaning down and dragging his tongue along the young man's tender skin. He could almost taste the salt of Nick's flesh in the back of his throat. He swallowed hard.

He wiped his hands clean on the towel as his gaze followed the sweep of Nick's back to that muscled, pert ass. Nick's narrow waist and broad shoulders begged to be framed by his powerful hands again. He imagined Nick's body arching up against him. A flash of heat flared between his legs and his eyes hooded. But then he saw the blisters that were the size of half-dollars. They were pink and shiny on Nick's back and his desire was tempered. His fault. If he hadn't made Nick feel like crap—*like his father makes him feel, yet another reason to hate Charles* — Nick would have taken better care of himself. He would have put on sunscreen and stopped work when he felt the burn beginning. But no, Nick had worked and worked and worked.

His gaze slid to the camera on the nightstand. He knew that Nick had taken some pictures already of the fountain. He knew he should wait until Nick was awake to be given permission to look at the photographs. But he couldn't resist. Besides, it would be better for him to see the photographs first, alone, so he could make sure his expression was neutral if they weren't any good.

But what is good when it comes to art? It is merely my opinion. It matters little.

Yet his mother had always said he had a good eye. He picked up the camera. His eyes slid to Nick's beautiful sleeping form guiltily. But when he was sure that Nick was deeply asleep and not about to wake up, he turned on the camera's viewer and began to scroll through the images. Every photograph hit him in the solar plexus like a physical blow.

Nick's photographs were *more* than good. They were *brilliant*. The photographs of the fountain's stone carving juxtaposed with the gorgeous blooms captured the wildness versus humanity's attempts to tame it. Bane was mesmerized by Nick's closeups of the flowers themselves. Even the weeds became beautiful and complex with the mixture of light and shadow.

Nick, you are talented. How does your father not see this? You should be encouraged. You should be allowed to spend every moment creating art. Forget business. Forget gardening. You need to be immersed in beauty.

Bane's head jerked up as he heard footsteps lightly coming down the hallway towards Nick's door. It was Devon's tread. He would recognize it anywhere. There was a sense in the footfalls that Devon was trying to be quiet so as not to alert Bane he was coming. Not that it did any good. With Bane's keen hearing there was no chance that Devon could sneak up on him. Devon was likely coming to "check" on Nick again. Except it wasn't Nick who he was checking up on.

What does he think he'll catch me doing with Nick being wounded like this? Does he believe I'm such an animal that

I'd demand Nick service me with a fever and weeping blisters?

Bane carefully turned off the camera and set it back down exactly as he had found it. He truly hoped that Nick would willingly share the photographs with him later. He was so eager now for Nick to spend time photographing every aspect of Moon Shadow. Forget scrubbing toilets! Nick needed to be focused on his *art*.

A whole year of Nick focusing on photography will be the best thing for him.

With that thought, Bane went to the door. He didn't wait for Devon to knock. He didn't want to risk Nick being woken. Instead he opened it just as Devon raised his hand to knock and stepped out into the hall, closing the door softly behind him. As he stepped forward, Devon was forced to step back.

"Oh, Bane! You startled me!" One of Devon's hands drifted up to his chest as if Bane had caught him doing something wrong.

"Devon, what is it?" Bane asked gruffly.

Devon's brown eyes widened and then narrowed. "I'm just checking on Nick. How is he doing?"

Bane repressed the urge to say that Nick was the same as he had been an hour ago when Devon had been there last, but that was unkind. Devon *did* feel badly for Nick, he was sure, but that's just not why he was here.

"Sleeping now. Dr. Trevelyan says he's mending, but still has a long way to go. There's a chance he might—might *scar*." Bane nearly choked on that word. His right hand fluttered up to his face, but he thrust it into his pocket instead.

Devon blinked. "That's more serious than I realized."

"It shouldn't be called a sunburn. It makes it seem like no big deal. It's a *burn* period," Bane stated emphatically.

"Well, yes, I can understand that. He did look awfully red last night and when he fainted..." Devon moved a hand through the air as if to express his realization about how injured Nick really was.

"Yes. He needs rest and quiet."

"Of course." Devon stood awkwardly, staring at Bane, as if uncertain what to say. "Would you take a walk with me? The day is beautiful."

Bane looked back at the closed bedroom door. He could tell that Nick was still very sound asleep. "I promised Nick I would be there when he woke up."

"Are you...well, we could both wait in the bedroom then. I'm sure if we talk low we won't wake him," Devon replied stiffly.

"No. He's just fallen asleep. I'm sure we can go out for a bit."

The beast would let him know when Nick was swimming back towards consciousness in more than enough time to be by his side for when he fully woke. Devon gave him a faint smile and put his arm through Bane's. They walked down the stairs. When Bane tried to direct them out to the back porch, Devon pulled him towards the front.

"I wasn't just checking on Nick. I was trying to escape Dean, Sloan and her phone," Devon explained with a theatrical sigh as they stepped out of the front of the house.

"Dean is awake?" Bane's eyebrows crawled up into his hairline. He had expected Dean to be in bed with a massive hangover for most of the day, or at least until the afternoon. It wasn't yet lunch.

Sunlight streamed down upon them. It was warm and welcoming, but Bane remembered what it had done to Nick's skin. They started walking along the gravel drive towards the gate. There was a path that followed the contours of the property that began there.

"In a manner of speaking. He's pretty much hidden behind a pair of sunglasses and grunting at everyone on the porch. Pre-verbal at the moment."

Bane nodded, but said nothing. He feared if he did that he would say something unfortunate. Dean's behavior yesterday was unforgivable. The beast agreed. It bared its teeth.

Devon reached out and lightly ran a hand down Bane's chest. "You should try to forgive him for last night. I know he was a drunken boor, but Nick handled him well. No harm. No foul."

Bane scowled. "He was nosing around Nick before he took his first sip of alcohol."

"And that's a capital offense?"

"Yes."

Devon let out a sharp laugh and gave Bane an even sharper look. Again, Bane recognized jealousy when he heard and saw it. But his brain would not completely let him accept it. Their relationship had always been casual. Suddenly, Devon was acting as if it was more or *should* be more. Or maybe it was his own reactions to Devon that were different. If he hadn't met Nick would he be so annoyed by Devon? Would he chaff at the man's touch and attention? No, he wouldn't. Something had changed in their relationship, but it wasn't Devon. It was him.

Devon said, "Handsy men like Dean are a dime a dozen. I'm sure Nick's had plenty of experience fighting them off considering how pretty he is."

Several retorts sprung to Bane's lips, but he bit them back. Instead he lowered his voice and said, "I can't believe *you* would be accepting of Dean's behavior. If I recall right, we met because of a man that wouldn't accept your 'no' for an answer."

Devon crossed his arms over his chest and looked away from Bane. "You punched him and I was grateful for it. Look, I'm not saying that what Dean said or did was—was *right*, but there's an explanation for the drinking, the groping and everything."

Bane frowned. "What reason would that be?"

"You know how he told us about how the Fairfaxes tried to take over his company, but he stopped them?"

Bane shifted angrily. "Yes, another Fairfax *attack*." He might like Nick, but he didn't like the rest of his family.

Devon's face became pinched, but then he said, "That wasn't exactly what happened."

Bane's brow furrowed. "What do you mean? What *exactly* happened?"

Devon sighed. "Dean approached the Fairfaxes. He wanted them to buy him out. But they wouldn't. Hermitage Pharmaceuticals is pretty much on the rocks. They didn't get the FDA approval to go ahead with that new cholesterol drug and...well, anyways, Dean is losing everything."

Bane drew up short. "What? Why didn't he say something to me?"

"What could he say to you? Not even you can fund the company until Hermitage finds some brilliant new drug, assuming they ever would. It wouldn't be his style to ask for a loan either," Devon said with a shrug.

"But the Fairfaxes would..."

"Sell off the company's parts and leave the employees in the lurch? Yes, but Dean wouldn't be left with nothing," Devon said. "He would have shared in the profits. But they turned him down flat."

Bane's lips formed a thin white line. "So he *hates* the Fairfaxes not because they were vultures, but because they wouldn't pick apart the carcass of *his* company."

Devon looked up at him and with sad smiled said, "Oh, Bane, once people are rich they don't want to be poor. Not ever. Thoughts about others sort of fly away. Besides, either way, the company is done. The employees are going to lose their jobs. It's all about whether Dean will have a pot to piss in."

"I see."

Devon stopped and turned towards him. "Do you?"

"I do, but I also see the hypocrisy."

"You can *afford* to have morals and talk about hypocrisy. Dean can't afford that any longer."

They started walking again. Trees shaded the path. Dappled sunlight fell on their shoulders. Bane imagined Nick walking alongside him. He wondered what they would talk about. Photography. Flowers. The fingers of their hands would intertwine. Nick's gray eyes would brighten with amusement. He would tease Bane about something. Then their steps would slow and they would kiss and kiss and kiss.

"Are you in a relationship with Nick?" It was Devon's voice that broke him out of his thoughts.

He thought about denying it. It would be the truth. They *didn't* have a relationship. "No, but I wish to have one with him."

Devon let out a mixture of a laugh and a sigh. He wasn't smiling any longer. Every line of his body was taut. "I see. I suppose I was hoping you were going to tell me something different. This is definitely new since yesterday, isn't it?"

"No, it's not really new. It's just that I'm admitting it," Bane said.

"What kind of relationship? Physical? Emotional? Both?"

"I don't think Nick would accept a relationship that is just physical."

"And you're okay with that?" Devon stopped walking again. His arms were tight around himself.

Bane studied his own emotions. "Yes, I must be."

"Why?"

"Because I can't seem to stop thinking of him." The words left Bane's mouth before he could stop them. He found himself saying, "From the moment I saw him I haven't been able to forget him."

"Love at first sight? You are ready to believe in that when you've always claimed not to believe in love at all?" Devon's eyebrows arched.

"I said nothing of love. Affection. Caring." Bane stopped speaking. These things sounded so clinical and *untrue*. "I don't know what I believe. I just know that I can't look away from him."

"And he feels the same?"

"He hated me yesterday. Today...he tolerates me." Bane shrugged. Those words hurt. "It's no more than I deserve."

"I don't understand." Devon shook his head.

"I treated him badly because I wanted him and thought...thought I couldn't have him. Now I might have made it impossible for anything to happen between us at all," Bane answered.

"I've never heard you talk like this about anyone. Not once." Devon looked thoughtful.

"I understand if you…if you don't…wish to stay…"

Devon tossed his head back. "Oh, no, Bane. This new *twist* to you makes me all the more determined to win you myself. I told you that I believe we are truly compatible. Far more than with this *boy* you've found an interest in. I'm not giving you up. Not by a long shot."

CHAPTER TWENTY-FIVE
MISTAKES

Nick woke up to the sound of purring. A warm, rumbly sound that made him feel safe and content. Did Bane have a cat? Or was he remembering his beloved Vaughn, a black short-haired cat, that had died when he was only eight? Vaughn had often slept on the pillow right next to Nick's head and would purr all night long, showing her contentment at simply being in his presence. He had often reached blindly for her and run his fingers through her short, silky fur. She would stretch out under his hand and the purring would increase in intensity. He almost reached for her at that moment, but at the last minute, Nick's eyelids cracked open and he saw where the sound emanated from: Bane.

 The beautiful man was sprawled in a chair by the side of the bed and the purring was coming from him. Bane's head was tipped back and his long muscular legs were stretched out in front of him. Bane's long dark hair had fallen away from his face for once. His dark lashes fanned against high cheekbones. His powerful jaw was relaxed and his full lips were parted slightly. Bane's body was utterly relaxed in sleep. He reminded Nick of a huge tomcat, purring with contentment. Nick had the ridiculous urge to stroke him. He imagined that the purring would increase if he scritched behind the other man's ears just like it had when he had petted Vaughn. The big man looked so different in this moment, so very young and almost fragile despite his massive size.

He must have been exhausted to have fallen asleep here. I wonder if he's dreaming. What would a man like Bane dream about? Conquest? Maybe. When I look at him like this he seems so sad and alone. Or maybe that's how I feel and I'm just projecting it on him.

The moment Nick thought that, he moved and pain lanced through him. His forgotten sunburn and the dull, throbbing, nearly constant agony it caused came back full force. He let out a soft hiss and Bane was immediately awake.

His Siberian blue eyes zeroed in on Nick. They were not sleepy, but instead had the full alertness of a wild animal disturbed from its nap. Nick froze. He wasn't afraid, but he felt like he had roused a very large, very dangerous beast from hibernation.

"Are you alright?" Bane's voice was husky with sleep and Nick could not deny its sensuality. Bane sat up fully though there was a languidness to his movements. He cracked his neck.

"I'm sorry I woke you," Nick said. "You looked so peaceful. Please don't get up."

But he needn't have said the last part. Bane was not moving, or at least, not moving to leave.

"I'm not going anywhere, Nick. Do not worry."

"I'm not worried," Nick said too quickly.

"Really?"

Bane stretched his arms above his head. There was a soft series of pops as his spine realigned. He regarded Nick with an intensity that would have had the young man squirming if it wouldn't have hurt so badly to move.

"I went for a walk with Devon, but I made sure I came back before you woke. You were the one that looked so peaceful so I decided to join you in a nap," Bane explained and there was something *more* in his voice that Nick couldn't interpret.

"I'm glad you came back," Nick admitted. "I really didn't want to wake up alone."

"I'm glad you don't mind me napping in here. I haven't slept this well in a long time." Bane cracked his neck and then leaned back in the chair.

Nick studied Bane's face. The big man's eyes were heavy lidded. He had sculpted lips and a powerful jaw. A noble nose. High cheekbones. A truly sensual brow. The scar could not take away from his innate beauty.

"It's nice to see a friendly face especially after the dreams I've been having," Nick confessed.

"What dreams?" Bane asked.

"I can't really describe them. I'm in a jungle. Someone is hunting me." The someone hunting him was Bane, but he wouldn't say that. Besides, in this last dream he had only sensed being watched, but the blue eyes could have been that of Bane or the white Bengal tiger that had infiltrated his dreams since he first came to Moon Shadow.

"Hmmmm," Bane said noncommittally. "I dreamt, too."

"About what?"

"I dreamt of when I got this." He gestured towards the scar.

Nick wondered if he would say more. He had been so very secretive about it. "It must be quite the story. It's such an *unusual* scar."

Bane made a movement to cover it up with his hair.

"Don't," Nick said. "You don't have to. You're still beautiful with it."

Bane froze. He slowly lowered his hand, leaving the scar uncovered. "You think I'm *beautiful*?"

"I think that *everyone* finds you beautiful. It's a *fact*, not an *opinion*." Nick laughed then winced because it hurt.

"And the scar doesn't detract from that? Doesn't draw your eye?" Bane asked with a slightly curious smile on his lips.

"It *does*," Nick said slowly. "But it just makes you more interesting. Because you can tell there's a good story behind it."

"A bad story actually," Bane corrected.

"Well, bad stories are good stories if you know what I mean."

"Yes, they make for *better* stories, I suppose." Bane's gaze went distant for a moment and then he began to speak, "There is a valley in India. It doesn't have a name. At least not a name that's on any maps. There is a village in the very center of it surrounded by thick, lush, steamy jungle. There were only a dozen families left when this happened, but the village has been there for over a thousand years, maybe longer. And for all that time they have worshipped white Bengal tigers."

Nick drew in a sharp breath as he thought of his own dream of such a beast.

"You are in pain." It was not a question, but a statement from Bane.

"No." When Bane gave him a sharp look, he said, "Yes, but that's not why I reacted like I did. I've just been dreaming of white Bengal tigers. That's all. Strange coincidence."

Bane's gaze fixed on him and the man didn't blink. "I dream of them all the time, too."

Nick blinked in surprise. He wasn't sure what to make of that. He wondered if Bane dreamed of him, too. Because tigers and Bane were synonymous in his dreams anyway. Nick mentally shook himself though and prompted, "But you were saying, there is the village in the valley?"

"The natives of this village believed that the spirit of all tigers inhabited a real white Bengal tiger. So long as their sacred tiger lived and was well all tigers would flourish, but if it were to die from *other* than natural causes the tiger spirit would be unable to remain in this world and all tigers would suffer," Bane explained. "The animal the villagers claimed contained this tiger spirit was said to be *magnificent*. And so I decided to kill it."

The starkness of that last statement had Nick staring at him with his mouth open.

Bane read the shock and dismay in Nick's expression. "You're not a hunter?"

"Uhm, no. I've never touched a gun in my life. And I would never want to shoot a *magnificent* animal with one," Nick said.

"No, you wouldn't." Bane looked at him fondly.

"Is the—the tiger rug downstairs the—the -"

"Yes," Bane paused and then continued, "Tarun and I—he had served my family for decades—tracked the beast to a watering hole. There it was. Big, beautiful, *perfect*."

"Did you shoot it then?" Nick found one of his hands curling against the sheets.

"It lifted its head. Whiskers wet with water. It looked right at me. It saw the gun. It *knew* what the gun was, but it didn't run. Didn't attack." Bane's gaze went distant and his hands flexed. "Why didn't it run or charge? Why did it let me kill it? Why didn't it protect itself?"

"Because it wasn't afraid of humans," Nick guessed. "It was worshipped, right? It was likely used to people being kind to it. It never would have thought a human would hurt it."

"Perhaps. But I believe—no, I *know*—that it understood what I intended." Bane's fingers curled against his thighs. "You see I wanted to destroy everything. Especially anything magnificent. Anything beautiful." Bane's gaze slid up to Nick's face and it felt like a physical caress.

"*Why?*" Nick whispered.

"Because I wanted the world to be as bleak and empty as I was. So I shot the tiger. Killed it. Right there. It was no challenge at all."

Nick felt sick hearing that. He looked away from Bane.

"There is a price to destroying something so beautiful and rare," Bane said. "It is a heavy, terrible price. As it should be."

"The villagers," Nick realized suddenly. He had forgotten that Bane was telling him about how he received the scar. "They did this to you. They burned you for killing the tiger!"

"Their priestess did. She *cursed* me for what I had done. Rightly so, but at the time, I already felt cursed. I thought it wouldn't matter if I were cursed again, but then she did this." He touched the scar this time.

Nick wondered if Alastair was the first curse that Bane was referring to, but he didn't have the nerve to ask. Instead, he said, "How did she do it?"

Bane gave him a mirthless smile. "*Magic.*"

Nick let out an uncertain laugh. Bane did not join in. Nick then thought of Omar. "Wait, Omar worships tigers. He said he came from a small village—"

"Same one. The priestess was his ancestor."

"What—what was the curse, exactly?"

Bane gave him a smile that looked more like a slash across his face. "She claimed that I would share my body with the tiger spirit. That I would be a *beast*. And the *only* thing that could free me from the curse is...*true love*."

It took Nick a few beats to actually *understand* what Bane had said. He didn't believe that Bane harbored a tiger spirit. That would be pure fancy! But the part about how to *break* the curse was terribly ironic and cruel. Omar's ancestor had taken the one thing that Bane claimed to not believe in and made it the centerpiece of his salvation.

"True love?" Nick repeated. "And you, a man that claims that he doesn't even believe in *ordinary*, garden variety love, let alone in *true love*."

"Do you believe in true love, Nick?" Bane leaned back in his chair, looking more and more like the tiger he was supposedly cursed to be.

"I—I don't know." Nick shrugged and looked away.

"You *do*." Bane actually laughed but not meanly. "Oh, you *are* romantic."

Nick blushed beneath his sunburn. "I admit that I've *never* see any couple who are in true love, but I guess, I, at least, *want* to believe in it."

"Yes, you would."

"Because I'm foolish?"

"No, because you have an *open* heart."

Silence, strange and weighty, fell between them.

"I'm not sure why I told you that story," Bane suddenly said and got up from his chair. His hair obscured the scar again.

Nick didn't want him to go so he found himself saying, "Because you made a mistake! You realized you did the wrong thing and you're sorry for it. You wanted me to know that you're sorry and not just about the tiger."

"Yes, I made a mistake with *you*, too," Bane said whisper-quiet. "And I *am* sorry."

"So am I."

"You have nothing to be sorry about."

"I'm sorry for what my family tried to do to you and Dean—"

"Your family did *nothing* to Dean."

"But I thought he said—"

"He lied." Bane's shoulders were tense. "Let us not talk of him. The very thought of him right now makes me angry."

"Oh." Nick was bewildered.

"And I would rather enjoy my time with you then think of Dean."

"I wish I were a bit more fun right now. This stupid sunburn is cramping my fun capability." There were blisters the size of golfballs on his upper shoulder blades now. They began to itch like mad. He knew though that he must not break them. They could scar or become infected. *Scar* ..."Thank you for telling me about what happened."

"You are the first person outside of Omar's family who knows the truth."

"I can see how painful it was to remember it."

"The dreams are always so vivid. As if I'm there again. As if I could actually make a different decision," Bane explained. He looked rueful. "But I *never* do."

"We can't change the past. We can just go forward, right?"

Bane rubbed his hands together and nodded. "True. It's just that the past is never fully passed, is it?"

"You just have to crowd it out with new, *good* memories."

Bane regarded him with a half smile. "Yes, I suppose you're right."

Now a comfortable silence fell. Nick's back though made it hard to enjoy the moment.

Maybe if I do something I won't be so bothered by it.

Nick said, "I should shower and then maybe help Omar downstairs—"

"You are *not* working," Bane said firmly. "Your only *job* is to recover fully."

"But I'm feeling better," Nick assured him even though the pain increased as he moved around. "It's—"

"I can tell from the fever in your eyes that you are *not* better. That fever will only burn hotter as night falls," Bane said. He glanced out the window. Nick followed his gaze It was nearly time for dinner. "You should shower though. I will remain here in case you need assistance. I will change the bedding and then bring you up some dinner."

"Oh, you don't have to —" Nick's mouth clamped shut as Bane gave him a look that said 'do not argue with me'. "All right, I'll shower and you'll—you'll *stay*. I assume that you'll eat downstairs with your guests, right?" Nick was shocked that he wanted Bane to stay and eat with him.

Bane looked quite reluctant. "I suppose that I should."

"I'll be fine. Don't worry."

As if to show him that he was perfectly fine, Nick slipped out of bed and padded slowly to the bathroom. He felt Bane's eyes on him so he forced himself to move fluidly as if he weren't in any pain at all. He didn't think he was fooling Bane. He managed to make it to the bathroom and then sagged against the sink as soon as the bathroom door was closed. His head was swimming. Bane was right that the fever was coming back. Maybe some of the dizziness came from not having eaten. But when he had a fever he had no appetite. He would definitely force himself to eat some dinner tonight though.

Nick looked up at his face in the mirror and winced. He had the complexion of a tomato. His lips were peeling. His eyes were still halfway puffed shut.

Not looking my best. Yet Bane doesn't seem to mind. He can't seem to keep his eyes off me. Nick snorted. *It's like a car wreck. He can't look away from the ruin. Unlike Bane, I'm not enhanced by being burned.*

He pushed off of the sink and tottered to the shower. He pulled open the heavy glass door for the stall. He managed to get the water going. The shower had a rain shower head. The hot water literally rained down onto the granite floor. He stripped off his boxers. A great deal of steam was already filling the glass-enclosed stall. He stepped inside and closed the shower door behind him. The steam wrapped around him like a lover. He wobbled on his feet and grabbed the wall.

C'mon. This is ridiculous, he told his body, but it didn't agree. He felt weaker and shakier by the moment.

The hot water caused him to hiss when it hit his back. He blindly reached for the faucet to adjust the temperature, but his head swam more than ever and he was falling forward. It felt like it was happening in slow motion. The stone floor rushed up to hit his head. He let out a cry of surprise and, suddenly, *impossibly,* Bane was there.

Holding him.

Saving him.

CHAPTER TWENTY-SIX
MOMENTARY WEAKNESS

"How did you get here so fast?" Nick gasped even as he nearly slipped through Bane's hands and onto the floor. His skin was slick with water.

"I was near the door. I heard you cry out," Bane lied as he held Nick tighter. The young man's legs were trembling beneath him like a newborn doe's.

He had been much farther away than just outside the door. He had been by the bed, stripping off the sheets when the beast had felt Nick's distress. He had moved before being consciously aware of willing it. And now he had a hold of Nick's waist. Nick's back was firmly against his front. Water was soaking Bane's clothes and shoes, ruining the latter, but he didn't care. He wished his clothes weren't there at all and then he could have felt Nick's skin against his own. The beast growled in approval, but he pushed it down. Now was *not* the time.

"You're getting wet," Nick laughed weakly. "Your clothes and shoes."

"I don't care. I'm not letting you go," Bane's voice came out gruff. "I'm not leaving you."

Nick half turned his head to look over his shoulder at him. Bane could see the firm line of it and the swanlike sweep of his neck. The beast rumbled in approval. Nick was beautiful. He saw the awareness of his position pass through Nick's eyes as he felt Bane shift against him. He was naked, Bane was clothed. He was weak, Bane was strong. In the attic, Bane had made it quite clear that he could do *anything* he wanted to Nick. Was Nick thinking about that moment now?

Bane wanted to curse himself for the millionth time. Every move he had made with Nick had been the wrong one. He had sowed fear not desire. He had made them enemies instead of friends. Somehow Nick had forgiven him. Mostly. But to be so weak and naked and reliant upon Bane's "goodness" would perhaps be a bridge too far.

"I—I think I can stand now," Nick said, but his legs were still trembling.

"Nick ..." His voice was only lightly chastising because of the lie. It was a lie with a good purpose behind it. Knowing that Nick wanted to be away from him, Bane suggested, "Perhaps we should get you out of the shower."

"No!"

Now *that* shocked him. "All—all right. What *do* you want?"

"I feel so gross. I really want to get *clean*," Nick begged.

"You can't do this by yourself though. You need help." All Bane wanted to do was stay and give Nick the cleaning and support he wanted. But Nick wouldn't want *him* doing it. "I could get Omar to help you."

Nick went still, considering this. His voice was low, "You. I want you. To help, I mean."

Though Nick was already red from the sunburn and the shower, Bane knew he was blushing as well as he lowered his head and his eyelashes fanned across his cheeks in embarrassment. The beast's tail whapped wildly. It was so pleased. Nick would let them groom him. That was appropriate.

"Let me clean your back. Is that all right?" Bane asked.

"Yes." Nick swallowed.

"Brace yourself against the wall. If you feel faint, tell me." The last was actually unnecessary. The beast was completely in tune with Nick's heart rate and breathing. It would know even before Nick did if something was wrong.

The young man put the palms of both hands flat against the cool tile. He spread his legs apart. His head lowered as the water from the showerhead rained down upon him. He was a vision like this. All long limbs, trim waist, pert ass and the posture of a willing lover. Heat built between Bane's thighs and he adjusted himself to hide his erection. His wet pants were like a second skin though, revealing everything. He reminded himself fiercely that Nick was not asking to be taken. He was asking to be *washed*. He had to remember that. The beast prowled in his chest.

Bane released Nick's waist and grabbed the sponge. He squeezed some of the shower gel that smelled of amber and almonds on it. His hands were steady as he brought the sponge gently against Nick's right shoulder and started to smooth it down the length of his spine. The water had already caused many of the blisters to break, but he kept the pressure on Nick's skin feather light nonetheless. The suds skimmed down Nick's spine. Some of them clung to his ass for a moment before falling onto the tile floor and being washed away. Others slid lower and trailed down Nick's inner thighs.

Bane had kept his touches to areas so far that were neutral. Nick's shoulders. Nick's back. Nick's arms. But now Bane gracefully got down on his haunches. The water squished in his shoes. His shirt was completely transparent and clinging to his chest. Now more water cascaded down upon him as he ran the sponge over Nick's pale buttocks. The young man drew in a sharp breath, but it was not from pain. The beast smelled Nick's arousal and Bane glimpsed his slowly hardening cock between the young man's parted thighs. His own erection ached, but he ignored it and continued to soap Nick up.

When he brought the sponge to the top of the parting between Nick's buttcheeks, the young man held his breath. Bane guessed that Nick was considering telling Bane that he could handle this part himself. But Bane did not give him a chance to protest. Instead, he drew the sponge firmly between the two ripe globes. Nick shuddered and rested his forehead against the tile. The scent of arousal grew stronger from him.

Bane slid the sponge between Nick's thighs and the young man's fingers dug into the tile. His breathing rate increased. Bane knew he was trying *not* to let on how aroused he was. Bane drew the sponge down the interior of one leg and then the other. These were long, slow strokes. Nick let out a hiss. Bane rose up. One of his hands curled around Nick's waist. He offered the sponge to Nick with the other.

"Do you want me to wash your front?" Bane's voice was a low rumble.

"I—I can do it, but ..."

Bane leaned closer, his lips just an inch above Nick's shoulder. "But do you *want* me to?"

"You know I do." Nick let out a rather helpless laugh. "You can *see*." He gestured down to his beautiful, erect cock. "But I..."

"Are you afraid of me? You are the one in control, Nick. I will do nothing that you do not allow." Bane lightened his grip on Nick's waist even as the beast surged forward, urging him to wrap his arms around the young man and kiss him and claim him.

"It's not that. Not exactly." Nick let out another uncomfortable laugh. "It's just that *this* is what everyone *thinks* is happening between us. That I *must* give you what you want, because if I don't...my family ...my family will be *destroyed*."

Bane froze at Nick's words. He wanted to say, "Do you think that I'm doing that? Do you think your family's livelihood is at risk if you don't let me touch you right now? Do you believe that of me?"

But instead his hands dropped from Nick's body and he was stepping back. The beast let out a bewildered whine. It wanted Nick. Why was Bane backing away? He should be stepping forward. He should be holding Nick. Touching Nick. Grooming Nick. Kissing Nick.

But Bane realized the position he had put Nick in. The young man was wounded, feverish, and completely at his mercy. Bane *did* have control of Nick's family. And he *had* taken advantage. He knew Nick was weak right now and yet he'd still done this thing. Were his actions any different than Dean's?

Nick turned around, bewildered. "Bane?"

"I'm sorry. I shouldn't have done that. I shouldn't have...You seem fine. I'll send Omar to you—"

Nick turned and reached for him, but Bane was already by the door. The young man called out, "Wait! I didn't mean—"

But Bane didn't hear Nick's words, instead he heard only his own internal curses as he raced from Nick's room.

CHAPTER TWENTY-SEVEN

YOURS AND MINE

"I'm fine, Omar. Really," Nick assured the Indian man.

Omar continued to fuss with the tray on Nick's lap. There was a bowl of golden broth. A perfectly roasted chicken breast with a velvety, creamy sauce and brussel sprouts with bacon. Instead of wine, Omar had placed a glass of ice water on the tray as well.

"Are you sure you have everything you need? Are you in pain?" Omar asked.

"No, I'm good." Nick caught Omar's nearest forearm. "You've done enough. I know that you still have to serve dinner downstairs."

"Bane is handling that," Omar answered with a quick glance at him.

Nick's breath caught at the billionaire's name. "O-oh, he is? That's good. I'm glad he's helping you."

Bane serving dinner. Now that is an image. If I hadn't said anything in the shower he would be up here with me though. Maybe he would be lying beside me in bed, spooning soup into my mouth. After dinner, he'd massage me until I fell asleep. God, why did I have to say anything? Why couldn't I just let him touch me and kiss me? I'm still aching for him.

"Did something happen?" Omar asked. "Up here, I mean. Bane came down looking...distressed."

"No, *nothing* happened. That was the problem." Nick gave out a pained laugh. He looked down at the tray when he asked, "He looked... *distressed*?"

"And subdued." Omar looked at him critically. "Something happened, didn't it? Nothing upset you, did it?"

Nick noted that Omar's question had changed from "if" anything had happened to "what" had happened. Should he tell Omar about this? Did he want Omar to know how he and Bane had nearly made out in the shower? He was pretty sure that would please Omar, but still it was a lot of information to share. But he needed to talk to someone about this and Omar was a really good listener. He took in a deep breath.

"I'm not sure. I think we almost kissed. Maybe more than that," Nick admitted and ducked his head with a blush.

"That's good!" But Omar's joy turned to uncertainty. "Or is it *not* good?"

"I don't know what it is." Nick sighed and rubbed his forehead. He grimaced. He was starting to peel. He had no idea why Bane had wanted to touch him at all. He was a red, peeling mess. "He confuses me."

"He is good at that." Omar nodded with a pleased smile.

"He can be charming. He can be thoughtful. He's...God, he's beautiful." Nick shook his head as the thought of Bane's beauty clung to his reason. "But when he touched me I kept thinking about the fact that if we—we *became physical*." He quickly glanced up at Omar even as his cheeks burned, but the Indian man didn't look nonplussed by the discussion. "I kept thinking that if things went *wrong* between him and I...well, my family's livelihood is at stake. And then I wondered if I really had a choice whether to do something with him or not."

"Yes, I can see why you felt all of those things." Omar let out a long suffering sigh. "He should not have approached you until he had ended this ridiculous *internship*."

"He's not going to do that, Omar. Whatever he might have started feeling for me isn't enough to stop him hating Fairfaxes as a general rule," Nick responded.

"Would you see him if—if the internship was ended?" Omar looked at him curiously.

"Like I said he's a mixture of amazing and aggravating. I don't know what I would do." Nick shrugged even as something in his heart *twisted* at the thought of not seeing Bane again. "If I had met him outside of all this there would be no question. If he showed his charming, caring side, that is."

"That, too, is quite understandable."

They both fell silent.

"You think that Bane really wants something more than just what happened in the heat of the moment?" Nick asked.

"Oh, I'm positive of it. It's why he brought you here in the first place," Omar said. "The whole internship was about him wanting to have you near."

Nick let out a disbelieving laugh. "Then why didn't he just ask me out?"

"Because..." Omar hesitated and met Nick's gaze and suddenly Nick understood.

"Because he found out I'm a Fairfax. And so he couldn't *like* me. Not *consciously*." Nick shook his head. "He's so stubborn."

"And foolish and proud and prejudiced. But he is many good things, too, thankfully. He can be so much greater than any of his failings if he has a reason to reach for his better nature," Omar said. "You can be that reason, Nick."

"Can I really be that, Omar? I seem to inspire strange things in him. Not all of them good."

And he inspires things in me that I can't explain.

"Well, do not think about this any longer now. Just eat and get some rest. I'll come up for the tray tomorrow so I won't bother your sleep tonight," Omar said.

"Thanks, Omar. For everything."

Omar bowed and left the room, closing the door softly behind him. Nick picked up the spoon and tasted the soup. It was delicious. The chicken was equally mouthwatering, but he only managed a few bites. The fever still plagued him and stole his appetite. Nick ended up setting the tray to the side with only a quarter of the food eaten. He would have to explain to Omar in the morning that he'd enjoyed the meal, but he was simply too ill to eat more of it.

He immediately turned off the light and curled on his side. His eyes strayed to the chair that Bane had fallen asleep in that afternoon. The curtains were not completely closed and a strip of moonlight illuminated it. He imagined, for one moment, Bane sitting there now. His Siberian blue eyes would be hooded and almost glowing in the moonlight. His large body would be sprawled languidly on the chair. Nick imagined reaching towards him.

"Please come back, Bane. I didn't want you to leave before. Please come to me," he would say to the man.

And Bane would gracefully rise up from the chair and prowl across the room in that tigerish way of his. Nick imagined him in only a black silk robe. Bane would kneel down on the bed and Nick's outstretched hand would curl around his hip. The silk would feel like cool water under his fingertips. Bane would make that growling pleased noise when Nick touched him. One of Bane's hands would drift down his shoulder, featherlight so not to hurt him, but letting Nick relish his strength at the same time.

"I would never leave you, Nick," Bane would rumble as he stroked Nick's arm and then gently cupped his face.

"Would you lay down with me? I want to feel your arms around me even if it hurts," Nick would murmur.

Bane would respond in actions and not in words. He would undo the tie of the robe and then let the silk run down his arms and float to the ground. His naked body would be heavily muscled. His cock would be as huge as he was and flushed a dark red. It would be jutting forward as if aiming at Nick. Nick's dry mouth would begin to water. The desire to taste Bane's cum would have him swallowing again and again.

Bane would lower himself to the bed and Nick would slide back to give Bane room. But the big man would catch his waist and gently push him onto his back. The cool sheets against his hot skin would feel good. And then Bane would be straddling him. Nick would draw in a deep breath as that heavy, male body pressed down on his groin. He would still have on his pajama pants, but Bane wouldn't let that stand in their way for long. He would rise up and Nick would squirm out of them.

Nick's heart would be beating hard and fast in his chest like a humming bird's wings. Bane would take one of those massive hands and clasp both their cocks together. He would slowly begin to stroke them. Up and down. Slow and sure. A firm hand on them both. His Siberian blue eyes would be slitted and definitely glowing now. Nick would be transfixed by them as his breathing became ragged.

Bane's fingers would snake down and roll his balls. Nick's hips would rise and his head would thrash against the pillow. And then Bane would be leaning down, still stroking them both. His mouth would cover Nick's and the kiss would have him moaning.

Nick hands would finally be able to move and he would run them through Bane's thick hair. Those soft, thick locks would slide through his fingers as their tongues delved into each other's mouths. He would pull Bane's hair when the big man ran his thumb over Nick's slit. His breathing would stutter-step as Bane twisted his wrist just the right amount and Nick's hips would jerk off of the bed. Any pain he might have felt in his back would be nothing compared to the pleasure.

He would writhe under Bane and drag his fingernails down Bane's powerful spine to his muscular buttocks. He would grip them and pull them apart then slide his fingers down between those firm cheeks. His fingertips would drag across Bane's anus and the big man would kiss him harder and stroke them in time to the frantic beating of their hearts.

Precum would squirt out of both their slits and make the slide of Bane's hand over their lengths smoother and silkier.

Nick would wrap both legs around Bane's waist and dig his heels into that magnificent ass. Bane would then be cradled against his body. Their kisses would become wetter and hotter and more desperate. Bane would rock up against him. Their balls would press against each other.

Bane would suck on his lower lip. His teeth would rasp over it and Nick would arch. Heat would bloom like molten flowers inside Nick's groin. Bane would stroke them faster and faster. Nick's fingers would dig into Bane's shoulders. Their mouths would fuse together as Bane's strokes became more frantic. Nick would keen against Bane's lips.

Their bodies would lift and rub together. Nick would feel his balls draw impossibly tight against his body. And then the orgasm would come. Creamy semen would gush out of both of them, painting their bellies with streaks of opalescent cum.

Slick with sweat, Nick would wrap his arms tight against Bane's body as the aftershocks rocked them both. Bane would cover Nick. He would twist them to the side so as to not crush Nick beneath him. As their breathing would slow, Bane would kiss him and Nick would kiss Bane back. They would be slow, aching kisses that soothed rather than enflamed.

Nick's eyes would slide shut and he would cuddle against his Bane's massive chest. Sleep would reach for him as Bane stroked his hair and told him, "You're mine, Nick, and I am yours."

Nick must have fallen asleep for real as he imagined that last part, belly still covered with cum, pants pulled down to his thighs, as the next thing he knew he was startled awake. His eyes were still bleary with sleep and the room was terribly dark. But he saw a masculine figure sitting on the edge of his bed. It was too big to be Omar and he thought—*hoped*—it was Bane.

"Bane?" His lips curled into a smile and he reached out for the big man.

The man caught his wrist in a sweaty hand and Nick caught the stale whiff of whiskey on his breath. He froze.

"No, sweetheart. Not Bane," Dean said, his voice slurred with drink. His head tilted down looking at Nick's exposed cock and balls. Nick hadn't drawn the sheets up over himself before he fell asleep. "Bane's with Devon. But I'm more than enough of a man to make you happy. Though I see you got started without me."

Nick opened his mouth to yell, cry out, but Dean slammed a hand over his lips. Silencing him.

CHAPTER TWENTY-EIGHT
THE TASTE OF ASHES

Bane had tried to lose himself in serving his guests. His mind though kept betraying him and remembering the feel of Nick's bare skin under his fingertips. He remembered Nick's clean, warm scent in the nostrils. He remembered the sound of Nick's voice saying his name.

Nick haunted him.

The beast, too, was haunted by Nick. It paced in his chest. At times, his own feet started taking him out of the dining room or kitchen and to the stairs to the second floor. To Nick. It had consumed all of his will to overpower the beast and turn away from those steps. These episodes left him shaking and coated with sweat. The beast had *never* been this hard to control this far out from the full moon and, even then, he could not recall the beast taking charge of him in human form.

Omar had looked at him strangely a time or two and the Indian man's hand had drifted up to the tiger amulet around his neck, but though questions filled his gaze, Bane said nothing to him of his struggles. Omar might become alarmed and think that Nick should be removed from Moon Shadow. In fact, after leaving Nick's bedroom, Omar had actually brought up the issue of the internship again in the kitchen, which would *ensure* that Nick left his home.

Omar had been dishing out chocolate mousse pie for dessert. "I think that Nick might stay on if you released him from the internship. I believe he likes it here."

Bane snorted. He thought of how he had clutched at Nick in the shower. He thought of that swanlike neck. "No, Omar, he wouldn't stay. He would flee and that would be the worst thing for him."

Omar turned to look at him. "Oh? How so?"

Bane fussed with the press pot of coffee he was preparing for Dean. The man was sloshed again and needed to be sobered up. "Because Nick is a very talented photographer and his father," he said *father* like it tasted bitter in his mouth, "his father has no knowledge of this. In fact, Charles routinely dismisses Nick's work without even having seen it." Like he had done, but he wouldn't mention that. "So if Nick were to go back home he would not be encouraged to practice his art. And if he were to strike out on his own he would have to focus on making a living not on his art again. Here he can be allowed to do so all the time."

"So no more scrubbing toilets?" A flicker of a smile appeared on Omar's lips.

"No more toilets. I think that we will have some more help brought in. You don't have the time to scrub toilets either."

Omar's eyes widened. "That is quite *considerate* of you, Bane. I know how much you value your privacy."

"Yes, well, Nick has *true* talent. It cannot be allowed to go fallow." He pressed the plunger down in the pot. "And I ask too much of you."

"You ask no more of me than I wish to do." Omar waved away his own heavy and extensive duties. "You will be Nick's *benefactor* if you go through with this plan of yours. I can see why this appeals to you. To give him the support that your mother never had. To support a *partner* in life—"

"Omar, I am *not—not* in love with Nick! He's a talented artist and he is beautiful and kind and..." Bane gripped the counter and closed his eyes.

Omar let out a snort of laughter. "Those are *terrible* traits. Not *lovable* at all."

"If I *believed* in love, Omar, Nick would...might inspire me to—"

Omar put a hand on his shoulder. "Bane, you will find that the heart wants what it wants. You cannot logic away what you feel."

"Even if *love* exists—which I do not believe—I destroyed that possibility with Nick with the internship. Ironically, now the internship is the *only* thing that keeps Nick here. So drop the rest of it. Please."

The unaccustomed "please" had Omar looking so sad. He nodded though and let the conversation go. Omar was a born optimist, but he hadn't heard Nick's words to Bane in the shower. Those words put into sharp relief how ungentleman-like Bane had been. He hadn't even been a *shadow* of a gentleman. So not worthy of Nick at all.

The rest of the dinner had been even more excruciating. Dean remained slobbering drunk even though Bane had pressed upon him the whole pot of strong coffee. Sloan's eyes had flickered among the group, seeing everything and recording it all in that clever brain of hers to be used at opportune—or *inopportune*—times. And Devon...

Devon had dressed in his most becoming outfit, which consisted of a pale green shirt with linen pants. It exposed the top of his well-defined chest and brought out flecks of copper in his brown eyes. He would lightly place his hand on Bane's nearest forearm whenever he spoke. He would lower his head and look up at Bane through his lashes whenever Bane spoke to him. He ignored Bane's silences and ill temper. He pretended that the night was going swimmingly.

Nick would not do that. Nick would have bitten my head off for being a bastard. He wouldn't pretend everything was all right ever. He would have stormed out of the dining room. And I would have apologized abjectly for my behavior and coaxed him back. If we were together... But then Nick's words were echoing in his ears about how he could destroy the Fairfaxes if Nick did not bend to is will. *Destroyer... That's how Nick sees me. As a destroyer and why would he not? I should just be his benefactor. That is all. I should distract myself from him.*

So when dinner—*thankfully*—ended and Devon put his hand on Bane's arm one last time, Bane smiled instead of grimaced and covered that hand with one of his own. He and Devon had then drifted out onto the back porch. The moon was at half full, but it shone down bone white and powerful. Bane went to the railing and tilted his head back to bathe his face in its radiance. Devon wrapped his arms around Bane's waist and leaned his cheek against Bane's back.

"What are you thinking about?" Devon murmured.

The two things he was thinking about, Nick and the beast, he could not discuss with Devon. The beast was snarling at him. Ears flattened, lips peeled back and sharp white teeth revealed. It wanted Nick. It wanted Nick now. And so did he.

But we can't. Don't you see that? We can't have him!

"Bane?" Devon moved around to his side to look up at his face. He didn't let go of Bane as he circled him.

Bane cleared his throat and lied, "I was just thinking that the night was beautiful. The moon is so bright even though it is just half full."

Devon's hands on him felt like leaden weights. Where before a simple touch from Devon had been pleasurable now it left him feeling dead inside.

This is nonsense. Devon is still as attractive as ever. There is no reason for me to not be attracted to him!

Devon smiled broadly, totally unaware of his mental distress, and looped his arms around Bane's neck. "It is a *romantic* night. One of those nights where kisses are magic."

Devon got up on his tiptoes and pressed his lips against Bane's. Bane just stood there and accepted the kiss. Like Devon's touch the kiss was dead, too. It tasted of ashes. Devon tried to deepen the kiss but Bane pulled away.

He'd heard something upstairs.

In Nick's room.

It was a muffled cry.

CHAPTER TWENTY-NINE
PROTECTOR

Nick wrenched Dean's hand off of his mouth and hissed, "Get out of my bedroom, Dean!"

With his other hand, Nick tried to grab the comforter and drag it up over his body, to hide his nakedness from Dean's lascivious gaze. His actions felt heavy and slow with sickness and sleep and shock. His back screamed in agony as he moved, but that didn't stop him.

Dean was a strong man. Not as strong as Bane, but stronger than Nick in his sick condition. Dean ripped the comforter out of Nick's hand and threw it off the end of the bed. Nick was now completely exposed. His pajama pants were twisted around his thighs. His cock and balls were out in the open for Dean to stare at eagerly.

"What the Hell are you doing?" Nick tried to squirm away from the bigger man. But his pajama pants hobbled him and blisters ripped open on his back causing him to hiss in pain and freeze.

Dean moved with surprising speed for a drunk man and hooked a meaty arm around Nick's waist and dragged Nick to him. The raw scent of whiskey licked up his face as a blast of Dean's breath gusted out of him. More blisters popped and

Nick bit down on his lower lip until it almost bled as nausea from the agony of his sunburn rolled through him.

"I know you want a strong man. You're needy. You're the type of boy who needs a protector. I'll be that for you." Dean's fingers dug into his bare thigh.

"Get off of me!" Nick cried, but his voice was weak and streaked with pain.

"You don't want that." He ran a hand through the dried cum on Nick's stomach. "I bet you fantasized about getting that sweet ass of yours reamed while you begged for it to never end." Dean leaned in, trying to kiss him with rubbery, wet lips.

Nick shoved him back, but it was like trying to move a mountain. More pain shot through him as his burned flesh was pulled. If brawn wasn't going to do it, reason would have to.

"Dean, do you honestly think this is going to happen?" Nick gestured between them. "All I need to do is call out and Bane will be in a flash. He does that. Moves so fast sometimes it seems impossible. So this thing you're doing here is so not going to happen. You need to just *go*."

Dean's hands slid up his sides and around to his front. He grabbed Nick's cock in one foul hand. "You scream to bring Bane here and I'll make *you* scream out of pain."

A ball of dread formed in Nick's stomach. Fever flared inside of him. His back felt like it was on fire. Dean's hand on his cock was cruel and could cause him yet more agony. Yet some part of him couldn't believe he was in this situation.

"You're not going to do that, Dean, because it still ends with you being at the wrong end of Bane's fists."

Dean let out a mirthless chuckle. "You think that *Bane* cares about *you*?" He let out an acidic belch at the very idea. "You're a Fairfax! And he *loathes* them more than cancer. Can you imagine that you're hated more than a disease?"

"He doesn't hate me," Nick said even he held himself very still. Bane did not hate him. But he had sent Bane away. When he compared Dean's actions with Bane's, he realized that he had acted like a fool in pushing Bane away. Bane would never compel him to do anything.

Dean's hand tightened on his cock causing Nick to hiss. "Oh, he does. *Everybody does.*"

"Right. Sure. Whatever. Bane hates me, but he still won't let you do this. He'll tear you apart. Let me go and I won't tell him that you did this—"

"He *owns* you! Tell me that he's not tapping your ass!" Dean's face was slick with alcoholic sweat. "You might not be as valuable to him if I've touched you. He might kick you out. Kick your family out of their home and onto the street. So you should be quiet and let me have my way."

Dean's mouth descended on his. Nick let out a muffled cry of disgust. He wrenched his face away from Dean's and let out another shout that was cut off when Dean sealed their lips together again. Nick raked his fingernails down Dean's left cheek, which had the man screaming and *yanking* on Nick's cock. Nick screamed, too, and black dots flashed before his eyes.

"You fucking little shit!" Dean howled. "I'll take you *dry* and make you *bleed.*"

There was a thunderous sound as the door to his bedroom burst open and Bane appeared in the threshold. For one moment, Nick saw Bane captured there in the moonlight like some kind of warrior king. Bane's hair flew back from his face. His mouth was open in a snarl showing sharp, pointed teeth. His blue eyes glowed like gas flames.

Nick swore that one moment Bane was in the doorway and Dean was on top of him. The next moment, Bane had slammed Dean up against the wall. Bane was holding Dean a foot off the ground by his neck. Dean was making these strangled sounds. His fingers scrabbled uselessly at Bane's clutching hand, but Bane smacked his hands away with ease.

He's so strong. God, he's...he's so strong.

"Don't," Bane hissed at Dean.

Nick expected Bane to be yelling, screaming, from the look of volcanic rage on his face. But Bane's voice was low and menacing. It caused a chill to run through him. It must have caused a chill to run through Dean, too, because he dropped his hands even as his face continued to redden and guttural sounds issued from his spittle-flecked lips.

"Give me one reason why I shouldn't *squeeze* and *break* your neck?" Bane asked, voice quiet and calm, but with a tone to freeze the blood.

Dean made a high-pitched couple of garbled cries.

"I know that you can't speak, Dean. It doesn't matter though. There's really *nothing* you can say to excuse yourself," Bane growled.

At that moment, Devon appeared in the doorway, breathing hard and holding onto his sides. He took in the scene of Nick half undressed and Bane holding Dean by the throat and bewilderment flooded his face.

"Bane! What's—what's going on? My God, what are you doing to Dean?" Devon cried.

"This bastard decided to rape Nick. Didn't you?" He slammed Dean against the wall once more. It caused plaster to flake off the ceiling and sprinkle on the floor.

"No! That's impossible!" Devon sounded shocked.

"It's more than possible! It happened!" Bane snarled and he shook Dean until his head was snapping back and forth like a doll's.

"Bane, you're going to kill him! Let him down! I'm sure there's some reasonable explanation for this," Devon babbled, reaching for him, but Bane shook Devon off and actually *growled* at him.

Devon took a few staggering steps back. His gaze flickered between Bane and Nick.

"There is *no* reasonable explanation other than Dean being a *pig*," Bane snarled and he moved to shake him again.

"Bane, don't," Nick rasped out. His voice had finally returned to him. He struggled to sit up. He grasped his pants with one hand and tried to cover himself as he got off of the bed. "Bane, he's not worth it. He's really not."

Bane went still. He didn't turn around to look at Nick. He continued to hold Dean up easily with one hand as if he weighed no more than a kitten.

"He *touched* you," Bane hissed.

Nick managed to drag his pants up. He felt the broken blisters weeping down his back. He took a step towards Bane. He took another and another. Every step he took towards Bane was agonizing, but he took it nonetheless. He reached for Bane.

"I promised you *safety* in this house and I could not give you even that. I brought the danger to you," Bane said, his voice aching.

"You're not responsible for him and you *have* kept me safe. You're here now." Nick placed one hand gently on Bane's back.

The big man shuddered but then pressed into Nick's touch. "He's a hypocrite, you know? Went to your family to see about them buying his business out. But they wouldn't take it. Trash. Not worth saving." He shook Dean like he weighed no more than a dead rat. "Like *you* are not worth saving, Dean."

Dean's skin was now purple instead of red. Devon made a gasp of fear. But Bane didn't seem to hear him at all. Bane seemed almost wild. That tigerish presence was huge in him. There was a cry by the door and Omar was suddenly in view. The only person not here now was Sloan.

"Nick? Bane? Are you all right?" Omar cried.

"It's okay, Omar. We just need to calm things down a bit." Nick put his other hand on Bane's back. "Please, Bane. Let Dean go."

There was another long moment, but then abruptly, he released his grip and Dean slid to the ground in a heap, coughing and taking in deep hoarse breaths.

"For you," Bane whispered. "I release him for you, Nick."

Devon dropped to his knees by Dean's side, trying ineffectually to help him. Bane stepped back. He turned to Nick. His blue eyes were still glowing. When Omar stepped towards him those gas lit blue eyes swung towards the Indian man and Omar stopped. His hand went up to the tiger amulet and clutched it. When Bane was sure that Omar would keep his distance, his gaze returned to Nick.

"I can *smell* your pain." Bane gently turned Nick around so that he could see his back. He let out a sharp gasp. "Your *back*. It will scar now. Oh, God, no ..."

Nick felt Bane's hands so lightly on his back then.

"It will be okay, Bane. Seriously," Nick hoped.

His back was *killing* him. The adrenaline had left him and now he felt weak as water and desperately wanted to sit down. Bane noticed and helped him sag down onto the bed. Bane sank down on his haunches before him and lightly pressed his hands on Nick's knees, gazing up at him. The wildness was still in his gaze, but there was a *pleading* look, too. Nick slowly reached and put a hand in Bane's hair. The big man's eyelids fluttered shut and he turned his head into that hand as if it offered absolution.

You saved me. You'll always save me.

"Bane, I think Dean needs a doctor," Devon called.

Bane's eyelids flickered open in an instant and his gaze was hard and voice imperious as he commanded, "Omar, we need Dr. Trevelyan here."

"Oh, yes, of course!" Omar seemed shaken out of his shock and he did his bobbing bow before he hustled out the door.

"Thank goodness! Dean, it will be all right," Devon said to the still choking man on the floor. "A doctor's coming."

"For *Nick*. For his back. Dean will *not* be here when Dr. Trevelyan arrives," Bane said not looking away from Nick.

Nick though saw Devon shoot a glance of absolute shock at Bane.

"Bane, I know that what Dean did was unforgivable, but he's drunk and your friend—"

"He's *not* my friend. He has *never* been my friend," Bane corrected, his gaze still on Nick. "He is no longer welcome here. He must leave. *Tonight*."

"But he can't drive himself! He's a mess! Won't the morning be good enough?" Devon protested.

Nick felt little good towards Dean, but now that Bane was here he was safe. "It's all right, Bane. He can stay—"

"No," Bane sounded implacable. "No, Nick, don't sacrifice yourself again for the unworthy."

"What do you expect Dean to do? Drive drunk? Get a cab?" Devon's voice rose up in anger.

"No, I expect that *you* will drive him back to Winter Haven," Bane said. "Since you *care* so very much."

Devon's expression darkened with anger and hurt. But then his face shuttered. It showed nothing. His voice was nearly expressionless as he said, "If that's what you want."

"That's what I *want*," Bane responded and Nick had this feeling that they were talking about something *other* than Dean. "Now get him on his feet and *out* of Nick's room or I will *throw* him out of it."

Devon said nothing more. He simply gripped one of Dean's arms and hefted the man up. Dean didn't look at Bane or Nick. He hobbled out of the room with Devon's help. The door shut behind them. Bane and Nick were alone. Nick's shoulders sagged with relief.

"Did he...how far did he..." Bane stopped. Words seemed to leave him as rage flared again.

"Just copped a feel." Nick shook his head to clear it. The fever was raging again. His head was pounding. "I'd like to lay down if that's all right."

"Of course. I'll get a cool cloth for your back and the ointment."

Bane lifted Nick's legs off the ground and onto the soft mattress. He then helped Nick onto his stomach. Nick's eyes closed and he must have actually dozed off for the next thing he knew Bane was washing him. At first, he didn't realize it was Bane and thought Dean had come back. He reared up with a strangled cry, but then Bane was murmuring soft words of comfort and safety in his ears.

"It's me, Nick. You're safe. It's just me," Bane soothed.

Nick laid back down again. As Bane smoothed the cloth and then the ointment over his back, Nick drifted off again.

He remembered vaguely Dr. Trevelyan coming into his room and looking over him.

"I am sorry to drag you out in the middle of the night again," Bane said apologetically.

"Don't be foolish. I'm glad you called. While I'm concerned about Nick's back, I'm more concerned about this attack. He wasn't raped, was he?" The elderly physician asked.

"No, thank goodness." Bane's arms were crossed over his chest and his expression grew thunderous.

"That is a relief. Still. He needs rest more than ever," the doctor said.

"He will have it. My final guest will be gone first thing tomorrow then it will just be Nick, Omar and I," Bane assured him.

"I'm not blaming you, Bane. The evil people do always astounds me, but so does the good." Dr. Trevelyan touched Bane's forearm. "You're looking unwell yourself, dear boy. Perhaps I should examine you, too?"

But Bane shook his head. Even in Nick's half-awake state he saw that the wildness was more pronounced in Bane's gaze and he shifted restlessly as if unable to keep still.

"I am fine. I will be fine. Once Nick is well," Bane's answers were clipped.

"Yes, yes, of course," Dr. Trevelyan said.

Nick must have passed out again, because the next thing he realized was that he and Bane were alone once more. Bane was sitting in the chair, eyes glowing, protecting him.

"Bane?" Nick asked, his voice thick with sleep.

Bane was immediately up and by his side. "Yes, it's me. What do you need? What can I get for you?"

"Lay down with me?" Nick asked.

Bane stilled and said nothing for a long time. "Are you certain? I don't want—"

"I'm safe with you. I want to feel you against me," Nick begged.

There was another moment's hesitation and then Bane toed off his shoes and laid down beside Nick. He kept himself very still, regarding Nick out of those Siberian blue eyes, and then he opened his arms and Nick went into them.

His head was pillowed against Bane's massive chest. Bane gently ran a hand through his hair. Nick let out a pleased sound and cuddled closer. He had never felt so safe, so...loved.

"Nick," Bane's voice was soft and deep.

"What?" He lifted his head to look at the big man's face.

"About the internship—"

"We don't need to—"

"It's *over*. I release you," Bane said with a sigh. "I release you."

Nick couldn't quite understand the words. "But what about my family? You won't send them packing—"

"No, no." Bane smoothed a hand through his hair again. "The deal still stands, but I am releasing you from your part of it. You are free to—to go."

Nick licked his lips and thought on that. He could go live with Jade just like they had planned before all of this had started. He'd have plenty of stories to tell from these scant few days here, but they would become distant and hazy. He'd forget all about Bane and Omar and Moon Shadow...except he wouldn't. He would never forget them. He wouldn't want to. Because though many parts of his experience here had been terrible, others had been *incredible*. Like nothing he had ever experienced. And he sensed that this was *nothing* compared to what would happen next if he stayed.

With a realization that stunned him, Nick knew he didn't want to go. The awfulness with Dean notwithstanding he wanted to stay here. He wanted to help transform Moon Shadow and document the progress with his camera. He wanted to laugh with Omar in the kitchen. He wanted moonlit dinners on the porch with Bane and perhaps something more...

"What if I don't want to go? What if I want to stay?" Nick asked.

Bane's hand froze in its petting of his hair. "You want to stay?"

"Don't sound so surprised!" Nick laughed and then let out an oomph of pain as it hurt his back to laugh. "I like Omar and Moon Shadow."

"Who couldn't?"

"Exactly."

There was a pause and then Bane asked, his voice low and smoky, "Anything else that is inspiring your desire to stay?"

Nick grinned against Bane's chest. "No."

"No?!"

"Don't yell! People are trying to sleep here." Nick was laughing harder then and his back really ached.

"Don't move. You will hurt yourself," Bane cautioned.

They were quiet for a moment. Bane went back to petting him. Nick's eyelids were sliding shut. Sleep was tugging him into her embrace.

"So...can I stay? With you?" Nick murmured.

"Yes, of course, yes, you may. I want you to stay." Bane gently kissed Nick's forehead. "Now sleep. I will keep you safe."

Nick was already falling down into velvety dreams and Bane's words sent him the rest of the way with a smile on his lips.

He woke one last time that night.

There was something soft beneath his cheek. It felt like the finest fur. He moved his head to brush his skin against it. It wasn't just his cheek either that was feeling such softness. His arm, which had been slung over Bane's waist was now curled around a furry middle. This furry middle was warm and moving beneath him as it breathed.

Nick's eyelids cracked open. He couldn't understand what he was touching. He had fallen asleep in Bane's arms, but now it felt like he was lying half on top of...well, he didn't know what it was. He lifted his head up. It was still night, but that slice of moonlight hit the bed just so and he could see what was lying beside him. He froze.

Bane was nowhere in sight.

X. ARATARE

A white Bengal tiger was stretched out on its side half beneath him. Its startlingly blue eyes opened and fixed upon him.

CHAPTER THIRTY
FLEE

Bane woke in Nick's bed feeling quite groggy and strange. He had felt Nick moving on top of him and had naturally awoken, thinking that the young man needed something from him. He focused in on Nick's expression and was startled. Nick looked...shocked, frightened, awed? Yet he was looking at Bane. So what would inspire those emotions?

Bane opened his mouth to ask what was wrong, but only a curious growl issued forth. Confused and uncertain, he reached for Nick, but the young man jerked back. His hand passed along Nick's left shoulder and red lines appeared. Nick yelped and the coppery scent of blood filled the air.

That was when Bane realized that he had extended a *paw* not a hand. A paw with claws accidentally extended that had cut through Nick's skin like a knife through soft butter. He could not speak, because the tiger's mouth was not made for human speech. He was the beast!

He jumped from the bed and landed on all four paws on the wood floor. The dresser rattled as his heavy weight came down.

How could this have happened? It's not the full moon! Why have I changed?

"N-nice kitty," Nick said, hysteria in his voice as he cradled his wounded arm against his chest. His eyes were huge and the scent of his fear was heavy in the air now, too, mixing with the blood. "How did you get in here?" Shivering with fear, Nick edged off of the bed so that the four-poster would be between them. The bed was not any sort of obstacle for the beast. "That farmer—Mr. Brennan—claimed Bane had a large... uhm, predator here. So are you Bane's pet? I know that Omar worships tigers so...are you nice?"

Bane again tried to speak, to tell Nick that it was all right, but throaty growls issued from his mouth. The smell of blood and fear started to overwhelm him then. The beast—who had seemed absent for a moment—suddenly surged forward. It was the one in control when they were in its form.

No! Bane screamed internally. He could not lose control when in the room with Nick!

He had a terrible vision of the beast launching itself at Nick who was still crouched on the bed. He imagined it fastening it's jaws around Nick's swanlike neck. He could almost taste Nick's blood as it flowed, hot and fresh, down his gullet.

"B-Bane?!" Nick called. "Bane, there's a tiger in here!"

The young man let out a choked laugh as his eyes were fixed upon the tiger that *was* Bane. Crimson dripped between his fingers as the wounds on his arm continued to bleed. The blood pattered on the comforter and the beast let out a low, rumbling growl. Nick trembled.

No! You cannot hurt him! I will not allow you to hurt him!

With all his will, Bane forced the beast to turn away from Nick. He pawed open the door and raced down the stairs, along the hallway and then he burst *through* the screen door onto the back porch. It collapsed and splintered under his weight. Bane kept running through the formal rose garden then into the long grass beyond. Though the beast took over from him once they reached the cornfields, they kept running *away* from the house, *away* from Nick.

Not safe, Bane thought with terrible desperation. *Nick is not safe anywhere near me!*

The rest of the night was a blur for Bane as it often was when the beast took control. He woke up in a cornfield, bare limbs covered in drying mud. Blood was smeared over his mouth, chin and chest. A mostly devoured sheep's carcass lay beside him. That told him what he had spent the night doing: chasing and killing Mr. Brennan's farm animals.

It could have been Nick's body lying there instead of a sheep's. His gray eyes could be staring up, sightlessly, at the morning sky, forever blinded by death.

Bane clambered to his feet. He was shivering, but it wasn't from the morning dew that covered his bare skin. The beast had overcome him not just once, he realized now, but at least *twice* outside of the full moon. That "dream" of going into Nick's room the other night had been real. Like himself, the beast was obsessed with Nick.

He wrapped his arms around his chest and walked stiffly back towards Moon Shadow. He knew what he had to do. He had to send Nick away. Far away from him. But the young man could only go as far as Winter Haven and that was not far enough. No, Bane had to leave, too. He had to fly out of the country and stay away until the beast settled again. Then, and only then, could he return here.

But I can never see Nick again. It's too dangerous for him. I must give him up.

The bleakness of that thought had him stumbling as he crossed from the long grass into Moon Shadow's formal rose garden. He caught himself at the last moment. He didn't care if he crumpled to the ground, but that would delay him getting away from Moon Shadow.

Will Nick realize it was me who was the tiger last night? No, people don't believe in magic any more. They certainly don't think a man can turn into a tiger! Except I'm both a tiger and a man. I have the soul of a tiger living within me. Some would say that I'm not a man at all.

"Bane!" Omar's voice called out to him from the porch.

Bane's head jerked up. The Indian man had been sitting on a chair on the porch. Waiting for him. And he wasn't the only one. Bane drew in a sharp breath as he saw that Nick was curled up asleep, under a blanket, on the porch's sofa. Nick was still ill. He should be in a warm bed, but no. Nick was out here.

"Bane, are you all right? Nick told me what happened," Omar said as he ran down the steps to Bane's side.

Bane's gaze could not leave Nick. His heart was pounding in his chest. He had not wanted to see the young man again. He had wanted to steal away before Nick realized he was gone. He planned to have Omar explain to Nick that he had been called away to Europe and wouldn't be back anytime soon. Nick could leave. He could go home. But now that plan looked to be in shambles. If Nick woke up...

"What did Nick tell you and what did *you* tell him?" Bane demanded to know, keeping his voice low as he did not wish to wake the sleeping young man.

"He told me about waking up beside a giant tiger," Omar said carefully. "He thinks it must be a pet that escaped from some area on the estate. Yet then when he couldn't find you in the house he started to panic. I'm not sure if he thought the tiger had harmed you or...or if he was beginning to figure out the truth. I told him that there was nothing to worry about. That you would be back in the morning to explain everything."

"What about his arm? I—I cut him. It was an accident, but—"

"Of course, it was an accident. They are shallow cuts. I bandaged it. Dr. Trevelyan is coming later today to check on Nick and that seemed like time enough for him to know about the cuts," Omar informed him.

Bane let out a mirthless laugh. "What will Dr. Trevelyan *think*, I wonder? First, a sunburn then attempted rape and now a tiger attack."

Bane's laughter continued until it started to rise up in a shriek. He immediately covered his mouth with one hand to hold it in. Nick was stirring at the noise, but he settled back down once Bane's laughter was swallowed. Bane focused in on the Indian man.

"Omar, I need to leave," Bane said. "Right now. I'm going to get a set of clothes and head to the airport. I'll call the pilot for the jet on the way."

Omar's mouth opened in surprise. "Leaving? But why? Nick needs to know—"

"What? What does Nick need to know? That I am *cursed* to turn into a tiger because I killed the tiger spirit's physical body over a hundred years ago? That your ancestor cursed me for all eternity to be this way?" Bane's voice was rising again and he lowered his tone as he said, "No, Omar, Nick doesn't need to be burdened with any of that."

"But if he is to remain here with us—"

"I am leaving, Omar. He is leaving, too. Send him home. The internship is already over. I—"

"He told me that, too." Omar looked proud. "But, Bane, think a moment. The spirit and you both care for Nick. The spirit is reacting—"

"The beast would have *killed* Nick last night if I hadn't stopped it. Do you understand? Nick is not safe with me. And I have to leave for *his* sake."

Bane did not wait for Omar to respond. There was nothing that the Indian man could say that would change his mind. He brushed past him, not even allowing himself one last look at Nick's sleeping form. He went to his room, showered the blood and mud off of himself, before he dressed and threw some clothes into a bag. He did all this in under fifteen minutes. He flew silently down the stairs and to the garage where he chose the Mercedes S-Class sedan that was black as midnight with red leather interior. The motor purred to life and he was pulling out of the garage and onto the gravel drive when Nick burst out of the front doors.

There was a white bandage on his left upper arm. A few spots of blood showed through it. His skin was more golden than red now as it was healing from the sunburn. His gray eyes were determined. He raced towards Bane's car.

"Bane! Bane! Where are you going? You can't leave! Please don't leave!" Nick begged, his voice muffled through the closed window.

Bane wouldn't look at Nick even as his heart cried out for him to do so. "I have to go, Nick. Please understand—"

Bane heard Nick try to open the door to the car, but Bane had locked it. "Bane, please! We have to talk. We have to—"

"This is for the best," Bane whispered and he didn't know if Nick heard him or not as he stepped on the gas.

The Mercedes' powerful engine soon took him out of Nick's reach and out of the gates of Moon Shadow. He passed by a girl with jet black hair riding a moped that was turning into the estate's drive. He guessed that would be Jade. That would be a good thing. Nick needed a friend.

Even as Bane drove to the airport with no expression on his handsome face, he felt as if a pit had opened up inside of him and was trying to swallow him whole. The beast, who had been strangely quiet, lifted its head and roared in pain. But Bane ignored the beast's cry. The only way to keep Nick safe was to leave him forever.

The scar on his face *burned.*

THE STORY CONTINUES IN CURSED 2!

Remember to get The Merman 1 FREE by signing up for our list!

The Merman is a 5-book gay paranormal romance series from Raythe Reign. This series contains psychic powers, a mostly-naked merman lover, an evil scientist, and true love beneath the waves.

Gabriel Braven's destined love is a merman, Prince Casillus Nerion. Problem is Gabriel doesn't believe mermen are real. And worse, Gabriel's parents died of drowning so he has no love for the sea.

But the sea is Gabriel's destiny in more ways than love. Caught by high tide in a cave, Gabriel drowns, but does not die. Casillus brings him to the surface, but tells Gabriel that he must return to the waves or perish.

For Gabriel is becoming a merman.

You can get read the full summary on our website, and get the first book free here:

http://welcome.raythereign.com/get-transformation-book-1-of-the-merman-series-free/

Printed in Germany
by Amazon Distribution
GmbH, Leipzig